MARCH OF THE DEAD

March of the Dead

Mountain Warriors
Book 3

R.J. BURLE

Pier House Books

To the true and original Mountain Warriors. The characters in the book are their own fictional characters, but the indomitable spirit of these real people inspired me. To Sean Kennedy the Asheville Ninja who started the camp out called the Mountain Warriors, Stephen Ledford, a great teacher, Spencer Bolejack, another great teacher and author of *Appalachian Ninja* (check it out), Stephen Opper, all around master of movement, Ben, Jeremy Till, Scott Flues, Elliot, Bryan Dietrich, Josh, Ira, Weston, Christopher, and many others. You all have taught me much!

| 1 |

Tommy Laurens sat in a plush leather chair in the heated comfort of his office located in the Safe Zone. He watched the scene unfold on his computer screen. Nothing deadly happened, but it thrilled him that he was watching the most dangerous area in the world, the South Eastern FEMA Sector in the Appalachian Mountains, also known as the Forbidden Zone.

The camera angle appeared from a drone that flew over the camp of the Mountain Warriors deep in a wild walled off area haunted by zombies, vampires, and other unimaginable horrors.

It was a busy scene that he watched. Under a dreary, early morning sky, the sixty members of the tribe of survivors packed up weapons, folded tents, gathered livestock and anything else of value as they prepared to leave their snow covered valley. At the moment, nothing stalked them, but the inhabitants moved with a sense of urgency because that could always change.

As Tommy absently watched, his mind kept wandering. His reality show called *The Mountain Warriors* had blasted through the sniping critics to become an overnight sensation among the viewers. His friend, Eric, had really pulled through. Tommy had not expected him to survive the week in the infested quarantine zone, but he had proved to have a resiliency beyond belief.

It would have been a challenge for anyone to survive, no matter the temper of their inner metal. Not only did they face death from the obvious monsters but also the paranoid survivors distrusted anyone one from the outside. You couldn't really blame the survivors for their distrust. They had been abandoned to the horrors of the Forbidden Zone no matter if they were infected by the zombie virus or not. After two years of barbed wire separating them from electricity, clean water, police protection and everything else a civilized person takes for granted, they were as hardened as Damascus Steel beaten and scorched repeatedly on the anvil and fires of hell. Only ten percent of the original inhabitants had survived. Pretty much everyone still alive on that side of the fence had had to kill multiple zombies and even other people. Few outsiders could ingratiate themselves into that bunch.

However, Eric, who had always been athletic before falling into a downward spiral of hopelessness, somehow had pulled through when under the hammer of the brutal life. Now with his filming, interviews, and narration, Eric had unwittingly delivered Tommy a major hit. Unfortunately, Eric would probably never experience the fruits of his labor as he was permanently exiled in the Forbidden Zone. In fact, Tommy made sure that Eric had no idea that he had access to the video and audio of Eric's interviews, and Eric certainly had no idea that his footage had been edited and been made into a reality show viewed and enjoyed by millions.

Tommy, for his part, had one major worry. Because of Eric's genetics, many in the Science Departments were attempting to turn him into a vampire with a bite from the vampiress, Abigail. Because of psionic abilities held in her strain of the vampiric virus, it was believed that if she delivered a bite to Eric that he would get her abilities rather than descend into madness like most vampires. The attempts were mostly covert because of Tommy's interference, but every moment of Eric's life was a blessing.

To save Eric's life, Tommy was tempted to give the final nod to turning him into a vampire. Besides adding another layer to the story of the reality show, the infection would give him a degree of immortality to survive in the gritty Forbidden Zone. Tommy also knew his friend well enough to understand that Eric and Abigail had feelings for each other that went beyond the alliance formed to simply survive.

Through his laptop computer, Tommy took control of the drone and searched the activity of the snowbound camp for his friend, and was shocked to see Eric, bare chested, sitting in a small pool of an icy creek that flowed through the village with two other Mountain Warriors. "Have they all lost their minds?" Tommy asked aloud to his computer screen.

Before he could ponder too much on the oddity of men sitting in an icy creek, he noticed a distant black speck on a mountain overlooking the creek. He zoomed in and among the white sheet of snow he saw a black hooded shape traversing toward the camp on a high ridge. The figure was a half mile away. Tommy felt the sudden profuse sweating of his palms as he realized it was a vampire. The hooded figure cast a glance at the drone. Tommy couldn't see the face in the blackened maw of the hood, but he had an idea who it was. In panic, he violently wrenched the controls to fly the drone away. There was only one vampire who was aware of drones at that distance and that vampire could mess with the electronics.

"Abigail!" he hissed like a curse.

Greenish hued static dazzled his computer screen and threatened to crash his drone. She had the mental ability to tap into the drone's wireless communications like she could into the neural pathways of another person's brain. However the drone flew at the extreme end of the vampiress' psionic abilities.

The drone flew higher and Tommy felt his stomach drop with the exciting sensation of flight as the drone swooped over the mountain. He watched the roller coaster effect on the screen as he flew the drone into a valley.

Tommy cursed again at what he saw. An army marched through the ankle deep snow toward the camp of the Mountain Warriors. There were enough to easily wipe out Eric's tribe. He squinted his eyes trying to tell if the army was made of people, zombies, or vampires. He could clearly see they had their weapons drawn and they marched with an aggressive sense of purpose Their obvious intent was to bring war to the unprepared Mountain Warriors, but the green static reappeared and his drone suddenly plummeted to the ground..

"Damn it!" he cursed as blackness blanked his screen. He clicked on the keyboard, but no other drone was in the immediate area, and Eric wasn't wearing his body cams in the icy creek. Tommy needed a camera.

Tommy searched and took control of a drone that was a few miles away from the mountain Warrior's ville. He flew it in that direction with haste.

Thousands of questions cascaded in his mind. What was that army made of? What was their intent? Was Abigail finally attempting to kill the tribe? Afterall, vampires were known to suddenly lose their minds. Whatever the answers, it would make great television, if he could film it.

"Come on," he coaxed the drone to fly faster.

***

"Let go and enjoy this, Eric," Bryan coached me.

I shot him a dirty look at his absurd suggestion.

Icebergs the size of my fist floated past me on the current as I shivered causing the water to ripple around me. I barely felt the hard stones of the creek against my numbed buttocks. I pushed aside the discomfort and tried to focus my attention on the beauty and activity around me as Bryan suggested. I caught sight of one of the drones passing overhead and wondered if my friend Tommy was watching, but I dismissed that thought. It was too early in the morning for him to be awake and alert.

The sunrise barely trickled through the cloud layer that covered our valley like a soaked woolen blanket, but the light lit up the camp to display what could pass as a picturesque New England winter wonderland. A patina of snow covered what looked like stone walls around the camp of sixty people, but beneath the wintery gloss over, the walls were not made of stone, but rather made of thousands of zombies that we killed in the week before. We wished for nothing more than to move to a new camp to get away from the carnage, but the traditionally fickle Appalachian winter decided to turn brutally cold and snowy, making travel almost impossible for anyone who wasn't born with paws like a snowshoe hare.

A few members still suffered from wounds sustained from the last zombie horde attack a week ago. One of the injured had an open fracture that had become terribly infected. For a few days we feared the man, Peter, would die and then we worried about amputation as the limb turned a sickening purple dripping with a greenish yellow pus. Now it looked as if he would eventually fully recover. These afflictions prevented us from traversing the rugged slopes even without the snow. We had to wait until the bone mended enough so that it wouldn't re-break at the slightest stimulus, such as dropping the poor wounded warrior on a slippery trail.

Adam, the wise elder of our group, assured us that the weather would warm today. This made us happy to leave. Our food supplies as well as the local game and wild plant edibles were dwindling. We also feared the warm weather would cause the rotten zombie bodies to spread their pestilence as well as its sickening stench of deathly decay.

The sixty or so people of the camp had been working in a scurry. Even in the early hours, the camp was abuzz with packing. Today we were moving out to a new camp about ten miles over the rampart-like ridge that towered above us, and into a river valley full of wild game. We had to move and everyone worked urgently.

I, however, was not helping with the work. I gladly would have busted my tail to avoid the tortures Bryan and the rest of the camp afflicted on me. It was their form of boot camp. They were more accepting of me now, but I feared that they would never fully see me as one of them. At this point, I wanted to learn as much from them about survival and self defense as possible so that I could go off on my own, relying on no one but me, if need be.

I looked past Reggie. His punishment for sleeping while on guard duty was to spend each night for a week tied to this stake. He was just finishing his last night and he looked miserable, exhausted and even more hollow cheeked than usual. It may have seemed harsh, but the other punishments for risking the safety of the tribe involved banishment or execution, and no one had the stomach for that in the tight knit group, but such disregard for the camp demanded payment. The protocol was followed no matter who you were. The laws ruled over the people of the tribe and were enforced by the chiefs who were equally subject to following the rules. Although I understood the necessity, the cruelty still hit me hard. It was one of the reasons why I wished to move on.

I had spent the days of the last week doing countless exercises, combat drills with sticks, swords, firearms, and bare hands as well as learning outdoor survival skills. I never got any down time other than when Shelley, the old herbalist, had me do some combination of yoga and relaxing pilates so that my overworked muscles could unwind. That wasn't out of sheer benevolence either but rather so I could keep training without injuring myself long after I thought I had reached my limit.

My schedule over the last week had me training before the sun rose and they didn't let me stop until after dark. The weather didn't halt the training, but only intensified it. They had me practice sword fighting on the ice slicked creeks where footing seemed impossible at first. Occasionally they'd make use of the snow for fun, but even when the kids were brought in, the playful snowball fights were built around learning tactics and strategy, speed and accuracy with throwing, and other combative skills.

Nothing in this camp was ever wasted. They had to value everything to survive; plants, animals, everything. Each bit of wild game was used for food or tools. Every bit of leisure was also used to train something. Nothing was disposable, including the two most precious commodities, time and life which became fleeting in this wasteland.

I didn't know if I was stronger, but at the end of the week, I found that when pushed to the limits and my muscles fatigued, they no longer hurt, but rather just refused to work. I would do push ups until my quivering muscles left me lying on my face, but I felt no pain. It was simply muscle failure. However after five minutes of doing sword drills or something different, I was ready again for push ups, where in the past, I would be used up for the rest of the day and sore for the week. It reminded me of a time I tried to learn to surf. The first day, I could barely paddle out past the line of waves. By the end of the week, I still couldn't surf worth a darn, but I could paddle on my board all day against the natural force of the sea.

We had also established that I was one of the best runners in the tribe, both in bursts of speed and long distance endurance. People were amazed that Bryan, Critter, and I had run back from the Lowboys town earlier in the week in such a short time in our escape as we battled the vampires. I still had a bit of leg strength and stamina from my time running track and field in highschool, and I was only getting stronger as the training awoke my latent muscles. My stay out here also kept me away from alcohol and other vices that weakened me. As bad as my situation seemed at first, I was truly living.

Currently, I shivered furiously. My breath raged in and out with ragged gasps through my chattering teeth. I sat in the creek with the near freezing water up to my chin. Bryan and Critter sat bare chested across from me. They smiled, looking as calm as if in a hot tub. I could see their lean but strong muscles standing out from the cold against their skin. Bryan ducked his head under the water, came up and shook the water from his longish locks and beard like a happy dog in a summer lake. I wiped some of the water that flew from his hair off my face. He smiled, leaned back and rested his arms on the snowy banks with the comfort as if he was in a luxury spa.

"Are we done?" I asked in a cold, choppy voice.

Bryan shook his head, no, and said, "Another minute Eric, but first feel where you're tense. The shoulders, hips, your breathing muscles, the diaphragm-- These are the muscles that will tense when you're scared and cause you to freeze when you need to either fight or run. That will lead to your death if you freeze in place during combat."

I nodded knowing I was prone to stand rigidly in place when I needed to act. I joked in a frigid, shaky voice. "However it's perfectly fine for you guys if I freeze to death right now."

"Trust me, brother, you'll live," Critter assured me with a wry smile. He ducked his shaved head under the water. He proudly proclaimed himself to be half Cherokee, half redneck. The balding man preferred to wear his hair long, but as with anything in his life, he accepted the receding hairline with stoicism.

I tried to relax like them, to control my breathing, but I didn't have the control that Bryan and Critter had.

I voiced that question to them, "How can I control--?"

Critter answered, "You don't control anything. You let go."

"When will I get to the point where I don't feel this torture, like you guys?" I asked.

Bryan said, "I feel pain. I just don't let it rule my reactions. Besides, this is not a pain. Your body is simply telling you that it's cold. You shouldn't suffer when your body tells you something, just accept it and let it go. Breathe."

"Well duh," I laughed. "Of course I know I'm cold." I joked.

"Then don't overreact," Bryan said. "Your own muscles and mental tension makes it more painful. Let your rational mind rule over your irrational instincts."

I realized that I had achieved this with muscle fatigue from push-ups, but it seemed each time that I conquered one thing, they hit me over the head with the proverbial monkey wrench.

With my humor frozen away, I said, "The rational thing to do is to not go in a freezing creek in the first place."

"The rational thing is that this will not kill or maim you," Critter said in an almost bored voice. "So relax. Quit overreacting, We feel pain. We just don't whine incessantly."

I nodded and breathed out rapidly a few times through my mouth like they had taught me to do when stressed. This freed the breathing muscles and unlocked everything else--supposedly.

Critter spoke up as he looked over the white blanketed hills, "Analyze the position of our camp like a military leader. Take your mind off your woes and focus on the betterment of your tribe. What are the pros and cons of setting up camp in this valley?"

I looked over the mountains. I had considered this already, so I said, "In this valley, we're screwed if invaders come down the slopes with guns. We're pinned down in this bowl while they have the high ground. However, the creek and access to food make this easier for the less fit among us to live. But where manpower is saved in gathering food, we lose it in having to have extra sentries patrolling to make sure we're not attacked at our vulnerable flanks. I've always suspected that you picked this place more in consideration for the comfort of the weaker members at the expense of the stronger of the tribe."

Bryan joked. "Eric may be the 'one.'"

I rolled my eyes. There had been rumors spreading of a messiah-like character coming from the outside into the Forbidden Zone. This tribe thought that rumor was propaganda put out by those in charge to install a puppet of theirs as a savior ruler. Bryan and a few others at first suspected me as being a plant sent to fulfill this "prophecy," so the joke stung me a bit.

As a side note, I found it curious about the un-inventiveness of the government when using words and phrases like the "one," or the "Forbidden Zone," a phrase used in *The Planet of the Apes*, but I saw it was less of lack of imagination, and rather, that the times and the moods of the populace were so dark that people naturally accepted these words because it had been in our language and mythos for so long. Because we didn't feel humorous, words that should have been mocked were taken seriously by many except for people like Bryan, or ignored with irritation by people like Critter.

Critter's brow furrowed slightly at Bryan's joke and went back to the conversation saying, "That's why I didn't want to camp here, but my vote was overridden. Saving man power on less sentries allows for more long hunters."

"You'll understand when you have a wife and kids to worry about," Bryan said.

I worked to conceal my shock as I looked at Bryan. Critter had lost his wife and children in the last two years. That was a horrible remark. I studied Bryan's face for malice, but he seemed to have distant concerns as his eyes stared at his own children as they played. They were thin, but not yet starving. I was tempted to call him on his callousness, but I kept my peace. This was between Bryan and Critter. They had an odd relationship to say the least.

I then turned my eyes to Critter to see his reaction, but the tracker seemed to ignore Bryan's remark. His face may have tightened for the merest moment if anything. Critter could stay calm through the worst of times and actually smiled when all hell broke loose, but I always wondered when he would let loose and explode. In the past, I had never quite understood the phrase that warned to be the most wary of the quiet person, but that was because I saw a lot of people who were quiet only because they were hiding their fear. Critter on the other hand was quiet because he was hiding his power. Critter let the callous remark go, maybe understanding that Bryan didn't mean it and drawled, "You know what I think of when I see that steep face of the hill?"

"No," I answered.

"How much it's gonna suck to carry everything up that trail when we leave in another few hours or so," Critter answered.

With the passing of whatever drama could have resulted from Bryan's callous remark, I smiled and said, "So you do whine."

Critter half grinned and added with pride in my accomplishments, "You'll make a good military leader, Eric."

"Really?" I asked.

Critter nodded and said, "You forgot your discomfort and are clear headed when strategizing and considering the needs of others."

As he said that, I remembered my predicament. At that moment, I was no longer cold. However, once I realized that, I went back to shivering uncontrollably. Critter chuckled as his eyes studied the far off forest bereft of anything green other than an occasional rhododendron bush.

"Alright," Bryan said. "Let's go to the fire. Walk slowly. Fearlessly. Heads up. Walk like royalty. Stay in control. Don't give in and run or tiptoe," he advised. I realized later that he spoke in incomplete sentences because the cold affected him too.

As we stood up, the cold water cascaded down our bodies.

I was satisfied to hear Bryan blow air rapidly through his lips. He suffered as well, despite his stoney façade.

I looked away as we passed Reggie, who was getting untied from the post. He was tired but relieved that his punishment was over.

Bryan and I walked inside his teepee of mismatched, threadbare tarps and gathered around his campfire in the center. A hole at the top let out the smoke. I began drying myself with a towel. I appreciated the warmth of the crude shelter. Once dried, I felt totally alive. It felt like every muscle in my body clenched and squeezed out every drop of stagnant blood and sucked in new blood. Yes, I really felt alive like I never had felt before. I was determined to remind myself that I always felt such elation after these cold water drills.

Bryan's eight year old son, Bradley, rushed in the teepee and excitedly greeted me as if I was a close friend he hadn't seen in years. He had a wide eyed curiosity and love of the world around him, and I found my heart breaking when I thought of him losing that openness as he grew older in this cruel world. I could see traces of the kid's zeal for life behind Bryan's eyes. However life in the Forbidden Zone had hardened his exterior.

Bradley started explaining the physiological benefits of cold water immersion using words that were better suited for someone with a body a few decades older and in debt for a few college degrees. His father quickly ruffled his hair and said, "Go outside and play. I'll be at the main campfire shortly for breakfast."

Bradley looked disappointed for a moment, but then excitedly ran outside as something else seemed to catch his attention.

I threw on some dry sweatpants and a sweater. It was amazing how the little things, such as warm, fresh clothes, could feel like the banquet of luxury. I was about to get a cup of hot tea when Bryan interrupted my intentions.

He looked alive as well and said excitedly, "Quick! Twenty push ups, twenty squats, twenty sit ups, and twenty leg lifts. After that, the camp's warriors will do some combat training."

I finished the exercises quickly in the tight quarters next to the fire and then left, walking back to my hootch, another teepee-like structure made with a couple threadbare tarps of faded, mismatched colors. There were about twenty such structures now. Half had been taken down in preparation to march to a new camp. I grabbed a military camouflage field jacket and threw it on, and placed my vest with the hidden body cameras over it. I wondered when Tommy would send a drone to pick up my footage. Supposedly he had no access to my personal footage because the internet access was cut off in the Forbidden Zone, but I had my doubts.

I walked back over to Bryan's hovel with my practice sword and two razor sharp battle swords. One of the combat swords was a short, two feet long wakizashi. The other was a longer katana like sword. It was an actual sword used by the vampires. Many here were envious that a newby like me had acquired one and worse, many questioned my story as to how I acquired it.

I arrived at the training area. The camp was small, no more than a half a football field in size. Our training area was within this boundary ringed by the walls of the slain undead. Bryan, Critter, and about half the camp took a break from packing to drill. I saw the twenty or so men and women look at the hills above as they discussed the travels that lay ahead today as they carried their weapons casually over their shoulders.

I was suddenly overwhelmed with the thought of the woman who gave me the vampire sword. Abigail, the vampiress. She had held the power of life and death over me at least three times in the past week, maybe more. I fought a daily battle with the psychic warfare inflicted by the vampires. The vampiric infection gave them the ability to pick up the electromagnetic fields from the central nervous system of others and even computers. I didn't find any of it to be mystical. The abilities of the vampires were as mundane as the technology behind walkie-talkies. I hated the vampires.

Abigail was different. She definitely had a kind of mystical power over me that was more similar to what women naturally have over men, only exponentially enhanced and that made her potentially the most dangerous to me. Each time I met her, my mind became overwhelmed with the thought of her. I could smell her sweet fragrance. I could—

"Eric."

I heard my name clearly but it was only as if I thought it. I whirled around with my hand on my sword. Bryan and Critter had theirs drawn already. The vampire stood behind us.

| 2 |

"Relax," the vampiress said out loud to all of us as we crowded around her in a semicircle but careful to stand at least ten feet from her..

"What do you want, witch?" Critter demanded. I could almost see his short hairs standing on end.

"I am not a witch," said Abigail. She stood before us with the fearlessness of someone taught to believe that she was immortal. I had my doubts.

Although she was slightly shorter than me, she stood on a rise in the terrain above us giving her a much taller appearance. Everything about vampires seemed to be show and illusion, but it was foolish to lose your fear and respect for them. It was well known that many people in the Forbidden Zone had succumbed to them. Some vampires had the power to take total control of your mind. She was one of them and probably the best, at least from the few vampires that I had had the misfortune to run into.

Her vampire's hooded cloak covered her head. The dark sunglasses on this gloomy day gave her true vampiric nature away. I didn't know if the sun could kill vampires, but even the defused sun beams that made it through on cloudy days annoyed them, even under their hoods and other protections like sunblock lotion. In fact, Abigail was the only vampire who was known to leave their caverns during the daylight. With her back to the sun, she removed the sunglasses exposing her deep, intelligent eyes.

Bryan sheathed his sword and ordered the others to do the same. His men hesitated. Bryan assured them, "Critter, Eric, and I are here because she saved us from an attack by the other vampires in her coven. I owe her." As they reluctantly put their weapons away or at least lowered the points, Bryan looked at her and said, "I guess I owe you a thanks." He bowed his head slightly in a gentleman's manner rather than submissively. "However, it's foolish for you to come here, especially in the daylight."

Abigail kept her eyes on the agitated and ever shifting tribesmen who surrounded her. We numbered about twenty warriors. She stood tall looking like a lioness encircled by a pack of jackals. Her dark cloak flapped around her in the breeze as she turned to face anyone who might advance against her.

"I came to warn you," she said, taking her wary eyes off the crowd and focusing on the camp's leadership.

Critter stood silent, but his eyes were full of distrust. "Is that a threat?" he finally growled. Although he was there the night her brood attacked us, he didn't witness how she had saved us and suspected that Bryan and I were possibly under her spell. I couldn't blame him. I wondered the same. In the last week, I sometimes had a hard time believing my own eyes and memories when recounting what I had been through on that dark night.

"No," she said. "I have never threatened you and you know it."

"Warn us about what?" Scott asked. "Warn us of your evil kind? We know about you all already." Scott showed a rare display of no humor, sarcasm, or hyperbole. Even his usually careless grammar was mostly correct.

"Scott, I owe her my life. Let her speak," Bryan said. "Especially if she has some intelligence that may save us."

"No, Scott, I don't warn you of my kind. You hold that fear already," she answered him with disdain. "I warn you of your own kind. A village of people. They outnumber you by over four times. They were chased from their homes and they mean to attack you. They are hungry, desperate, and ready to kill."

"Chased by what?" I asked with heavy skepticism. She could see that I suspected the other vampires.

Her intense eyes were upon me and I was sure that even if I closed my eyes I could still feel hers burning on me "No, Eric. It wasn't us. You wouldn't believe me if I told you what drove the people from their homes."

"Tell us," I said.

She sighed heavily and said, "An army of zombies ran them out. The survivors escaped and now they are looking for a new place to settle. They haven't eaten since they left their stronghold days ago."

Bryan raised an eyebrow. "How were they chased out?"

My question exactly. We knew first hand how a horde could get the best of you, but Abigail made it seem intentional, which wasn't a zombie capability.

"The zombies wielded swords and marched in formation," she said. "As if they were programmed to fight."

"Holy hell," Scott laughed. "You came out in the daylight, all this way, to BS us."

She looked at him long and hard before saying, "You have been warned. Those refugees will be here in less than an hour. Also, do not go up this hill when you leave—"

"How the hell did you know where we were going? Do you--?" Scott started to ask, but Bryan shushed him.

She cast Scott a sharp look and continued, "A small formation of the zombie army will be waiting for you at the top of this hill. I recommend that you devise a plan to take out the zombie army and the creator. He is an evil man. He lives in a valley to the Southeast--"

Tomas, one of the twenty people who had remained quiet, scoffed and interrupted her, "If you want us to take out the creator behind the army, I can only suspect it's because the vampires see him as a threat."

Abigail glared at him and sternly said, "No. He is an ally of the vampires against you. I am risking my life delivering this message."

An explosion of skeptical snorts and laughs erupted, but Bryan cut in, "She's proven to be an ally in the past. But we're going to have to worry about some evil boss man and his zombie army later. We're a little busy at the moment. Maybe later when we are settled in our new camp."

"The time of the coming fight may not be up to you. I suggest you prepare." She said as she looked to the thinning clouds in the sky above. I could see her brow crinkle at the annoyance of the diffuse sunlight. She announced, "I need to go before the sun breaks."

She stood tall, put on her sunglasses, and for a dramatic moment, I expected her to bring her cloak up and to disappear behind a cloud of smoke and explosive fire, but instead, she calmly turned away from us and started to walk up steep ravine that led to the hilltop that she had warned us not to traverse. I noticed that she was careful to stick to the shade provided by the steep mountain side as much as possible.

"The hell we'll let you go, you blood sucking witch!" Tomas yelled as he raised his sword.

"Let her go," Bryan said to him and then he called to her, "and thanks for everything."

She looked one last time and nodded to the group and then specifically to me, "You're welcome."

I started to follow but Bryan grabbed my arm.

"Abigail," I called.

Scott laughed, "Abigail? You're on first name basis with a vampire chick? She's you're drinking buddy now? A literal bloody drinking buddy."

"Shut up, Scott!" I said. My mind was in turmoil. Not just from her physical presence, but somehow she had some telepathic connection with me that I thought was impossible a mere week before. My mind, body, and spirit felt like she had stirred them to a hot scrambled mess.

"Alright! You heard her," Bryan said. "We gotta get our defenses set. It looks like our morning training drill will be a real fight."

Scott said confidently, "I always preferred game day to scrimmage."

"You believe that witch?" Tomas asked, still angry. "We should have killed her. We may never get such a good chance again. She is out in broad daylight, for heaven's sake. We should at least have interrogated her."

"She slashed another vampire to allow Critter, Eric and me to leave when the others of her coven had us dead to rights," Bryan said.

Critter and I nodded our agreements, although I felt guilty. Abigail had originally only tried to save me. Critter and Bryan were to be on her coven's dinner plate. She only saved them because I refused to leave, preferring to have died with them.

"Alright," Bryan said. "If our attackers are an hour away, we need to get busy."

Scott laughed ruefully, "And give them a welcoming reception."

"Bryan, I have to speak to her," I said as I saw her about to round a bend.

He glared at me, but I took off running to catch her. "Be careful, Eric!" he commanded.

He was about to say more but I heard the people around him asking for directions for fortifications of the camp's defenses.

I ran and Abigail turned to face me, well within Bryan's view. In fact I could feel his suspicious eyes watching me as I spoke to her. To be with her out of sight would make people suspicious as to whether I had been bitten and infected.

Abigail gave me her supercilious smile. "I know you dream of me at night. It really is me in there with you, you know. I told you that our minds are connected."

"Be serious, Abigail. What's going on? What is your game? You could kill me, yet you help me. I wanted to--"

"Thank me?" She smiled as she read my face. "I told you that I can read your mind."

"Yes, but it means more to me to say it face to face. Also, I can sense things about you. Behind your smile, I sense sadness." It was a forward statement on my part, but I needed to know if what was in my head was real or if the stress of the last week was pushing my limits of sanity. Was what I felt between us real? Were we communicating with our minds in my sleep or was it all a nightmare?

We stared at each other for a moment. Even behind the dark glasses I felt like I could see into the depths of her soulful eyes.

I warned myself to be careful because vampires have a well deserved mystique. Beyond the obvious psionic abilities,

Abigail had an unconscious power over my primal urge. Vampires when hungry for blood have a ravenously hungry focus in the eyes for something mysterious that will not ever satisfy. When a man sees a vampiress looking at him with that hunger, his mind of course delves deep in the wellspring of lustful desires. The ego propelled sex drive is stoked as a man feels that she wants his sexuality rather than his life blood.

Abigail's appeal was even stronger. In the moment, I didn't consider why nor even suspect the reason why because the urge was so primal and so repressed, but she never cast those hungry eyes on me. They were always distant eyes, looking for something desired yet so far out of reach. I wanted to be her white knight. I told myself that that was foolish. She was a vampire, but my gut continually battled my reason.

We stared at each other for long moments where time lost meaning. "What is it you want?" I finally asked.

For an almost unnoticeable moment her smile faded but came back stronger. She spoke in a sarcastic tone as if mocking her past naivety, "I loved life once. I studied in college to be a naturalist. I wanted to be at peace with the world but they turned me into this, a vampire. I love my life, but I hate what I have become. Is that what you want to hear from me? Happy?"

"As happy as one can be in a zombie apocalypse while pursued by vampires but it seems you play games." I said with playful sarcasm that turned bitter and acidic. I started to say more but she interrupted.

The smile left her face, "I will be honest. Being given an immortal life that I half despise, half relish, I succumbed to nihilism, until I met you. No games, Eric. I want you to live, but we live in separate worlds. Go back to your people. You are in over your head. Never trust yourself this close to me when we're alone, especially at night, but for now, that scientist and his zombie bots will be your biggest threat, and I am expected to fight against you to protect that monstrosity. I will die if I refuse, but that may be my only option," she finished by biting her lower lip with her front teeth while keeping her fangs out of my sight behind her red lips.

"Abigail," I started to say something more.

"I really do have to go," she said as she turned her back to me and walked off. She appeared very blunt, but I didn't know what to believe from her.

I went after her, wanting to catch up to her before she rounded the corner in the ravine where she'd be out of sight of the camp, but I heard Bryan calling me.

"Get back here, Eric! The camp will banish you if you turn that corner and go alone with the undead."

Abigail called over her shoulder, "I am not undead. I am infected but very much alive."

"Abigail!" I called. I sensed she had information about the cause of the infection and those who were behind it. I needed that information for the documentary I was supposed to be making. I also really wanted to know her better. I didn't see her as just an ally, but also, despite the vampirism and her warning me not to be alone with her, I considered her a good person and maybe even my friend or the closest thing to a friend out here. Among these tribe's people, I felt less like a member of this tribe and more like an eternal defendant.

"Get back here now, Eric!" Bryan commanded in a tone that I didn't dare to disobey.

I jogged back and he gave me instruction to help reconstruct a spiked wall to defend the small camp. I nodded and ran to perform the duties.

As I got to work, I was already wondering if Abigail's visit was only a dream. She had a surreal effect on me, but her visit was evident by the fact that everyone was working to get ready for the invading force. I could see the urgency on the faces and in the movements of those working around me.

As people set up spiked fences and other fortifications, Adam, who was pretty much the head chief, ran up to us clearly dismayed. He was an older man in his early seventies yet very vital.

"What the hell are you doing?" Adam demanded as he watched people constructing defenses that we had torn down just hours before. Bryan really should have consulted Adam before launching into readying the tribe for battle, but I could see the urgency in his eyes.

As Bryan started to explain what he had heard from Abigail, I heard someone run through the village alerting, "Invaders! Invaders! Invaders!"

I recognized the man as someone who was on sentry duty on a ridge top, a slender fellow with a long, prematurely gray beard.

Adam streaked over to the sentry at a speed I never imagined a seventy year old capable of achieving and I watched him grab the sentry by the arm. I followed behind the old leader barely as fast.

Adam and Bryan questioned the man. Critter stood by and listened. The sentry reported an itinerant tribe that approached from down the valley, the same direction of the zombie horde from the week prior. At over one hundred fifty fighters, the number of the invaders easily quadrupled our own. They were followed by a slightly slower group of the non-combatants of their tribe that numbered at least one hundred strong. Although this last group wasn't capable of conquering us, they were capable of wiping out our remaining food supply in less than an hour once their army took control.

The sentinel further reported that the invaders started running toward our camp as soon as they realized that they were spotted. The sentry figured that they meant to attack as soon as possible, hoping to catch the camp unaware in the early dawn.

Adam nodded his agreement, "It's what I would do if I were them."

The sentry had spotted the invaders from the top of a hill, and he took a shortcut across the ridge. The invaders, following the winding valley, were fifteen to thirty minutes away if they continued at their current fast pace.

"Quick," Adam said loudly for the camp. "Reset the stakes used to slow the zombies. Gather—"

Bryan interrupted. "That won't slow an assault of even semi-rational men. We can't fight off a larger force in this camp. We need to set up cover to protect from gunfire and work on a retreat. We have no--"

I had to agree with Bryan. The stakes that Adam ordered to be reset were about five feet long, stuck in the ground at a forty five degree angle, and spaced about six inches apart. They were designed so that the zombies would impale themselves. It would barely slow a full charge of regular warriors with an IQ above that of a stone.

"Do it!" Adam commanded.

Bryan grimaced but nodded his submission to the older man. Bryan turned to the tribe and issued Adam's orders in a deep commanding voice.

The camp got to work as Adam took Bryan aside and explained the strategy. I couldn't hear all of the words clearly, but I could see the explanation calmed Bryan's furrowed brow a little. Although still worried, the younger man smiled as the plan seemed to now make a little more sense to him.

As I worked setting up the defenses, I noticed that I was actually working up a sheen of sweat on my skin. I could feel a pleasant warmth on my face. It was very welcome after the dismally cold days of the last week. The sun had broken through the clouds and I realized that the snow would probably be gone within an hour. I hoped the battle would be resolved and we would be on our way before the zombie bodies were exposed again after the snow melted off of them. The sight was bad enough, but unfrozen, the stench of human decay is worse than anything you can imagine. I really feared that a battle would pin us down surrounded by unfrozen bodies for a few days. Bryan had told me of one such incident that he had suffered through about a year ago.

We were far from ready when another sentinel reported that the invaders were about to round the final bend in the ravine. They would be in sight within five minutes.

Adam scowled as he looked over the poor defenses. Even I knew there was no way to hold off a larger force from our current position. Were I in charge, I'd tell the weaker members to take flight into the hills and the stronger to execute a fighting retreat. I'd leave some type of loot (probably food and alcoholic beverages) to satisfy the invaders temporarily. Granted that would only buy a little time, but we could then retreat to a place where I could strategize a good defense or lead an offensive, most likely at night.

Adam and Bryan then began to direct us to the positions with orders barked as if from the throats of savage dogs. Their plan surprised me at first, but it shouldn't have. I had thought of it already earlier in the day, but didn't think of how we could implement it against invaders.

"Five minutes! Hurry! Get in place. Make sure they can't see you!" Adam ordered.

"If the enemy sees you, you will ruin our plan!" Bryan shouted.

We hurried.

3

When Abigail had turned away from Eric, her smile immediately disappeared as she walked from the tribe. Despite her confident exterior, cringing from the sunlight made her want to cry. Even the small creek sparkling with reflected life-like light that used to enliven her spirit now pained her eyes even through the dark sunglasses. Abigail walked in the dark shadow formed by the towering cliff to her right. When the terrain leveled enough so she could climb the mountain, she stepped off the trail and made her way above the village of the Mountain Warriors. After climbing above the shadow, she lowered her head so that the hood would protect her skin from the scorching conflagration of the winter sun.

All her life she reveled in the outdoors. Even at her young age she taught wilderness survival courses at many of the Southeastern primitive, reenactment, and outdoor gatherings. In college she graduated with a bachelor's degree in primitive technology. When she discovered that the degree was only good for getting a job as a waitress, she decided against further schooling and instead set off to live in the woods for a year and write a book not just on the physical but also the spiritual aspect of living close to nature. When escaping to the woods, it wasn't that she hated society, but rather that she loved the outdoors. Indeed, her goal was to be a modern, female version of Henry David Thoreau.

She cursed the day of the zombie apocalypse that destroyed her loved ones and her dreams. On top of that, she killed a vampire and attracted the attention of Richard, the head vampire of the local coven. As his attention focused on her, she found that she was able to sense his thoughts. At first she thought that she was insane as strange and abhorrent thoughts haunted her mind, but the things she knew in her mind felt as clear as if she read them on paper. She actually could mentally communicate with the vampire leader. She could also shut off the communication at will. She knew when they would attack her. She knew when to fight them and when to run based on reading their thoughts. Somehow their mental probing and attempts at mind control had opened something in her own mind. She knew how to use these abilities better than most of the vampires who had only developed psionic abilities with the help of a virus-like entity.

A few vampires, who lost loved ones to Abigail's blade and bullets, desired her death as revenge, but many of them didn't want to kill her. They wanted to turn her because of the natural psionic power that she had. The virus that caused vampirism was originally developed to cause or enhance psychic ability. Vampirism was simply an unexpected side effect.

Eventually she was captured and Richard himself turned her with a bite to her neck as she teetered on the brink of death from an unrelated injury.

As she walked to a perch above the coming battle, she thought of how Eric Hildebrande had the attention of the coven and especially Richard, the head vampire, who was also the top scientist in the field of vampirism and psionic technologies. Eric had shown the ability to withstand Richard's psionic power, but not Abigail's. Due to her mental intercession, which the coven was unaware of, the people around Eric seemed protected from the mind control as well. They mistakenly believed it was Eric's protection, but Abigail knew that some suspicion was beginning to get directed toward her. She was caught in a bad position. People naturally distrusted her and her coven was beginning to turn on her.

Vampires tended to either become absorbed into a hive like mind or they went insane. Abigail's curious nature of wandering out of the cave for daylight hikes, reluctance to drink human blood, her preference for animal blood, and other minor acts of rebellion had attracted the unwanted attention of Richard and The Specter.

Because of both her psionic abilities and to test her loyalties, she was sent to stalk Eric for the last week with orders to turn him. At night she had haunted the forest above the village, slowly passing through the trees and around boulders, always with eyes upon Eric's tent. At times she even entered the camp at night, placing the sentries in a trance. She walked among the dwellings confidently as if she lived there with the people. Although she did not enter his tent, she entered Eric's mind in his dreams.

Under her psionic control, he would have come to her in a sleepwalk like stupor and taken her bite on his throat. She had that power. That is what she was ordered to do, but she could not go against her good conscience. The Specter's thin patience was running out. She faced a death sentence if she ignored her order to turn Eric much longer.

The Specter's threat was not the only prompt that goaded her to deliver the bite. In the deepest hollow of her psyche lurked a loneliness. Not necessarily the lustful search for a mate, but the desire to have a comrade who shared her abilities and rebellion against what was being established. The goal was to have the vampires rule the Forbidden Zone.

Abigail found a shaded overlook and sat down removing her hood so that her long hair fell over her shoulders. Even in the shade and sunglasses, she squinted her eyes through the harsh sunlight that seeped through the thick gray clouds. In the daylight she saw everything as black and white with eerie shades of gray, green, brown. Only blood stood out as deep but bright red.

However, she loved her enhanced vampiric vision at night, because she never needed a flashlight even in the deepest recesses of the Vampires' Caverns. In the before, she could only listen to the night creatures scurry around her tent. Now, Abigail was one of the creatures of the night. She watched owls swoop from a high perch and catch scurrying mice, bobcats chase down rabbits, and she herself stalked and hypnotized deer and other animals for their blood. She was the mysterious creature who worried people as she softly crunched through the leaves past their tents.

She looked down upon the Mountain Warriors' camp as she absentmindedly ran her tongue over her two inch fangs. In the last few months she had not gotten used to them but constantly felt them with either her tongue or fingers.

She watched the figures below scramble with a sense of urgency. She wasn't sure about their strategy. Observing the people below her perch was her only way long term to interact with humanity as she realized that she would always be an outsider. Despite appearing to the people in the daylight when she was at her weakest in order to show her peaceful intentions, they still wanted to kill her. Only Bryan and Critter stayed the violence of the mob, and only out of the sense of repaying a debt for her rescue.

She let go of her thoughts and studied the activity of the tribe. The villagers below seemed to be moving the more intact zombie bodies that were frozen as stiff as half century old hickory trunks. As she was trying to figure out the reason behind their tactics, she caught her breath as she watched the invading force round the bend in the valley. She gripped her sword debating whether she should join the defense or just watch. Joining the defense may solidify their trust in her, or they may attack her.

If she was accepted in the tribe, Abigail could help them greatly. She was a natural night watchwoman, she could lure wild game to their camp with her psionic power, but she was sure that would never happen. She remembered a short story by Lovecraft where an eldritch creature was tortured by its desire to rejoin mankind. Her myth always preceded her. In their eyes and flightful imaginations, she was the embodiment of the female eldritch horror, a witch, a vampiress. Were they wrong, she wondered. Right now, despite her discipline tempered in morality, she hungered when she smelled their life giving blood thundering through their arteries. She would always smell the nourishment that they would provide her if she sank her fangs into their soft throats. She would always have to fight the urge. Human blood intoxicated a vampire in a way animal blood couldn't touch.

As she stood with indecision about whether to join the Mountain Warriors in their fight or just observe, a mental image of Richard's stern middle aged face flashed through her mind with the message from him, "You need to return to the caverns, immediately. The Specter demands it."

"Consider it done," she mentally replied. She cut off any further discussion with him from her mind. She could sense thoughts as physical objects that she could move to different sections, eject, or block.

Her breath deepened as she watched the opposing group start to run at a full charging speed toward the Mountain Warriors' defensive line. She swore as it looked hopeless for Eric and his crew, but she had to follow The Specter's command. However, it was for the best. The scent of blood from the battle would drive her crazy.

| 4 |

They positioned me and everyone else except for Bryan and Critter higher up on the hills surrounding the camp. We sprinted up the slopes to rocky cover, finding hiding spots with a sense of urgency. I found a nice spot sheltered behind a chest-sized boulder that would protect me from potential incoming gunfire and made myself comfortable lying prone and ready to return fire with my rifle. From this vantage point, I watched the coming battle from about fifty yards above our snow covered tents. As I kept my eyes on the coming battleground, I started to notice the smell of earth, and appreciated the sun warming me and the surrounding land. I would rather have sunbathed than prepare for battle, but as Critter said, "Such is life."

The warchief of the band of invaders ran with his larger army of mostly men and a few women behind him. This hard charging group was made up of only their fighting force which numbered about one hundred and fifty as our sentry reported. I was amazed how the sentry knew the number. I couldn't count that fast. I found myself overwhelmed at the surging sight of violence coming at us like an incoming tide. The non-combatants of the band were a few hundred meters behind. Their fighting force would easily inundate our tribe as we only had about thirty-five people who were able to fight.

Although the invaders were strong and well muscled, the slight hollowness of their cheeks and eyes told the story of a few days without food, but they weren't emaciated or weak. Their eyes blazed with a hungry energy to fight. It wasn't just the sheer numbers, that was bad enough but also desperation that gave them a much greater edge. It fueled their light jog on the snowy ground. The rhythm of their run seemed to suggest that they were holding back to release a crescendo of a charge. I felt my body tense in anticipation.

Aside from the fire in their eyes, everything else seemed to droop. Their ragged clothes hung from their bodies like Spanish moss. Even their scraggly hair and beards seemed to accentuate the dismal frowns etched into their faces.

Contrasting their downtrodden appearance, their swords pointed at the sky as if challenging the very gods above. Their guns were slung across their shoulders, backs or at the holsters on their hips. I guessed that they didn't want their gunshots to attract a zombie horde. Zombies immediately followed gunshots. A gunshot advertised an easy meal that was wounded or freshly dead. In the Forbidden Zone, firearms were used as a last resort. Another reason for shying away from gunfights is that after two years without contact with the outside world where all things were manufactured, bullets were more scarce and far more valuable than gold to a survivor.

It looked like the invaders believed that the Mountain Warriors village would agree to those unspoken terms of limiting the fighting to blades. I figured they could see our hooded guards standing with swords at the ready behind the tribe's defensive walls. I just hoped they didn't guess our secret.

On the village's front lines, I watched as Bryan leapt up and stood tall on a mound of frozen zombie bodies still covered in snow, a grizzly lookout post. To the invaders it surely looked like a force of twenty hooded men stood guard next to Bryan, ready to fight, but they were decoys. All the living except Bryan and Critter were in the surrounding hills, holding our gunfire until the command.

Bryan shouted in a voice that echoed off the walls of the valley to the invaders, "Halt. What is your intent?"

The leaders, two compactly built men with similar droopy mustaches, long viking-like braided beards and horned helmets, ignored Bryan. The older of the two raised his sword in a silent signal to launch the charge and their combat shuffle raged into a full attack sprint.

"Attack!" The leader then commanded and was echoed by his twin companion. The invaders raised their swords, machetes and warcries to the skies and charged toward the camp. Any sign of weakness from hunger was left in their wake. They sought conquest, victory, sustenance, and nothing would stop them.

Bryan jumped off of the pile of zombie bodies and ran behind a large rock outcropping. With less than one hundred yards from the charging front line of the attackers, Critter and Bryan peeked around either side of a boulder. Bryan raised a battered AR-15 rifle to his shoulder and Critter aimed his AK-47 variant called a MAK-90 and shot a half dozen of the invaders before ducking behind their cover and retreating further into the camp past the decoys propped up to look like defenders of the camp. Bryan and Critter picked out their retreat carefully to avoid piles of zombies slaughtered from the week before. They didn't want to seek shelter behind the wall of zombie bodies for fear that a bullet might ricochet off of a frozen body of the undead and penetrate their skin. causing them to turn into the monsters themselves.

The two men kept to rocks and trees for cover, ever firing at the charging line and retreating further into camp as our camp's decoy "sentries" stood in place. The decoys were simply the frozen bodies of slain zombies propped up to look like defenders. The real defenders, like me, ringed the camp up on the hills above.

At first, I was surprised that Bryan and Critter had opened fire. Usually that was reserved for desperate times. Zombies had the uncanny ability to follow the sound of a gunshot for several days, but because we were leaving in an hour and had just killed off most of the zombies in the area, we didn't observe the usual rule to reserve shooting for only dire emergencies.

The army of invaders continued to charge, leaping over their fallen comrades. Infact, their charge became more driven after the gunshots. They quickened their speed, screamed their war cries louder as they rushed onward. Now it wasn't just to raid and gather food. They sought to avenge the deaths of their brothers and sisters in their group who lay fallen in their wake across the snowy valley.

In mid charge, many of the invaders sheathed their swords and machetes and armed themselves with firearms in response to the gunfire from Bryan and Critter. I gripped my own gun a little tighter, just waiting for the command to shoot.

Having reached the first line of our zombie body defenders, the leader of the invaders wearing a horned viking helmet swung an oversized broadsword at one of the hooded figures. He realized the trick as his steel struck deep and became stuck in the hard flesh that was obviously frozen.

The leader watched for a moment as the hooded figure that he had struck with the broadsword fell to the ground and broke into large bodily chunks. By the gray rotted skin, soulless eyes and mouth locked wide open in a death howl, he could see it was the frozen body of a slain zombie.

The leader of the invaders swore loudly, and warned his fighters in a panicked scream. "The men guarding the line are decoys! Dead zombies!" With desperation, he looked ahead and saw more propped up and slain zombies guarding the tents. In the fog of war, I guess he didn't realize that they were more decoys. It was also the direction where Bryan and Critter had retreated.

"Attack those in the camp!" He screamed. With a savage wrench, he yanked the broadsword from the toppled zombie and shouted, "Open fire on the villagers! In the center of the tents!" The followers looked at him in fear. I could see terror blazing in their eyes. Now that they were below us and in my rifle sites, I guessed this by the way they then scrambled to attack with more urgency. They had more fear of their leader than they did of the battle. I also noticed that the followers were leaner, but the two men screaming the orders were well fed by the standards of the Forbidden Zone. The leader clearly led them with an iron fist.

As I watched, I wondered if they were scared and why didn't they rebel against the two men? As I waited for Adam's command to open fire, I found the journalist in me pondering the questions of humanity, and pondered what drove those below us, what drove the tribe I was with and what drove me.

My wonder was cut short as the invaders ripped the air with gunfire at the center of the camp. The rounds of ammunition slashed into the tents and slammed into more hooded defenders that were only decoys as well. Other invaders attacked anything they could with swings and slashes of swords, machetes, and staffs.

I could see on their faces that they were perplexed that the two men, Bryan and Critter, who had offered initial resistance by opening fire, had long disappeared. No one shot back. The invaders realized that they were surrounded by the frozen bodies of the propped up dead zombies. After sheathing his broadsword, the leader of the invaders shouldered his rifle and bellowed, "Fire your weapons at the tents! That's where they hide!"

The fusilade had to deafen the attackers. In their frustration and to unleash their rage, they fired at anything resembling a person or target. Bullets slammed into the tents and decoys.

I could see the horror in the leader's eyes as he saw that all the only occupants of the camp were long slain, frozen zombies. They stood stupidly taking each round of ammunition. If anything, they stiffly fell to the ground and broke. Otherwise the zombies stared back with masks of horror. An eerie terror overcame the invaders that was soon displaced by frustration and fear of a trap.

Desperate invaders kicked their way through and tore into tents, ripping fabric from the stakes and poles to reveal nothing but barren ground beneath. The tents were empty of anything of value. They swore and threw a tantrum by kicking down and firing upon propped zombies, tents, or anything that they could take their aggression like their leader had done.

Their guns finally clicked on empty. The valley was eerily silent as the echoes of gunfire died down. All of the invaders looked to the leader for guidance. They appeared to be too stunned to even start to reload as their opponents had vanished. Their faces were not quite as blank as those of the long dead zombie decoys. The deepest primitive part of the leader's brain had to be screaming at him: Trap! However he couldn't run. He was frozen with the sudden fear as he stared gape mouthed at the surrounding slopes.

The leader of the invaders spotted a virile older man, Adam, standing on a boulder the size of a cottage. His jaw tightened as all of us aimed our guns at them.

"Fire!" Adam's bellow echoed up and down the valley.

The hills then exploded with gunshots and the invaders fell around the leader. His ranks were quickly decimated. There was no place to take cover as they were in the open and had the low ground. They fumbled to reload, but even if they could fire back, we had the cover of the trees and the boulders above. All the leader could do was swear as his people ran in panic and collapsed around him from gunfire.

I shouldered my rifle as I hid behind a boulder about fifty yards away and up the hill. It was a Winchester 30-30 lever action. It was the type of gun that I had seen in old John Wayne movies. I probably fired only twenty shots for practice over the last week, and contrary to the limited training, I did not (or could not) aim at any one individual. Instead I fired at the mass of the running invaders. I knew that was wrong, but I had read about soldiers doing the same in wartime. It was too much for me psychologically to place the sight on another person's chest and to squeeze the trigger from a distance.

I was sure I could point and shoot at a person who was swinging a sword at my head from the distance of five feet away from me, but from the safety of fifty yards behind a rock formation, my good conscience just wouldn't allow my finger to pull the trigger with the sight on a man or woman's chest, no matter how much I tried. This instinctive morality would change quickly. You don't survive in the Forbidden Zone with archaic civility.

In the past, I thought the horror would come from fighting zombies, but they were already dead. The people below, although enemies, had eyes clear with desires to feed their families. They were people trying to survive like me. People who believed that they had to attack us to survive. Even if they meant to kill everyone in the Mountain Warriors' tribe, (which was common in the Forbidden Zone) they did it out of what they saw as a necessity. However, to lose myself to being ruled by mercy was to die and to live without compassion was to live a pointless life. I realized I would have to walk the razor line between keeping my life and at the same time keeping my humanity.

After three or four unaimed shots that only kicked up dirt, I quit shooting the rifle because I was wasting precious bullets and instead watched what my tribe was accomplishing. Adam had turned the camp's weakness for the villagers into a trap for the invaders. We lured them to the low ground as we took the high ground and fired from cover. While the tribe calmly fired their weapons at the invaders, the invaders were in a state of confusion. Not seeing anywhere for cover, many were frozen with fear like an animal caught in a headlight. We could have wiped them out in another couple of minutes, but Adam nodded to his second in command, "Take control, Bryan."

"Hold your fire!" Bryan yelled. Others echoed his command and instantly obeyed aside from a few sporadic shots that quickly died down. No one else seemed to have the stomach to shoot the easy targets trapped in the ravine below us, but it may have been less brutal than what we were faced with next. It shocked me to my core

Bryan then looked down into the camp and commanded, "Drop your weapons, get on your knees, and interlace your fingers behind your head. Now!"

The invaders hesitated.

"We will finish all of you off if you don't comply!" Bryan roared.

The invaders complied. We had a complete advantage. Some looked angry. The desire for vengeance marred their face. Others looked fearfully docile. Most had shifty eyes. Some just stared ahead with unblinking terror.

The warriors of our camp marched down, guns trained on the conquered. I stayed near Critter and Bryan as I felt like I was their apprentice.

It was horrible to my relatively new eyes seeing the dead and wounded people, not zombies. The dead were bad enough on my psychological core, but the twenty or so wounded cried or moaned in pain. They reached for me and begged for help that I could not give. That was almost too much to bear. Only a brute could not be touched by their calls. That will always haunt my dreams: The cries of the wounded, the last moans of the dying, and the final gasp and wild eyes as someone gets dragged down into death's cold embrace.

A man wept on his knees as I stood above him holding my rifle. His hands reached up to my chest as he whimpered for mercy. I feel bad for having done this, but I shoved him away from me and barked an order for him to be quiet like the other Mountain Warriors were doing. Seeing the group as a whole from the safety in the hills above was one thing, but to look in the man's weeping eyes drove me so far to pity that I was about to weep. However, I realized I could never cry in front of an enemy or my tribe, so I reacted with anger inspired by the battle. I stepped away from the defeated invaders, nearing the point of feeling overwhelmed with a mix of pity and hatred. I almost felt insane dealing with this emotional rollercoaster. It probably made me look arrogant, but I kept my vision above the heads of the defeated. It was too much.

The villagers didn't appear to share my feelings of mercy. These invaders endangered their children, threatened their lives and might still be capable of killing them with some means of trickery. The other side still had hidden weapons and there was another group arriving behind them.

In this land, there were no jails, as there were no means to feed prisoners. On the way down the hill, Bryan grimly explained to me that we had a choice, let them go so they could regroup and possibly attack again or the Mountain Warriors could kill them as they knelt. I had heard that this was a common dilemma after a battle in the Forbidden Zone, but I never thought I'd witness it. It was denial, but denial helps an individual keep his sanity as everything around him falls apart.

The first option could lead to our death because we only defeated this much larger force this morning by trickery. I couldn't live with myself if we performed the second option, but killing an opposing tribe on their knees was commonly committed by other tribes in our area. It's likely that these invaders might have committed the same atrocity against us. If the Mountain Warriors killed them in cold blood, I knew that I could not live with them anymore. I felt my stomach heaving and I feared vomiting in front of everyone. I didn't want to be associated with such an atrocity, but didn't see a way out surrounded by vengeful tribesmen. I hoped that the invaders could convince our tribe that they would just move on and never bother us again.

The villagers used their booted feet to nudge the dead and injured, looking for anyone faking the degree of their injuries or hiding a weapon. I watched Critter shove a motionless, prone man with his moccasinned foot. The man was playing possum, and rolled over, pulled a handgun that he had concealed beneath his chest. As the possum took aim, Critter stomped on the faker's gun hand and savagely kicked him in the face with his other foot, knocking him unconscious. As the man lay still, Critter kicked him in the crotch to test if he was actually out or was playing unconscious again. The man shuddered, but otherwise did not react. Critter grabbed the handgun, pocketed it, and then dragged the faker by the scruff of his neck into the center of the village and plopped his now unconscious body on the ground.

God above, I swear that I wanted to stop him, but I found my heels frozen to the ground. My stomach and chest coiled, released and recoiled. I was afraid that I would collapse and worried about a heart attack from the tight feeling, but I was expected to stand strong.

"Who's the leader of this pathetic mob?" Bryan leveled a withering glare at those kneeling around him. He shot a few side glances at the two leaders in the viking helmets, but they showed no reaction.

We towered above the vanquished as they knelt before us in their defeat. They indeed looked pathetic, even more so than when I first spotted them. The fire and life was stricken from their eyes as they awaited their fate, praying for mercy but expecting vengeance, most likely in the form of a death sentence. Mercilessness was the usual law of the land. Without Abigail's warning, had they attacked us when we were completely unaware, they would have wiped us out, completely. I had heard that in a lot of the warfare in the Forbidden Zone, the only ones kept alive were those deemed useful as either slaves, warriors, or concubines. They knew this and it showed in their eyes.

I always believed that I would protest such harsh measures. I'm not making excuses for my weakness, but as a new guy who was constantly under everyone's suspicion, I found that my courage evaporated away as quickly as fog in the morning sun. I could only hope that the combat maddened Mountain Warriors could keep their humanity.

The kneeling survivors answered Bryan's question of who was in charge by lowering their heads closer to the ground but were otherwise silent.

"Tell me who rules you or you shall all face retribution. Immediately!" Bryan roared. Even I felt a tremor of terror from his stern booming announcement, and it was not directed at me. He cast an eye in the direction of the two men in the horned helmets and scowled as the men remained silent.

Bryan could be ferocious when pushed, but I also knew he was a man of good character, but nothing made him more vicious than defending his family. I knew he was struggling with what to do. So did everyone else, but that struggle seemed to make him meaner. My shoulders tensed as I pondered the next move. I could see that the conflict inside could drive him to cruelty.

Bryan pulled out his handgun and pulled back the slide and let it go to chamber a round with an ominous clacking sound of metal on metal. Bryan had once told me that when he did this, he already had a bullet in the chamber. In such situations, he'd secretly palm the bullet as it was ejected and loaded a new one. The purpose of the little charade was that Bryan believed there was no sound in the world that terrified a person more than the mechanical clacking sound of a bullet getting chambered, other than an actual gunshot of course. I had had guns pointed at me quite a few times in the past and had to agree.

"Tell me! Now! Who is incharge?" Bryan thundered.

"Randall Mussellmann and his brother Reginald led us here against our will," a thin, pinched faced invader accused, pointing at the compactly built men with the viking horned helmets.

"Thanks, Rat Man," Bryan immediately nick-named the fink. Bryan walked over to the kneeling leader and his brother who looked similar with drooping mustaches, beards and horned helmets.

Bryan looked at Randall and scowled. "Your tribe looks hungry, yet you and your brother look well fed. Besides being hungry, they look afraid of you. I hate bullies."

Randall Mussellmann looked up and ignored Bryan's accusation. Instead he asked in a good natured voice dripping with insincerity, "Are you Bryan? We were warned that you and your tribe are strong and not to mess with you. Damn, they were correct."

I noticed that Randall's eyes kept darting to his broad sword that lay on the ground at his side.

"Cut the crap! Why didn't you come in peace?" asked Bryan.

"My people had no choice," Randall pleaded.

"Shut up!" Bryan commanded. Then he replied in a low threatening growl. "I have the power to execute you all. All of you! And I should. What's stopping you from turning around and attacking us tomorrow?"

"No. Please." He pleaded as Bryan aimed his hand gun at his face.

I watched his brother Reginald reach quickly into his pocket like a man with nothing to lose. I knew he was going after a gun.

"Bryan!" I warned.

Bryan then aimed at Reginald as he pulled a handgun from his pocket and scrambled to his feet. Bryan's shot rang out across the ravine followed by the sound of Reginald's body plopping to the ground. Blood leaked from the man's forehead from a neat round hole between his eyes. The horned viking helmet smashed to the ground, cracking in a few cheap and sharp plastic pieces. For me the sound of a limp body hitting the Earth at freefall speed is one of the most sickening sounds in the world. It's something I will never forget.

Adam kept a stoney face despite the violence, his eyes hidden by his reflective glasses.

Critter roughly nudged the body with the toe of his boot and then patted him over and pocketed anything that he wished to keep. I had seen him deal with the dead before and he was usually respectful. Bryan's callousness and the utter disregard for the deadman made me wonder if they were purposely provoking a rebellion to justify a slaughter. In my heart I knew that I could never justify it. I would turn into a different person if I did.

I tried to remind myself that although defeated, they still outnumbered us by well over double. To imprison them was out of the question. We had nowhere to hold them and no way to feed them. To let them walk was almost equally out of the question, because nothing was stopping them from a second try at conquering us.

I saw a tribe member catch the wavering look in my eyes. He shot me a scornful glance and looked away, shaking his head in disdain. I either had to voice my protest or walk away from the camp and never return, but I found my knees weak and my voice absent. My heels were still frozen to the ground. I never imagined that people could turn this savage with only two years away from civilization, and from what I had heard even in Craigsville, the Mountain Warriors were more merciful than most tribes.

"Hey!" Randall Musselmann exclaimed as Critter took a necklace and a locket from the deceased Reginald's neck. "That locket is a family heirloom."

Critter winked at Randall.

Bryan holstered his handgun and smacked Randall across his stunned face. A taunting smirk creased Bryan's face. "Your brother was a dumbass."

Randall lunged and grabbed the broadsword that Bryan had left within his reach. Randall drew it from the scabbard, and launched himself at Bryan with a savage war cry.

Bryan drew his two katanas and blocked the descending broadsword with an X block and simultaneously moved to Randall's side and kicked him hard in the ass. Randall stumbled a few steps past his opponent and Bryan kicked Randall's heel causing him to trip and slam on his face.

"Fool," Bryan said. "You're just as stupid as your dead brother, but clumsier."

Randall jumped to his feet and charged screaming at a full sprint, swinging across at Bryan's throat. I knew how irritatingly smug Bryan's smile appeared in the heat of combat. I had faced it in training. In those moments, I hated him. Bryan simply ducked the sword stroke, and stood back up with arrogance. His smile seemed to announce that he could not be brought down. Randall took it as a challenge.

Bryan remained impassive other than his confidence as the broadsword whistled downward toward the top of his skull. He stepped aside, parried with one sword as his other sword collided with the rushing Randall's neck. His head flew off, landing at the Rat Man's knees, who screamed in shock and edged away as Randall's still blinking eyes stared at him.

Bryan wiped the blood from his sword on the deadman's clothes and asked, "Who's next in command?" No one wanted to claim that title. "Answer me. Are you third in rank, Rat Man?"

"My name is—" he started to protest.

"Your name is what I say it is and you're Rat Man from now on," Bryan said with a finality that the Rat Man didn't care to contest. Bryan then announced to the defeated invaders, "To answer my question to you, I am now in command of your group. I defeated your leaders in fair combat. You will answer to me. Is there any argument?"

The invaders were thoroughly defeated and unled. In this wild land, many times a strong man would rule strictly by brutality and once he was taken out, a battle ensued to fill the void. The void would be filled with the next most terrible warrior. In their eyes, Bryan was as bad a choice as any and they really had no choice anyway.

I reminded myself that I knew Bryan. Underneath it all, I knew he didn't like having to execute the leaders, even in one on one combat, and this deed wasn't done out of retribution. At least, I hoped. His main intention was to make the invaders a leaderless mob so they couldn't reform and launch another attack. I'm not defending Bryan's savage choice. It seemed very brutal to me, even in retrospect. However, I wasn't sure if there was another way in which our village could survive. In Bryan's mind, executing the leader was necessary so he wouldn't have to execute the entire force. It seemed provoking the Musselmann brothers to fight made it easier for him than simply shooting them.

"What will you do with us?" asked the Rat Man.

Critter slapped the man across the face causing him to fall to the ground. "Shut up, Rat Man!"

"Get back up. I didn't tell you to fall," Bryan commanded. "And remember that we ask the questions. Do you understand?"

The Rat Man just stared at the ground.

Critter kicked him from behind, sending him sprawling again. "Funny," Critter drawled. "He babbles when he should shut up, but when asked a question, he plays dumb. Get up, Rat Man!" Critter added as he kicked him in the butt again.

I tried to remind myself that I knew Critter, too. There was a good reason behind all this. I had to believe that.

The man crawled back to his knees wiping his freshly bloodied lip.

Bryan then repeated, "I asked you a question. Do you understand English?"

"Yes. Yes, sir." the Rat Man stammered.

Adam cleared his throat, he said too calmly for me, "Gentlemen. May I have a word."

Bryan, Critter, and I stepped out of hearing range of the defeated tribe to speak to him as the rest of the camp kept their rifles trained on them.

Bryan sighed heavily and then said, "The survivors... Do we?" he let the question hang for a moment. "They still outnumber us. They could regroup and attack us again by the end of the day. They're within a day's march of our new camp."

"They are defeated on the inside," Adam said. "This attack was their last gasp. We completely knocked the wind out of them. Without their tyrannical leaders, they have no will to fight." It was clear to see that he was right once he said it, but in the fog of combat, it took the older wiser man to see and express it so clearly. The rest of the camp was still adrenalized from the fight.

Bryan and Critter sighed with relief. So did I.

"Look at them," said Adam.

I saw our outlying sentries escorting the non-warriors into the center of the ville. They were mostly the elderly, new mothers, children, or infirmed. Some of them ran to embrace those on the ground who were dead or dying. The non-combatants were ordered to kneel as well. They slowly obeyed. I cringed knowing that could have been me were it not for Abigail's warning. I was even more pathetic when I came to the Mountain Warrior tribe last week than this group that knelt before us. As I felt my mix of revulsion and pity, I vowed never to be at the mercy of others ever again.

When the non-combatants saw their two leaders dead they didn't look horrified or grief stricken, but simply demoralized. The brothers who led them were obviously not loved, but the invaders entrusted them with the survival of the band.

"Sir!" yelled the Rat Man guessing what the conversation was about and guessing they were about to open fire on all of them. "This is not a question!" he blurted as Critter glared at him. "Don't execute us. Let us join your band. We can help you survive. We have skills."

"Absolutely not." Bryan retorted.

Adam said, "Maybe some of the women, if any of our men would care for them."

It was a seemingly odd pronouncement from Adam to civilized ears, but the men outnumbered the women in our tribe. Adam had been trying to set Critter up with someone. There were rumors that Critter had a secret crush for Anna, Bryan's wife. Whether it was true or not, that was not a good rumor to be floating through the camp, and the old man wished to kill any hard feelings promptly before a fight broke out. In these stressful times, tensions even among friends could run high. The Rat Man's tribe was heavier on the female population. There were also tribes in our area running slavery rings, including sexual servatude, and I hoped he wasnt implying that. I had only been here for a week and still wasn't sure how degenerated the Mountain Warriors were after living outside of civilized society for two years.

Critter shook his head and grumbled contemptuously, "They are all weak stock. Not a warrior among them."

Adam, Critter and Bryan further discussed something that I couldn't hear. Critter turned scowling and said, "Come here, Rat Man!"

The man stood and took a few steps.

"No. On your knees, Rat," Bryan barked.

The Rat Man got back down and wobbled across the rocky soil on his knees

"Now! Hurry!" Bryan commanded.

The Rat Man's breaths came out as whiny gasps as he moved as fast as he could over the rough and rocky ground that brutalized his knees.

They interrogated him out of the hearing range of his comrades. The questioning went quickly. The Rat Man had nothing to hide nor the courage to withhold anything. The invaders were completely at the mercy of the Mountain Warriors. The Rat Man told a sad tale of starving through the winter and of the tyranny of Randall and Reginald Mussellmann's leadership.

The Mountain Warrior's chiefs mostly let him talk until he answered their question about why the invaders had left their homes.

They had lived undisturbed in a valley that had been a secluded Boy Scout camp.

"Why did you leave?" Bryan asked, finally losing his patience.

The Rat Man's eyes widened in terror as he recounted, "An army of zombies marched in on us."

We all looked at each other, remembering Abigail's warning. Bryan's forced mocking laughter echoed around us, "You mean that a horde shambled upon your town, Rat Man."

A formation of a disciplined zombie army was too much for anyone to believe.

"No, no!" the Rat Man said, looking up at the men from his knees. "I was in the United States Air Force. I know a formation when I see it. They marched in. I mean they really marched in an actual formation, in lock step. Were it not for the stench of decay and ragged skin, I would have thought they were actual army. They were armed with machetes, swords, and sticks. They could fight. Not just devour. They moved as if following orders, but they were brain dead zombies."

Even the usually morose Critter chuckled.

"Brain dead zombies in formation," Bryan laughed. "Must be some jarheads."

Scott, a former Marine, stepped into the conversation and elbowed Bryan good naturedly. "Hey now…"

"I'm telling the truth!" cried the Rat Man. In his anger, the fear left his face as he tried to defend his statement.

Critter slammed the Rat Man back to his knees. The Rat Man accepted his kneeling position but his eyes were ablaze. "I'm not fooling around. We've survived out here for two years. We don't run from the shadows."

"If you've seen the shadows we've seen, you might," Critter said cryptically.

Adam sighed as he took it all in and looked at the Rat Man, and said. "Stand up." When the rat hesitated for fear of consequences from Critter, Bryan said gently, "Stand. You may walk back to where you were with your people and then get back on your knees. We'll probably let you all live, but we need to discuss something first."

The Rat scurried back and whispered the news to his comrades. They showed only minor relief. They might not be executed, but they were still starving in a winter wasteland.

The usually goofy Scott looked worried as he said, "A bunch of Bryans marching in formation." Bryan shot Scott a quick dirty look for using his name instead of using the word zombie. "What the hell? The vampiress was right after all."

I was unaware that a group of Mountain Warriors gathered around us, and I was startled when Tomas said from behind me, "She's in on it. Those vampires can direct the zombies."

Critter said, "They can't direct them in disciplined, orderly ranks. What the hell's going on?"

"Yeah," Scott agreed, "Vamps will send a horde in a direction, usually away from themselves. Even the vamps have enough class not to want anything to do with those rotters."

Adam shrugged and looked as if he heard that a harmless garter snake was in his backyard. "Who knows," he said with another shrug, "but here is what we will do today, or rather what we will do with the invaders."

I forced my face to remain neutral. What Adam suggested wasn't horrible, but it wasn't a nice thing to do to a group who was already defeated and hungry.

| 5 |

The remaining tents of the camp were quickly taken down and loaded on the backs of the strongest members of the defeated tribe. We left some of the tarps as the invaders had ventilated quite a few with bullet holes. However the invaders accepted the holey tarps as if they were gold, franchensens, and myrrh.

The strongest of the invaders loaded our gear on their shoulders and began to porter the camp's equipment up the long steep hill. The wounded and the weaker noncombatants were left behind at the campsite. Carrying the heavy load was a job no one in the camp was looking forward to doing, so this was part of the defeated payment. Besides, tiring them out would ensure they wouldn't have energy to do anything atrocious to us in the near future.

The line going up the hill spread out for a few hundred meters. A few of the invaders loaded down with packs were interspersed with a few Mountain Warriors keeping an eye on them. It reminded me of a line of worker ants as they toiled single file up the steep and winding trail.

Toward the front of the line, Scott walked with his AR-15 casually pointed down, but his eyes were alert. His Louisville slugger was sheathed on his back like a ninja sword. Still, he didn't pass up a chance at smartassery. He smiled goofily as he walked up to Rat Man who led the porters with my backpack on his back.

Scott called out to him, "Hey Rat Man, old buddy! Thanks for stopping by with your chums."

Scott got a weary look from Rat Man as he trudged, weighed down with my backpack, up the mountain trail. Large rolled up tarps were tied down on the pack. I guessed it weighed about sixty pounds or more.

Rat Man blinked a few times to get the sweat out of his face but said nothing. Whether his silence was due to exhaustion or fear of a deadly reprisal for rising to the taunt, I didn't know, but I could see that beneath the fear and exhaustion simmered a growing hatred for us. I wanted to tell Scott to back off but I didn't have the spine. I was less of an outsider than the Rat Man's tribe, but still an outsider none-the-less.

Scott roughly slapped the back of the Rat Man's backpack with his hand as if roughhousing with an old chum in on a joke. The slap almost caused the Rat Man to sprawl face first into the slope as he staggered to keep on his feet. Scott then said, laughing at his own joke as usual, "You can always tell a good friend because they show up for a moving day, and here you are, my dear, dear buddy."

The Rat Man picked up his pace causing him to pant heavily to get away from Scott. Scott then started taunting the next man in line. No one but Scott seemed to think he was funny. However, that never stopped him.

"Scott, leave them be," I said with a weaker voice than I meant.

Scott was about to say something smartassed to me, but again, Tomas startled me as he spoke up behind me, "Eric's right, Scott. Let them do their job."

Scott was about to retort but Adam's booming voice echoed from ten people in line behind us, "Scott! Leave them to their work."

Scott nodded and taunted no one for the next few minutes, a surprisingly long time for his smart ass.

As we continued up the hill I could smell the campfire below us and could see the weaker of the invaders tending the cooking fires.

Not able to carry everything, we left some of the acorn gruel that we usually fed to the egg laying hens or ate ourselves in times of extreme and desperate emergencies. I remembered clearly the first time I'd eaten that gruel. It wasn't great, but it wasn't bad either. It was similar to grits but it stained your teeth brown and we had no access to butter or cheese. The thought makes me shudder now. The feeble, non-combatant invaders started to cook the gruel, but we refused to let the porters eat until they carried our gear to the top of the ridgeline. The hour and a half wait for the gruel was their punishment for attacking us.

I could see a spark of motivation in the eyes of the defeated. This would probably be their first full meal in a few days. The tepid smell of the flavorless gruel brought life to the starving tribe.

About thirty minutes into the trip and pretty high up, the trail narrowed as it skirted a cliff and we had to walk carefully. Ahead of me on the trail, one of the invaders slipped and fell back on me. His burden, consisting of a large backpack and an armload of sleeping bags, was too much for him to control and the two of us rolled toward the cliff. I slammed into a boulder, grabbed a root of some blessed tree and caught the man's outstretched hand before he could fall. It probably would not have been fatal, but it could have resulted in a broken limb, and a broken limb was sometimes a death sentence in the Forbidden Zone.

I numbly watched as the sleeping bags fell onto the rocks at the bottom of the cliff.

"Thank you," the saved man said.

"You should have let the bastard fall," Critter interjected before I could tell the man that he was welcome.

"One less," Critter growled.

I glared at Critter. I knew we had to play heartless, but I was starting to wonder if he was playing.

Critter kicked the fallen man in the butt as he scrambled back to the trail. "Move your ass," Critter drawled. "You're holding everybody up."

The guy stood up, staggered under the weight of his remaining backpack. His hands were now free without the sleeping gear.

"Let's go," Bryan yelled at the men who stopped to stare blankly at the accident.

"Move it!" A few others in our group echoed to remind our temporary servants of their status.

I stepped off the trail to catch my breath and calm my nerves. I watched some of the caravan pass.

My adopted tribe followed behind carrying nothing but weapons , kids, or anything else that wasn't to be entrusted to the outsiders. One of our tribal members carried a small cage of egg laying hens, who continually clucked in protest. The carrier valued the fresh eggs and hens more than he would gold of the same weight, and he didn't trust the enemies to carry them. It would have been intolerable for the chickens to get stolen or accidentally dropped off of a cliff.

At the far end of the line a few people kept an eye on the herd of goats. The milk provided by the goats was priceless. The people guided them with staffs to keep them on the straight and narrow path. A few goats bleated their protest. A bleat sounded from the front of our line. I whipped my head in that direction confused because no goats had been up there. I shook my head and grinned when I saw that it was just Scott joking around.

Even without the heavier burden carried by Rat Man's tribe, most of us were winded from the steepness of the climb. I found myself feeling some pity for the porters.

The Mountain Warriors were by no means well fed. Before I came here I would have considered them near starvation, however the invaders, with their hollowed eyes and cheeks, looked like they were a few days closer to meeting the grim reaper. Not just that, but the lights in their eyes were dimming, just like an oil lamp will dim when the fuel is moments from burning out.

It took about two hours to crest the ridgeline. The sun had warmed the mountains to the point that we were all sweating. However I smiled through the sweat as I noticed that the snow had melted. The white blanket was replaced with the covering of coppery leaves. The warm sun was one of the few things that day to bring a smile to my face.

Bryan shouted, "Alright, porters! Set your loads down carefully. Do not break anything and you are free, with this warning, if anyone from your group attacks anyone from our tribe in the future, it is an automatic death sentence for your entire village."

The porters gently placed their gear and backpacks down. Some of them collapsed into the coppery leaves with exhaustion.

"Get up!" Bryan ordered in a commanding voice. Other warriors of the tribe echoed the command with the pointing of swords and rifles to back their words.

Bryan continued, "Your women and children await you down below! Move!"

They proceeded back down the hill, trudging like a defeated army.

"Damn, I don't blame them for their reluctance. They have some ugly women to return to," Scott laughed. "Uglier even than some of the men here."

That wasn't completely true. Tomas, one of the villagers, who I trained with on occasion, had a pretty woman at his side from the invader's group. They hit it off on a conversation up the trail. It amazed me how quickly people not only hooked up, but would seem to devote themselves to one another in the Forbidden Zone. Tomas and the woman seemed like a married couple already in the way they stood together.

When the defeated army had left, Adam ordered a break. There was an abundance of fallen trees with fresh dry wood and a seep nearby with deliciously clear drinking water.

"Our breakfast was interrupted down there, let us have a brunch and then continue on our journey," the old man said. "We should get to our destination before dark and we have much work to do setting up camp."

We split into smaller groups to eat. Everyone kept their weapons nearby and at the ready.

Critter invited me to dine with him. He had saved up some eggs from his hens and he cooked them with bear fat stored in a pint sized jar. He added some greens that I think were called chickweed and some solomon's seal roots which tasted like potatoes. With a pinch of salt, some pepper, and a splash from a bottle of Carolina Reaper hot sauce, it was the best breakfast that I had ever had in my life. Indeed it had been well over a week since I had had an egg, and the long walk up the mountain made me appreciate the breakfast even more.

We mostly ate in silence. I only spoke my gratitude.

"Thank you so much," I said for at least the fifth time as I was finishing up the omelet.

He smiled at seeing the way the appreciation lit my eyes. He just nodded his head and went to clean up his cooking utensils. From the taciturn man, that was like a hug and a kiss on both cheeks.

I started to lie back on the soft brown leaf carpet. I was thoroughly warmed by the sun, food, and the hot sauce. I stared at the stunningly clear blue sky above us, but just as I felt a contentment wash over me, I looked at Critter and asked what gnawed at my gut.

"Did we have to be so cruel to them? They were hungry."

I expected an angry rebuke, but he looked at me with sympathy as he said, "I asked myself that as well, but that omelet that you just ate…"

After a few moments of silence, I prompted him with a, "yeah?"

"They would've shot you in the back and used your lifeless chest as a dinner table to eat it. Our 'cruelty' to stop them was nowhere near the cruelty they would have used against us, and we didn't start this fight!" His eyes blazed then he sighed and smiled graciously at me. "Now appreciate your full belly. It's a rare luxury these days."

I nodded still laying in the grass. What he said didn't sit right with me, but I tried to just enjoy the feeling of a rare full stomach, but before I could relax too much, I noticed Critter stare off into the distance.

Critter's lips compressed. The way he slowly stood up reminded me of a serpent uncoiling, readying to strike. I noticed other men and women slowly standing, swords at the ready.

"Hell," Scott swore, dragging the word out into two syllables. "Them zombies march more like Sailors, not Marines." He finished, remarking on Bryan's earlier verbal jab at Marines.

I looked along the ridge and was astonished to see a formation of thirty soldiers marching three abreast in a formation along an old fire road. The line went about ten soldiers deep. There was no one calling cadence or any communication. They all moved exactly alike as if by some magnificent cosmic coincidence. They were armed with swords and machetes. I watched the ranks as they approached from a hundred yards away. The forest of mainly hickory trees at the top of the ridge was thin enough to see for a few hundred yards, especially with the trees bare of leaves in winter. As the formation neared, I saw the problem, and the problem was that they were all zombies. The greenish, gray rotting flesh, the slack jaws exposing the rotted teeth, as well as the dead look in the eyes gave that away, and then the smell of rancid flesh when the wind blew just right removed any doubt.

I rolled and came to my feet, sword in hand and ready to follow any orders.

About thirty warriors from our group advanced beyond the cook circle to defend those unable to fight. Although we were slightly outnumbered as far as the fighters went, we normally had little fear when facing zombies. A person who knew what he was doing could easily take on a few at a time if he was armed with a sword, bat, or machete. The secret was to attack their remaining nervous system. A blow to the head or spinal cord could do it as well as a shot through the heart.

Adam, Shelley, and Bryan believed that somehow the zombie disease wiped out the nervous system except for the motor skill that unnaturally propelled them. Their sense of smell, sight, and hearing appeared to be amplified, but their sense of touch and feeling was totally gone. If they could feel pain, it only seemed to anger them, causing them to roar a putrid stench of air from their rotting lungs.

However, we were worried because we had only recently seen armed ones and certainly never disciplined in ranks.

"Form ranks," Bryan ordered.

The thirty warriors formed a wall reminiscent of the Roman legions. We carried some rudimentary shields made of wood, metal or woven branches in one hand and a sword or machete in the other. The goal was not to let the zombies attack any of us from behind or to flank the formation.

Bryan, Adam, and Critter stood in front of our quickly formed formation. Instead of a sword and shield, the three armed themselves with two swords, one in each hand. They were purely offensive.

Bryan ordered over his shoulder. "March behind us and don't break formation."

We marched along the fire road slowly, shoulder to shoulder to meet the zombie formation. From our own ranks, I watched Critter and Bryan maintain an almost painfully slow pace. That helped to settle the nerves. Despite marching toward the formation of zombies, my adrenalin demanded that I rush. The deliberately slow pace instilled order and discipline that was crucial for our group.

From behind our formation, some of our tribe's noncombatants hurled stones from slings and shot arrows from bows into the approaching zombies. A few of the undead fell from shots to the head and heart, but it did not slow their overall progress. They simply stepped over the fallen with no more concern than an automaton. Some marched on seemingly unaware that arrows fletched with turkey feathers now jutted from their abdomen and limbs.

When we were within ten yards, Adam broke off and stood to the side to give commands and fight in reserve wherever needed. He also watched our rear and flanks as tunnel vision overtook us. Also, Adam could jump in with his swords better than almost any man half his age.

Bryan and Critter, left the formation and charged in a full sprint and headed like a juggernaut at maximum steam into the zombies' ranks. Their flailing swords threw the zombie formation into chaos like two wrecking balls hurtled into a line of bowling pins. The formation that I was in marched on and hacked at the backs and the sides of the monsters left in Bryan's and Critter's wake. It seemed that whatever held them in formation suddenly released them to their natural zombie instincts. They left their orderly rows and now attacked, growling and shrieking at whatever was near without a plan. Although they did wield swords and other weapons, they did it with a lack of training. Not savagely, but rather almost mechanically. They resembled robots whose only program was to hack down or from the sides, repeatedly, but it was deadly none-the-less. I heard a woman in our formation let out a scream of pain that bespoke a wound, but she stayed in the formation. I hoped I would have the fortitude to keep fighting and watch the flanks of my brothers and sisters if I received a potentially deadly wound like that female warrior.

I pressed on with our group. I slashed and killed one with a single stroke. Another zombie pushed the dead one out of his way as he fell and rushed in slamming his machete into my sheet metal shield leaving a six inch gash. I pushed him back with the shield and hacked through the top of his head. The undead fire that lit his eyes instantly went out as he fell to the ground.

We were now stepping on or over the fallen zombies as we pressed on to kill. I kept flicking my eyes to the zombies on the ground. Even with their heads cut off, their jaws still snapped hungrily at our ankles. Getting bitten by a severed head could turn you just as quickly as getting bit by an intact zombie. Because of this, I tended to aim for their heads to brain them and kill them completely. I slashed a thin female zombie splitting her head. She was no more than five feet tall and about one hundred pounds. Just a week ago, I struggled with the idea of killing a female zombie strictly out of a sense of chivalry. Critter even pushed me at one to demonstrate that it was either kill or be killed. These things were evil, no matter who they were before getting the disease.

The battle was over within minutes. We immediately stepped back from the carnage and checked everyone over for potential bites. We were very fortunate. This was the second battle of the day and so far we suffered no casualties from either one, aside from the woman I had heard cry out in pain earlier. Luckily, hers was a flesh wound at the hip from a sword slash rather than a bite, but she wouldn't be a reliable fighter for a week or two.

Usually one person armed with a sword could take on a few zombies at once, but I would be worried about going one on one with any of these things. I hoped we didn't run into a whole company of these guys. This small platoon put up a decent fight.

We took care of our weapons by cleaning them of disgusting zombie goo. Then we studied the zombies. Adam and Shelly bent over two slain zombies side by side.

"Bryan," Adam said with concern in his voice.

"Yes sir," Bryan said with genuine respect for the elder.

"Look at this," Adam said as he pointed.

Bryan squatted and studied the backs of the two heads. "Whoa. Is that?" He didn't finish his question as he looked at a third, then fourth and then a few more slain zombies.

"They all have stitches at their temples," Bryan said.

I looked and saw that it was true. The stitches held two severed pieces of scalp together. There was no sign of healing. It was like the sutures performed on cadavers.

Critter cut open a suture with the tip of his razor sharp sword. Despite using the large, cumbersome blade, he had the delicateness, precision, and agility of a surgeon with a small scalpel. He exposed a small black box embedded into a cut out section of the skull. Electrical wires left the box and disappeared into the brain.

"Someone's controlling these things," Critter said.

"You think?" Bryan said with slight sarcasm.

Robert, the teen with computer and electronic talents, pulled on some latex gloves and with a multi tool from his pocket opened the black box still attached to a zombie's head. He flicked a switch and one the zombie's eyes lit up and it tried to bite him. Critter's sword flicked through the undead's eyeball and into the brain ending that.

"That's fricking nuts," Scott said.

"At this point I have no other explanation for their behavior," Adam said.

Bryan spoke up, "Let me take half our fighting men and women and trace the trail of this formation. Abigail warned us that we would have to eliminate these guys."

Adam shook his head. "We are not setting tribe policy on the words of a vampiress."

"It's not just to eliminate them, but we need answers as to why," Bryan retorted. "If someone is raising such an army, we need to end it now or at least gather intelligence to ally up with some other tribes to end this."

Adam shook his head again. "No."

Bryan said, "It's not just the zombie army that I fear in itself, but also the panic that it's causing among the survivors in this area. That invasion this morning was strictly because of these things."

"Abigail's warnings have always proved to be reliable," I reminded them.

"I don't trust her," Tomas said.

Critter walked to Bryan's side. He said nothing, but I could see by his firm posture as he stood by his friend that he was in full agreement.

"I'm not sure," Adam said. "We're heading a few miles in the opposite direction. We need everyone to set up the defenses for the new camp."

"A few miles is nothing for an army of zombies," Critter replied.

"I don't know," said Adam who normally tried to avoid conflict as opposed to his hotblooded second in command.

"You're saying that strictly to be contrary," Bryan told Adam.

I did notice a bit of tension between them. Bryan made the statement respectfully but as if it was fact rather than taking on a tone of accusation.

"Maybe," Adam said, "but our tribe has been through a lot today. Two battles..."

"Let me trail them and just recon what's going on. I promise to avoid a fight, and I'll be back before sundown," Bryan requested. "I think whoever sent these things is protecting something potentially hazardous to us nearby. A formation of zombies like these is not something you send on a three days march."

Critter nodded.

"That's reasonable," Adam said. "Although, I will take the remainder of the camp towards the river. We need to get some traps set to get some meat ASAP, or we'll soon be looking like that sorry invasion force that we met this morning. You can take fifteen men with you."

"Thanks!" Bryan said with noticeable surprise as he received more people than he was expecting. Then he assured Adam, "We won't be long. I'd like to bring Critter for his tracking skills."

"Tracking skills," Adam scoffed. "With the tracks left by that zombie army, even Eric could follow that trail. We need Critter's food gathering skills when we arrive at our new home."

Bryan replied, "We won't be gone long and besides, it's not just following, it's reading what the signs say. I can tell you where someone went. Critter can tell you if the quarry was scratching his butt at the time and how bad his hemorrhoids hurt."

"Alright," Adam chuckled and said, "you young uns have your fun, just be careful."

"Of course," Critter said with a wry smile.

"Seriously," Adam said, "be careful."

Bryan snapped a salute to his forehead that was more friendly than militaristic in nature and then he pointed to about fifteen people, including me. Among the fifteen, he picked Tomas who spoke his mind very bluntly and was an aggressively skilled fighter. Scott the older smart ass who wielded a bat rather than a sword to avoid zombie fluids from a cut. Robert the nineteen year old kid who was a whizz with computers. A woman named Kristy with hair so red that the others joked that her hair color would give away our position like a flare. She was also our best sniper and carried an antique looking scoped rifle. There were others who I hadn't gotten a chance to know well in my short stay, but I knew that they were all solid fighters.

Bryan said, "let's go."

We immediately began our journey. Critter led our scouting party down the trail. We traveled light with weapons, and small packs with a day's supply of food and knick knacks such as large trash bags for shelter and light blankets for an emergency overnight stay. Adam was right. Even I could follow the trail the zombies took. The zombies had stuck to a trail worn deep over the centuries. Critter told me that these were once buffalo and then Cherokee trails. Later it was turned into a fire road that could easily accommodate a fire department's light pick up truck or SUV. Although the trail was embedded in the mountains, debris such as leaves and branches covered it from lack of use, and the tread of the zombie formation disturbed the leaves enough so that I could follow them as Adam claimed.

Bryan wondered aloud whether it was possible for the undead to veer off and march through the rugged terrain of the mountains. The formation that they marched in would most likely be severely disrupted by the rocky, hilly ground. He guessed that the trail from the formation would follow the road and lead back to whatever twisted headquarters concocted such morbid soldiers.

Bryan proved to be right. We marched for a little over an hour, as we followed the trail along the ridge line and stopped to study an overlook that towered above a narrow but deep valley below. A walled compound sat at the bottom. There was a large two story brick house and a large steel building that could have been a garage for three eighteen wheelers and their trailers. Distant ridges and mountains ringed the valley like the walls and turrets of a castle.

The fifteen men and women of the Mountain Warrior tribe sat in the leaves and rested as Bryan and Critter planned our further actions.

I watched Kristy scope the area out with the optics on her battered sniper's rifle.

Bryan pulled out a small set of binoculars and glassed a small rock formation that sat high on the opposite ridge. "That doesn't look like natural stone to me."

He let me look through the binoculars. To me, the rocks looked like any other boulders, but I nodded my head in agreement.

"Let's go. Be stealthy," Critter said. "I think it's best we go off the trail."

"Hold up. I don't think there's any need for stealth," Bryan said. "Whoever sent those zombies probably had drones or some means of following them. Someone had to be controlling them. They know we destroyed their army. They're probably watching us now."

We eyed a drone in the distance.

"What do you suggest, brother?" I noticed Critter addressed Bryan as "brother" whenever he grew irritated with Bryan contradicting him.

"We walk in standing tall, friendly, but on high alert."

"Friendly?" Critter questioned. "We just wiped out their troops. Who were sent to kill us by the way."

Bryan shrugged and said, "They were zombies, not brothers in blood."

Critter argued back, "Anyone sick enough to create these zombie bots, probably loves them as much as a normal person loves his dog."

"It's probably some scientist," Bryan said. "One of those types who doesn't have emotions. All logic and no feelings."

"A mad scientist with sick, insane feelings," Critter stated.

"OK, maybe a mad scientist, but a mad scientist who is already aware that we're overlooking his valley," Bryan said as he eyed a distant drone again.

The drone maintained a range of two hundred meters. I could barely hear the whine of its four small rotors, but it was aware of our presence the way it circled with its camera on us.

"So what's the plan?" Critter finally asked knowing that Bryan was set in his way already.

"None really. We investigate. Our plan is based on how we're greeted. We'll let them know we're either friend or foe. It's up to them."

"Then let's do both. You lead half our people out in the open down that trail, and I'll take the other half through the woods and sneak up from behind," Critter counter offered.

The faces on the fifteen men and women spoke volumes of their lack of desire to walk off the trail on one of Critter's wild adventures. A trailless venture through the Appalachian Mountains involved cliffs, seemingly endless and nearly impenetrable briars, mountain laurel, and rhododendron patches, and on top of the natural obstacles, who knew what else in this wild age of scientific monstrosities lurked in this forest. Only a keyboard commando who had never trekked these woods would think anyone would wish to take that hike off trail. Fifteen people couldn't be stealthy crashing through the thickets.

"I'll let you take Eric and no one else. He's a good long distance runner," Bryan said. The rest of the men and women sighed in relief. "And I'll give you a head start."

Critter pressed his lips together making them disappear in a thin slash across his face. I wasn't sure if he was disappointed that I was following him or that he wished he had more men at his back. "Come on," he finally said to me and went off the trail after he watched the drone disappear temporarily behind a high ridge.

I started but stopped when I heard Scott yell, "Hey, Eric."

"Yeah, Scott?" I said as I saw him still sitting there with a smartassed grin.

"Don't hook up with any questionable vampire chicks in the woods this time," he drawled with a laugh.

The rest of the crew laughed. I smirked and flipped him the finger.

"Come on, Eric," Critter said again with impatience.

"Hey, Eric, one more thing," Scott called as I started to follow Critter again.

I ignored Scott and walked alone into the woods with Critter. Scott didn't say anything else.

We took off at a light trot downhill through a dense forest. Although there were no leaves on the trees, we still had briar patches to push through. It wasn't too bad wearing a winter jacket, but it still slowed things down. I quickly found myself envying the rest of the group walking on the road.

I was expecting to go straight down the hill toward the compound, but Critter jogged, in a roundabout way. When I asked him why, he pointed down hill to a spot I couldn't see due to the undulation of the steep decline.

"There's a large patch of rhododendron bushes that's pretty much impossible to pass through."

"How do you know? Were you here before?" I asked, keeping my voice loud enough to be heard over the crunching leaves beneath my boots but quiet enough not to echo through the valley below.

"No."

"Then how do you know?" I asked.

He opened his mouth to answer, looked around for a moment, and then he looked at me and said, "It's hard to explain. The smell, the lay of the land, I don't know. I just know."

He turned away from me and ran, continuing to lead our way down into the valley.

Despite the rough land, Critter and I jogged at a good pace. Our speed increased as the gravity of the decline continued to pull us. Critter wanted to get there long before Bryan's crew did so that we could find a good spot to launch a surprise attack from the flank if things went south for Bryan and our tribe.

Due to the vegetation and topography changes, I soon had no idea where we were or where we were heading due to the seemingly erratic nature of Critter's path. I caught no further sight of the compound below nor the rock formation that had caught Bryan's eye. I scolded myself for not paying attention to the details of the craggy spires of the mountain peaks that I could have used as reference points. If Critter was taken out and killed somehow, I feared I could never find my way out to safety by myself.

After thirty minutes of running mostly downhill, I guessed that we were nearing the bottom of the valley. Despite the lack of leaves, the trunks of the trees obscured my vision beyond fifty meters. Critter raised a hand and we slowed to walk. The ground leveled out, relative to the rest of the area.

After a few minutes of walking in a combat crouch, he raised his hand at his head level and closed his fist. I came to a stop about ten meters behind him.

"Breathe," he said quietly.

I let out a pent up breath.

He kept his head facing forward and without looking at me, waved me to him. I went to him and saw that we were on the edge of the forest. A small grassy area separated us from the walled compound. At the backdoor of the complex, I realized the compound was much larger than it appeared from the high vantage point.

I was captured with awe not just with its size and formability, but only a week ago, if someone told me that I would be stalking an enemy compound preparing for a counter attack or ambush, I would have laughed at them. Back then, I had just been an out of work journalist in the Safe Zone. Now... All I could say was, "Wow," to myself.

Critter silently pointed above at the lower portion of the mountain and I saw Bryan leading his warriors down the road. They appeared to be the size of ants, and I guessed that they were about ten minutes away. They looked friendly enough in their approach. A week ago I would have assumed they were out for war based on the fact they were armed for one, but everyone who wasn't a zombie was armed to the hilt in the Forbidden Zone. What determined belligerence was more of what was presented on the face, the tension in the body, and actions of the armed person. Bryan's group looked as friendly as you could get. Their walk was casual and they stood straight, tall, and proud, rather than hunched with anticipation, aggression, and fear of a confrontation. Their swords were in their scabbards, rifles strapped to their shoulders. If a weapon was held in the hands rather than holstered it was held without aggressive intent, rifle barrels aimed and sword tips pointed at the ground.

"Stay still," Critter ordered as he pointed at two far off drones in the sky. Their focus however was on Bryan and his men. I slowly looked around and could see no other drones. I guessed that Critter and I had the advantage of surprise.

"What now?" I whispered.

"We wait."

"For what?"

"We shall see for what. I currently have no agenda other than to watch Bryan's back," Critter replied in a bored tone. "What you and I do is entirely dependent on what Bryan and the inhabitants of this compound do."

I nodded, watched, and waited. I tried to relax as much as Critter. He had once told me to think of a spider calmly sitting in its web as it awaits a fly. I tried to clear my mind of worry. It wasn't working so I simply relaxed the muscles in my face, including my tongue, and shoulders and pretended to be relaxed. That kind of helped. Critter had told me that to hold tension in those muscles of anxiety simply wasted energy and gave away a person's intent. Tensing those muscles also triggered a release of adrenaline, which always over inundated my body with nervousness.

I watched as Bryan and crew disappeared in an undulation of the landscape and reappeared five minutes later only a few hundred meters away.

Critter swore.

I followed the direction in which he looked and swore as well. Behind a fold of land, away from Bryan's line of sight, I watched a large gaggle of zombies armed with long blades slowly move into ranks from the enormous garage. The zombies outnumbered our crew five to one and had surprise on their side. Bryan wouldn't have time to form the men and women into defensive ranks because they would not see where the zombies were hidden until they were right on top of them. We had killed off thousands a week ago, but these armed zombies could probably wipe out our ranks, easily in a head to head match, especially if they ambushed us.

"OK," Critter growled. "Get ready to attack."

"The zombies?"

"No. They're merely the fist. We're after the brains."

I could see Critter breathing fuller, deeper, but steady and relaxed to ready himself for combat. I copied him, inhaling through the nose and exhaling through the mouth.

"Let's go. Don't be seen," he directed.

"OK."

Critter took off in a sprint toward the wall and scaled it easily as a monkey and disappeared over the top. I struggled to make it up and fell down the other side with a plop. I stood up and looked for Critter but couldn't see him. I wondered if he rushed into the backdoor without me.

"Psst!" I heard him hiss from somewhere.

I looked up and saw him on a sloped first story roof over the brick house. He waved me to him. I ran to the house as he started to climb up a gutter toward the roof. I was out of breath as I started to climb up to join him and feared that I wouldn't make it up. Around the side, I saw the zombie army lining up in formation and ready to move against my tribe. That helped to power my muscles, but I feared that I was too late.

| 6 |

Bryan had just marched his troops up the last undulation and looked ahead to the compound's wall, now a mere fifty meters in front of them. As they came over the rise, the full expanse of the compound rose before him, but the fully formed zombie bot formation lay hidden behind the protective walls that ringed the house. On a second floor balcony of the building, Bryan saw a thin, diminutive man who moved with an agility that bespoke of hidden strength in his wiry limbs. The white coat he wore weakly fluttered in the lazy breeze. A laptop computer rested on the railing in front of the man as he looked up over his spectacles as if mildly irritated by the disturbance of the approaching warriors. A solid eight foot high opaque steel wall loomed above them and separated the warriors from the house. Bryan stopped his contingent in front of a large closed gate in the wall.

"Good morning, sir," Bryan yelled loud enough to be heard, but not threatening. He waved a hand as if greeting a friendly neighbor. "It's turned out to be a lovely day. For a while, I never thought that the snow would melt."

"Get out of here or you shall surely die," the scientist yelled dramatically in a high, nasally voice without looking up from his computer..

Despite Bryan's friendly demeanor, the Mountain Warriors behind him milled nervously.

Bryan chuckled at the bluntness, "That's a harsh way to address a neighbor out on a friendly visit."

"Friendly? You and your men killed my precious pets, my guardians," he replied in a calm and reasonably sounding tone. There was more than a touch of arrogance in his inflection.

Again Bryan laughed, more because he had no other response. "So those were your zombie bots?"

"Why do you laugh?" asked the scientist as he looked up sharply from his computer.

Bryan's laughter ceased and he was deadly serious in his reply. "You are aware that your precious pets are zombies that are wired and armed to kill anyone in their path, correct? In fact they displaced a village that attacked ours. People have died today because of you and your 'pets.'"

"I have monitored the situation. I believe that no one from your group has died. Now quit complaining and wasting my time. Be gone," said the scientist as he looked back at his laptop, muttering to himself as if the conversation was over.

As the silence wore on, Bryan looked at his warriors, slightly confused. Tomas shrugged his shoulders in reply. Bryan looked around with distant, but searching eyes and took in an uncertain breath. He wondered how to deal with a lone unhinged man. Despite the solitary presence, Bryan had been around enough in the Forbidden Zone to be aware that not everything was as it first appeared and that when a situation seemed harmless, death was just on the other side of the door or a wall in this case.

Bryan looked back to his tribe who looked back to him expectantly for leadership. He took in a sharp inhalation and said to the scientist, "Listen, many of our group could have died from the two attacks this morning, from the zombie bots themselves, and the displaced tribe, earlier. Second, because of you, I had to kill a few men this morning to defend those I love. That is not something that sits lightly on my psyche."

"Yeah, yeah, yeah. Such melodrama," the scientist scoffed with a snicker.

Bryan blew out some air, demonstrating his loss of patience, "What the hell is the matter with you?" Bryan glared at him with a stare that had caused people much larger than him to back down as he awaited a reply.

The scientist ignored him and typed something into the laptop. Then tossed his head back in a showy laugh. It seemed like he purposely tried to sound like the typical mad scientist from archaic movies but his voice was almost too high pitched and nasally to be taken seriously. However, Bryan had no time to mock. Suddenly the Mountain Warriors tensed as they heard an electronic solenoid click in the gate, as ominous as the sound of a gun being cocked. They nervously looked around as the gate gave a quiet metallic whine as if ready to move.

Bryan and then the others slowly stepped back in anticipation of the gate opening outward. However they leapt back suddenly as the eight foot high solid steel gate collapsed right where they had been standing a split second before. A platoon of zombies immediately marched at them over the fallen gate.

Bryan's warriors were caught flat footed and outnumbered. The zombie bots approached within ten feet of their position. The zombies had their arms cocked back with swords and were growling from their bared teeth. Bryan looked around in panic as his brain took in the threat that rushed at him. Within a split second a plan took hold, the confusion left his eyes, and he issued his orders with surety and authority.

"Follow me! Scott, cover us with the shield!" he ordered and began to run straight at the enemy formation over the fallen gate. His warriors followed as Bryan ignored the zombies and sprinted around them, toward the scientist on the balcony. Using a police shield, Scott slammed his bulk into the zombie formation, knocking a few over and restraining their attack long enough for the Mountain Warrior fighters to slip by into the walled yard. Then he dropped the shield and ran with the others toward the balcony.

The scientist was taken by surprise at the bold and sudden action and didn't have time to turn the formation to fight the Mountain Warriors as they ran through the gap between the zombies and the upright section of the wall.

The speed that Bryan launched himself with could have easily propelled him onto the balcony to attack the white-coated man at the controls, but the scientist laughed again.

Before Bryan could start his rush and ascent, another platoon of zombie bots marched in front of the Mountain Warriors from around the corner of the house. The scientist on the balcony pressed a few buttons and the zombies disbursed and reverted to their natural savage behavior. They broke formation. As the zombie bots charged with their swords and hatchets raised and swinging in a violent fury, their fangs sought the soft, warm necks of Mountain Warriors.

Bryan and his warriors were surrounded. They fought fiercely, slicing down the evil remnants of humanity but they were getting compacted together from the sheer press of the numbers from both sides.

In the heat of the fight Bryan didn't have the room or time to clear the rifle that was strapped to his back. Grimly, he looked up to the balcony trying to judge the distance for throwing one of his swords at the scientist. He was just at the end of his range of power and accuracy, but Bryan instinctively wanted to take out the brains of the zombie army. He had no other hope. His people were cornered, restricted and outnumbered. He didn't want to lose his sword while under attack, but he felt that he needed to take the only chance he had. There was little hope in him as he reared his arm back to throw, but he kept his sword gripped firmly in his calloused hand, as he watched the scientist. Bryan hardly believed his eyes.

***

I followed behind Critter across the roof of the fortress. Down below, the zombies surrounded our tribe. I watched Critter sheath his sword and draw a handgun. He then leapt down to the balcony, landing behind the scientist with the gun to his head.

Contrary to his panther-like movements, I more of scrambled down from the roof than jumped, but nonetheless, I supplied some back up for Critter.

"Call off your preciouses, geek." Critter growled as he ordered the scientist. Critter's handgun poked at the man's head. I held my handgun pointed at the scientist as well.

The scientist let off a whine like a spoiled toddler being deprived of pulling his sister's hair, but he pressed a few buttons on his computer and the zombies backed off and reformed into stoic motionless ranks as they awaited further commands.

The mad scientist screamed as Bryan's men attacked the compliant zombies. It was a slaughter as the zombie bots stood still with the order to attack canceled.

"I will destroy this whole place including all of you if you don't call off your dogs!" the scientist screamed at Critter. "This place is wired with explosives! All I need is but to hit a button on this computer. Call off your dogs now," the scientist screamed with desperation at Critter.

Critter yelled at Bryan and his warriors, "Back off, my friends!"

I was always surprised how loudly the usually quiet Critter could bark an order. His voice pierced the battle fog that drove the bloodlust of the fighters.

"Form into ranks, Warriors, and honor the truce," he called.

Bryan's men and women relented of the attack and formed into ranks with Bryan at the head. In this formation they were all but impervious to a zombie attack, natural fatigue from a prolonged conflict was the only weakness.

"Let them in," Critter ordered the mad scientist. "We just want to talk."

"Oh," he whined again. "Are they housebroken?"

"Better than your pets. Now let them in or you lose your head," Critter commanded as he pushed his gun's barrel against the scientist's skull.

"Anything for the famed 'Mountain Warriors,'" the scientist answered in an odd sing-song voice with sarcasm coloring his tone. For someone we just met, he seemed too familiar for our comfort with the title "Mountain Warriors." He then hummed a cheesy guitar riff, and ended it with a giggle as if he was the only one in on an inside joke. He pressed a few keys on his computer. In response, most of the zombies marched backwards letting the Mountain Warriors walk past them to the house. A contingent of zombies remained behind, standing ramrod straight in formation, awaiting electronic orders.

The Mountain Warriors behind Bryan still had their bloody swords at the ready as they walked within a few feet of the slavering mouths of fleshy automatons. The men and women maintained their discipline, but I could see the tension in their faces and bodies.

The scientist led Critter and me off the balcony through a sliding glass door, into the second story room lined with bookcases and with gadgets and gear stacked to the ceiling. We exited the room onto a landing overlooking the first floor with a vaulted ceiling. We walked to the staircase and started to descend to meet the rest of the tribe at the front door. However, I stopped on the second step from the top as the contents of the first floor room held me in awe.

There was not a single decoration. The walls were lined with bookshelves, gear, and experiments. Everything was strictly for a utilitarian purpose, most of it appeared to be (at least to me) arcane scientific equipment and computers from various dates but mostly looking sleeker than the latest technology that I was aware of. There were various machines whose purposes I could not guess, some had robotic arms with humanlike hands that wielded weapons including blades and guns as well as scientific gadgets. There was a plethora of chemistry equipment. Measuring containers for liquids and devices for weighing the many colorful powders and potions that lined the walls on the bookcases.

On the wall opposite from the chemistry equipment was a massive shelf full of all kinds of biological experiments. There were dried mummy-like human bodies in various stages of dissection. The head of a once beautiful woman in a gallon jar of formaldehyde looked at me with long dead eyes and a mouth wide open as if in a scream. The terror I felt while looking at the head went beyond mere morbid horror. Something about the woman's head still held a hint of vitality. I swear that I saw the eyes subtly following my movements. I also saw other large jars of animals and human remains preserved in jaundice yellowed liquids. Some specimens seemed to be a hybrid mix of human and animal.

As I looked over the place, I got the feeling that the scientist wasn't a jack of all scientific trades but rather a master of them all. His work blended biology, chemistry, computer/electronics, as fluently as the Spanish and English languages blended on the Texan/Mexican border.

I realized this room was his whole life. He even lived in there. His personal area had no clear boundaries between his work and leisure space. The scientific equipment mixed freely with his few personal items. A small cot was stashed in the corner with a wool blanket and a single pillow, but a couple laptop computers, a few bare circuit boards, and wires took up most of his sleeping space. Some food stewed in a beaker above a Bunsen Burner set on a low simmer. The coffee maker was the only thing from his life that was uncluttered with his work.

The entire place was lit by electricity. Oddly, in a land of extreme scarcity, there seemed to be no attempt to conserve the rare energy, so I guessed he had a large supply from hydraulic, solar, and/or wind. I had seen some solar panels and wind turbines on the roof and we had passed a dam on the creek that looked like it had turbines under the water's current.

We reached the bottom of the stairs as Bryan opened the door and entered from the opposite side. Bryan looked like he was about to charge and slice the scientist when he saw him.

"Relax," said Critter, in his emotionally detached voice.

With the full crew inside surrounding the scientist, Critter put his handgun away in his appendix holster.

The scientist did not seem to realize the tension in the air. His smile beamed like a star struck fan as he approached Bryan.

"Ah Bryan! I have been looking forward to meeting you," said the scientist as if they were old buddies. "How's your three kids, I might add?"

Bryan stopped in a moment of shock. There was no recognition on his face as he studied the scientist who was way too familiar with him.

The scientist waved a dismissive hand and said. "You do not need to answer, I have seen that they are all fine. They are descending down the opposite ridge top to the river as we speak."

Bryan tensed like a coil ready to spring. Then he sighed and asked, "What's your game?"

"Really nothing, other than perhaps an autograph from the second in command of the infamous 'Mountain Warrior,'" he sang Mountain Warriors as if it was a famous cheesy jingle in a commercial. Then he sang, "The Mountain Warriors!" in a voice dripping with sarcasm and added a guitar riff, "The Mountain Warriors, dun dun dun," he then laughed in his high pitched, nasal voice.

The way he spoke with familiarity among us and laughed as if he expected us to join in his joke caused a pause in all of us. His demeanor unsettled us as we looked around the tribe. He should have been terrified, surrounded by our fiercest warriors who scowled in a foul mood. Each of us made eye contact with each other to see if anyone in our group was in on the joke. All of us were equally perplexed.

"But what I would really like is to meet your wife, the voluminous Anna," he said, holding his hands suggestively before his chest.

Bryan sheathed his sword with anger and clenched his fists. It actually inspired fear in us because the way he put away his sword suggested that he was ready to tear the scientist apart with his bare hands. Bryan walked forward and a cloud of his anger almost physically enveloped the room. The very atmosphere seemed to compress as he clenched his fists.

The scientist smiled and walked up to Bryan unperturbed. He reached forward as if expecting to shake Bryan's hand, "By the way, I'm Dexter. You can call me Professor Dext."

Bryan reached to grab the scientist by his skinny neck. However, the little guy stepped to the side and with a wrist lock wrenched Bryan's arm with one hand and threw him over his back into a table that crashed beneath his weight. The papers on the table flew everywhere.

Bryan cried out more in surprise than pain as he slammed to the floor and rolled to his feet into a standing position ready for war.

Scott immediately grabbed Dexter from behind in a full nelson but somehow the little guy seemed to shimmy his way out and threw Scott's big bulk over his shoulder and onto the floor. Air burst from Scott's lips in a scream of shock and pain. Critter grabbed Dexter and placed him in a standing armbar that he had taught me the day before. When Critter did that to me, I thought he was going to break my arm. However, Dext rolled his wiry arm and shoulder, dropped his body to the floor, and rolled out of the arm lock on the ground. He sprang to his feet like an acrobat reversing the hold on Critter. Bryan then tried to wrestle him but the little guy was like an eel and rolled away. He did a combination of jumps, rolls, and ran through four or five grasping people before he did three somersaults in a row and rolled under a table by the wall, disappearing.

"What the hell?" yelled Scott. "I swear that guy must dress up like Spiderman and save the world on the weekends."

Robert shook his head no and said, "More like dressing like the Riddler and destroying the world."

Whatever," said Scott. "He moves like a greased cat with lightning shooting out its butt."

I didn't spend any time trying to figure out Scott's weird comparison.

Critter approached the table with his handgun leading the way. He squatted and looked under, swearing.

I squatted next to Critter, looked and saw a large entrance to a pipe that was about mid thigh in height at the floor level. It was just the perfect size for Dext to roll through. He was long gone into the darkness below. We listened and could hear nothing echoing up from the blackened maw of the passage.

"Holy Jiminy!" Scott swore. "I ain't taking my fatass through that. You're skinny Eric," He laughed as he pushed me at the hole. "How 'bout you go down there and bring him back."

I tensed against his hand. A flash of a giant spider with a clown face from a Steven King novel sitting at the bottom shot through my mind. The fear went beyond fiction into what was a real horror of flesh and supernatural. I drew my fist back instinctively to punch him.

Scott laughed at my jumpiness and stepped back, "Calm down, brother. You might have fun down there. You never know until you try. Can't be any worse than getting jiggy with a vampire chick."

"Leave him, Scott," Critter ordered. "None of us are going into that pit to hell. There could be a legion of those zombie bots to take us out one by one as we emerge from the pipe."

"Or a deadly gas," Scott said as he farted.

"Hell," said Critter as he pushed Scott away from himself. "I'd rather follow Mad Poindexter than wait for that fart to take effect."

"I'm quite proud of my hang time," said Scott.

"Shut up," muttered Bryan, broodingly quiet as his eyes stared off into space.

We all stepped away from the pipe as well as the evil mist that Scott had left in his wake as it started to permeate the area.

"What now?" asked Critter.

Bryan looked around the great laboratory. "Let's see what we have here. Be careful of booby traps."

Everyone nodded and started to glance around the room as if deciding what to do first.

"I want to see who this guy is and what he was up to," Bryan said, looking lost in thought. "We need to know if he's acting alone or if he's with somebody else. Maybe the Lowboys, The Specter, or even Governor Hildebrande's government?" Bryan pointed at a wall of video screens that relayed hidden camera and drone footage. "I have a suspicion that the drones aren't his but rather he has hacked into or was given access to the government's apparatus. He knows a lot about us, so maybe we can tap into some answers ourselves. Let's explore and see what we can find, but be careful."

"What about his threat to blow up the entire house," Tomas asked.

"I don't think that he would destroy his work," Bryan said. Then he shrugged and added with grim humor, "If he does, it'll be the quickest, most painless death that one could ask for in the Forbidden Zone."

Robert walked over to the coffee maker with excitement on his young face. Dexter had bags of various gourmet coffees which were always a treat in the Forbidden Zone.

Scott joked, "Careful, son. That coffee maker is probably some secret space age ninja weapon."

The brilliant, but somewhat gullible teenager, was about to touch it. Wide eyed, Robert nervously stepped away from it as Scott laughed, pushed his way forward, and then started making some coffee.

I walked over to a laptop. I suspiciously looked over an office chair before plopping down in it at the computer. Although even the Lowboys didn't seem to have internet connections, I wasn't surprised to see that Dext had full access. The government had supposedly blocked any internet transmissions in the Forbidden Zone. I wasn't sure if Professor Dexter had overridden the block or if he was actually part of the government and was purposely given special privileges.

I was tempted to log into Facebook and say, "Hi," to my girlfriend Jennifer, but I really needed to work. We were surrounded by a literal army of zombies and I needed to focus on finding information. That was my real job as a journalist. Besides, Jennifer had sort of broken up with me before I was banished and I was now forever exiled from the Safe Zone. So in reality, we would most likely never see each other in person again, unless some major changes took place.

Before entering the Forbidden Zone—that term, Forbidden Zone, no longer sounded hokey to me now—I assumed all the tragedies were a catastrophically unfortunate accident, but an accident none-the-less. I believed that the high ranking officials took draconian measures with the best interest of the people in their mind, and my initial research was based on that premise. I wanted to see what was happening, but mostly I wanted to get the human perspective of day to day life rather than an expansive overview of politics, science, or conspiracy theory. Now, no one knew the difference between news, propaganda and conspiracy theories.

As my fingers flowed over the keyboard, I began to restart my research from a more conspiracy theorist's perspective. Unfortunately, on the internet, I could only access state approved articles that I was limited to back in Washington DC. After a few minutes of frustration, it dawned on me.

I looked at Dext's search history, then his bookmarks tab which was an odd mix of deep scientific research and outlandish and abhorrent pornography. I finally checked out his saved files. I swore as I was inundated with information. At first, I scrolled through the headlines. As a journalist myself, I was aware that most long winded articles tend to give no more information than the headline. Many links were shown that were deleted by some bureaucratic internet censors. I then found a treasure trove of articles of the deleted news stories that Dexter had screenshotted and saved. I then shut down the internet and strictly kept my search to Dexter's hard drive. I briefly skimmed some of his personal writings.

What I read was like the rants of the most outrageous ravings of a conspiracy theorist who long ago fell off the edge. His writings combined the latest scientific research with apocryphal writings of Revelation from the Bible, and occult writings of Von Juntz and Abdul Alhazred. Ancient texts that I was allowed to view when I attended journalism school at Miskatonic University. I saw references to the "one." To me it was obvious that the prophecies of the chosen one, the messiah of the Forbidden Zone, was indeed a creation of those in power. I skimmed through Dexter's writings and saw that he had schemes to siege this mantle for himself.

My eyes widened when I saw a file for "VAMPS." I clicked on it and a number of photos appeared. My heart skipped a beat and I felt sweat bead on my brow as I saw a photo of Abigail staring back at me from the screen. From his pictures, I could see he had quite a fetish for the vampiress. I looked at them, even in the still photos, her eyes were as expressive as when she hypnotized me in the past. There were so many more important things to look for beyond my silly infatuation with a woman who may be after my life, and who even through the photos seemed to have a spell over me. I felt that I could swim in the deep pools of her eyes and would almost gladly drown. The logical side of my mind was horrified at my fancies.

I skimmed more of Dexter's insane writings and could have shrugged it all off, except I recognized the names of people I personally knew such as my friend Tommy. I saw references to someone who had to be me, but no mention of my name. I saw my uncle's name, the governor of this fema sector and too many times I saw the phrase, "Hildebrande bloodline." Unfortunately it was written with such familiarity that I couldn't gather much other than they probably wanted to see how I would react to the vampiric virus.

I felt like I was finally on the brink of the answers of those questions that I could not even put to words just a day before, but my concentration was dashed. I found a video of Abigail, the vampiress, when she gave me the vampire's sword. She was supposed to kill me the prior evening in order to pass a test. She could have killed me then. Both times, I was hypnotized and placed under her spell. The video was uncannily blurred, but it totally had my attention. I strained my eyes to see if there was any malice on her face as she stood with her lips and bared fangs near my neck, but in the grainy video, I couldn't decipher her demeanor as I was at her mercy.

In the background of Dexter's laboratory, I heard Scott call Bryan to look at a computer screen. I was vaguely aware of hearing the cheesy jingle of "Mountain Warriors!" that Dexter had sung with the heavy metal guitar making a, "dun dun dun!" sound.

I should have paid more attention to what they were talking about, because it almost led to my death, but I was locked in my work. I assumed that they were seeing drone footage of themselves but did not realize the significance of them singing the song that Dexter had sung.

"Hey. There's a picture of me. Damn, I look good!" Scott, the goofy fat guy, boasted with a laugh.

This too should have captured my attention but I was studying a video that professionally combined the footage from my vest camera with that from a drone when Abigail confronted me in the woods alone. My jaw fell open as I realized that my footage and audio was transmitted. I had always believed that Tommy would have to pick up a chip with my video through a drone, but it seemed someone with internet reception could acquire it.

But my anger disappeared as I was captivated by the video. It was blurry. I wondered if Abigail's psionic abilities affected the electronic equipment. My eyes widened as I realized that the footage was when Abigail met me in the woods while I was alone just after relieving myself. It was when she hypnotized me and gave me the sword by placing it in my belt.

I gasped as I heard the words we spoke clear as a plucked guitar string. I was mesmerized as I saw myself in her trance. I saw myself standing there with my eyes closed as she calmly approached. In the video I was totally under her power. She glared at the drone, then her eyes softened as she placed her hand on my forehead and whispered.

"Eric. You are a good, strong man. You need to see that you are painfully naïve."

She looked so concerned for me. Her angelic heart was concealed by her vampiric black hooded robe.

I actually slapped myself across the face as I worried that I was falling under her spell simply from watching the video. My worried mind was suddenly inundated with wild suspicions of conspiracies. I wondered if I was purposely supposed to see this video so I would trust the vampiress. Was her concern for me in that video just a well acted scene on her part? It seemed far fetched, but the Forbidden Zone was loaded with so many insanities, I couldn't blame my suspicions of anything.

I watched the video as she placed the vampire sword and scabbard in my belt. She smiled. I was almost taken back to that moment as I sat there and touched the very hilt of that sword at my hip.

I wanted to see if they had the video of Bryan, Critter and me fighting the vampires at night. That moment was so full of confusion when we felt lost in a cloud of evil magic and illusion. We had attacked each other fully under the spell of the vampires. I wanted to see if the cameras and recording equipment picked up anything supernatural.

I didn't find that, but I froze in terror as I saw a green hued video taken late at night with night vision drones. I recognized our camp and then my tent. I saw a dark shadow at the edge of the camp. I blinked as I swore that I saw it move. It did move. It seemed to morph into a human-like form in a black hooded cloak as it crept closer to the communal campfire. It moved easily past the guards standing their post, and the sentries were oblivious to the black ghost-like apparition. I was sure the thing had them in a trance. As I watched the feline grace of the phantom's movement as it headed to my tent, I realized that it had to be Abigail. The dark figure stopped in front of the entrance to my tent. It lowered its hood, spilling her hair over her shoulders. She brushed it back and I saw Abigail's face. She ran her finger over my tarp as she looked like she was deeply considering something. Her eyes then sharply turned to the filming drone. Her vision bored into me from the computer screen as I watched.

As her brow furrowed with hatred at the camera, the picture warbled and then turned to static. The footage cut out completely. I sat looking at the computer for a few moments as I calmed the terror that had grown in my heart.

I rubbed my suddenly weary eyes for a moment before I clicked on other files. As I was locked into my research, I was mostly oblivious that everyone else was suddenly interested in a video on the other side of the room. I was unaware about its contents.

I looked up from the computer as I heard Critter's uncharacteristically loud voice boom in surprise. "What in the unholy hell?"

The men in the other room laughed raucously out of shock, but the outburst quickly calmed to reverential swearing.

"Da-yam. Lucky you, Bryan." I heard Scott swear in a joking manner. No one laughed, now. Not even Scott who was infamous for laughing louder than anyone at his own jokes.

Bryan cursed savagely causing my short hairs to stand as taut as the Marine Guard before the President. I heard the smash of a fist on a computer and the shattering of plastic and glass as the machine was knocked to the concrete floor. "Where is that dog?" Bryan raged.

For a moment, I felt sorry for whomever Bryan sought. Despite his usual agreeable nature, his anger could be swift, violent, and fatal.

Bryan dispersed his quiet woodsman's steps. I heard his heavy boot stomp headed in my direction. I stood and turned to see what caused the commotion as he loomed before me. His anger seemed to have grown both his bulk and stature as it seemed like he filled the entire room. His eyes were filled with homicidal fury.

Before I could ask who he was after, I realized his scorn was directed at me. His fingers flexed claw-like at my throat level as he pinned me with a glare that bespoke my murder. The fact that he held no weapon told me that whatever had enraged him had made him disregard training and sent him to an atavistic level of tooth and claw.

I backed up until the computer desk would not give another inch and it crashed beneath me.

A few people feebly attempted to hold Bryan back but failed as he raced at me. I don't think they tried either, they seemed to believe that his unbridled fury was righteous.

He lunged in a savage leap and locked his hands around my throat as he slammed into me like a tornado. His thumbs honed into my carotid arteries. I felt my blood pulse thundering under his pressure. The cessation of blood to my brain caused instant dizziness.

I could only croak as I tried to ask him, "Why?"

As the room rippled with my obscured vision, I distantly heard Scott say to me, "You really screwed up this time, Eric."

Then everything went black.

***

"No! No! No!" Tommy Laurens screamed, gripping his desk.

He stared helplessly into the screen of his laptop computer and watched the live video feed as Bryan choked out Eric. Tommy then felt an icy terror as Bryan looked over Eric's vest and then his eyes picked out and locked on a hidden camera.

Although they were separated by one hundred miles and an electrified barbed wire barrier, the intensity of Bryan's glare through the computer screen made Tommy feel like he was making direct eye contact with a killer inches from his face. He had seen Bryan kill many times from the drone footage in the past. This was the first time he felt the intensity of the warchief's homicidal stare. Tommy muttered, reminding himself that he was safely in his office.

From the way the footage tumbled as if he was looking into an operating clothes drier, Tommy could tell that Eric's body was getting turned over and searched. Whether he was dead or unconscious, Tommy could not tell, but if Eric lived, Tommy could tell by Bryan's murderous oaths that he wouldn't be alive much longer.

It looked like the vest with the four embedded cameras was removed and stuffed in a desk drawer. Tommy's computer went black and as silent as a profound abyss with the final sound of the drawer getting slammed shut.

Tommy then started clicking on drone footage from the area desperately trying to find something that could give him a status update on Eric's life, but nothing came through.

In a panic he grabbed his cell phone and called his right hand man.

"Yes," The Specter answered on the first ring from the Cavern of the Vampires, deep inside the quarantined Forbidden Zone.

"I need you to go to Dexter's fortress. Take some of the vamps with you. If Eric is still alive or can be saved, I want him turned into a vampire immediately!" Tommy had fought the idea earlier, but he figured that an undead Eric was better than a dead Eric.

"You got it," The Specter replied and hung up without saying anything else.

Tommy swore. Just last night, he was given an award for his documentary taken from the drone footage in the Forbidden Zone. People had seen the full effects of the zombie hordes, but last night at the awards show, he presented two episodes of his new Mountain Warriors series. It was seen through Eric's POV and the public instantly fell in love with Eric's presentation that showed the human aspect of the survivors. In the Forbidden Zone, Eric was as green as the average viewer in the Safe Zone. He was the perfect POV character, but in the last week, he had demonstrated a courageous change that gave the average Joe the feeling that he too could survive a zombie apocalypse. This was key, because so many people feared a breech in the wall. The series was literally an overnight success.

And now, Eric was most likely dead.

Tommy wondered if he could contact Byan in the odd chance that he might take Eric's mantle as the documentarian if Eric was indeed no more.

***

Abigail entered the cave of the vampires and removed her hood. She instinctively checked the sword and handgun at her hip. She had taken her time getting back and knew that she would catch hell for that and the fact that Eric was still human rather than a vampire.

She followed the crystal passage into the bowels of Shining Rock Mountain. Many fears and uncertainties turned over in her mind. Many of them conflicted with each other. She tried to push the worries aside as she had to focus on responses to anything that The Specter and Richard might throw at her.

With her mind in turmoil she walked past countless failed vampires. Their numbers had been increasing as vampires were biting and infecting humans. If the human victim didn't die, they usually lost their minds as they turned into vampires. Vampires should be using the sterile dagger to drain people without infecting them, she thought. No, she corrected herself, they should be consuming animals instead of people, like she was doing.

She ignored the faileds as some stared dumbly at her and seemed only capable of drooling on their cloaks. Others stared psychotically at her as if trying to determine if she was food or not, but they would not dare to touch a vampire of the inner circle. Just as she relaxed inside, one of them charged her suddenly with a horrifying screech. With its wild hair and unkempt appearance Abigail couldn't tell its gender. With a quick draw and flick of her sword, Abigail sliced through its neck. She stopped the slice just inches past its neck and with a twist and a thrust of her hips launched the point through its heart. The psychotic fires extinguished from its eyes and a dumb look of horror dawned on its face as it realized that it was dying.

Abigail withdrew her sword from the thing's chest and with two more quick flicks of her sword, wiped her blade clean on its robe before it hit the cavern's floor, dead. She guessed that it smelled the faint scent of the Mountain Warriors on her cloak.

"Take this thing to the pit," she ordered two other failed vampires who looked intelligent enough to follow the basic order.

The pit was a shaft that went deep into the Earth. Something down there ate any vampire that was thrown or went down there on its own volition.

To give herself a confident and in control appearance she quickened her pace and assumed a purposeful stride as she neared the communications room. She walked to a solid crystal wall without slowing. The quartzite wobbled and seemed to turn the consistency of gaseous liquid. She passed through as if it was merely smoke.

Her confidence fled as she stood face to face with five of the intelligent vampires and The Specter. They were dressed and armed, ready for war rather than asleep for the day in their chambers. Their eyes told her the story that she feared. She kept her hands away from her weaponry, but made plans to grasp her handgun quickly when needed.

She held her head up and looked back into The Specter's eyes. Through the skull faced-mask, his eyes didn't blink as his dark pupils glared at her.

As his mouth started to open, she blurted out, "I apologize for my tardiness. Eric's psionic abilities are powerful, but I believe that I may be able to crack it within a week and turn him. Which is better than the nine months it took to turn me," she said, holding her head high as she reminded them that she had flummoxed all of them in a task that was dumped solely on her shoulders.

"Quiet," The Specter growled.

Abigail was tempted to say something just to press his buttons but kept her peace. Everyone in the room was deadly serious.

When Abigail finally nodded her head in submission, The Specter said, "We have more pressing issues. Those idiots are destroying Dexter's army!"

Abigail repressed a smile as she forced her face to look innocent, "Who is destroying them?"

"Those Mountain Warriors! We need to leave now. When we arrive it's shoot or slash first and ask questions later. Dexter is to be protected at all costs. He is the only man alive who can rebuild the zombie bot army that has been decimated. Eric is a secondary concern, but he is to be killed to protect Dexter and his scientific work if needed. If Eric does fall into our hands alive, you, Abigail, are to bite him immediately. Senior Director Thomas Laurens has finally given the go ahead, not that we needed it."

"But what if Eric doesn't consent? He may go insane?" she protested.

"It doesn't matter! The games are over! Turn him!" he ordered. "Let's go!"

The other vampires took their eyes off of her and began to follow The Specter, as did she.

The Specter knew that Abigail was changed without consent. If a person did not willingly take the bite, they were usually overwhelmed with the sudden overload of extra sensory input. Even when willingly changed, it was terrifying as the human brain began receiving input from other brains and even electronic equipment. Many people died almost instantly of insanity. Those who did survive usually became either blood-crazed zombielike vampires or drooling idiots. In both cases these vampires were called faileds.

Abigail's case was a rarity. Instead of succumbing to hypnosis before her capture, the mind control that Richard attempted to use on her had the opposite effect. Her mind understood and adapted to it. In this way she was able to read their intentions and avoid their attacks.

When they finally caught her, it was only because she had an open fracture in a leg bone and was delirious with fever from the infection. As death scratched at her door, Richard delivered the bite as she was barely conscious, but she turned with very little problem. Eric's mind worked similarly. Abigail was sure that he would turn with no problem, even if he tried to fight it. However, she resisted turning him strictly based on her morals. She did not wish the vampiric life on anyone and was determined to find a cure for herself if there was one.

| 7 |

Light slowly seeped into my vision as my consciousness rippled in a void like I was swimming to the surface from the depths of an abysmal ocean. My eyelids burst open when Critter slapped my face pretty hard. The panic from having my circulation cut off from Bryan's attempt at my strangulation flooded me with anxiety. However, I saw concern in Critter's eyes as he looked into my own. I relaxed only a little as I realized that I was laying on my back on the hard tiled floor of the mad scientist's laboratory. I wasn't dead, yet, but neither was I out of the fire. Critter was only restoring order.

My instincts kicked in and I looked up and sought out Bryan. Scott and Tomas held his arms as another man stood in front with his hand on his chest. They kept him in place about ten feet from me. He didn't struggle against them, but I could tell by the snake-like coldness smoldering in the depths of his eyes that he was willing to bide his time until he could exact his revenge. I also noticed that the vest with my camera equipment was gone. All eyes focused on me.

As I sat up, I instinctively adjusted the ball cap with the remaining hidden camera. It had stayed on my head but was askew.

The concern left Critter's face when he saw that I wasn't injured. He was all business now. "Were you sent to spy on us?"

"What?" I asked.

"Don't play stupid!" Bryan growled, causing Scott to restrain him with a little more muscle.

Critter held a hand up towards Bryan and said, "He may be innocent. Let's hear his side before passing judgment." Critter only temporarily kept the peace. The tone of his voice was clear: If I didn't do a good job explaining, I would face the fatal wrath of our tribe.

"How did you send them your video?" Bryan demanded.

"I don't know what you are talking about," I protested feeling vulnerable in a sitting position as they towered over me like lions waiting to pounce. Their eyes were as hungry and piercing as vultures.

"Get up." Critter ordered.

I fearfully stood up expecting to be attacked as soon as I was standing upright. It seemed like some macho etiquette to have a man on his feet before killing him.

Instead Critter led me, with a hand tightly gripping my collar, to a computer. "Robert," he called. The young man was at his side and Critter directed him, "Get that video up."

Robert messed with the keyboard and started the video at the beginning. Next to the computer was a smashed screen where Bryan had evidently already vented some anger.

I watched as an episode started with Tommy dressed impeccably as usual. Before an audience, he soberly introduced the show called "The Mountain Warriors.". His cocky smart-assness was totally absent in his delivery. He had the same concern on his face as a talk show host of one of those trash TV shows when he's about to announce who the real father of the baby is after the DNA test. You see the compassion on the host's face but anyone with an ounce of intellect or true compassion knows that beneath the facial facade he's excited about the hell that is about to erupt on stage.

Tommy's presence was unneeded. I could tell he was there purely to stroke his own ego by being on nationally viewed video. He spoke with serious concern, but I couldn't hear his words. My mind was on my own fate.

"That guy is a real piece," said Scott.

"He is my best friend," I reluctantly admitted. I swore a curse at him and corrected myself. "That bastard was my best friend." I bitterly emphasized "was."

Scott laughed, "You couldn't see the grease and slime dripping off that guy? You gotta be the most dumb assed guy in the world, boy."

I barely heard Scott.

On screen, Tommy stepped away as the episode began to play.

I cringed as the intro song played. It was the same tune that Dexter had been singing. The song engaged the worst of all the latest trendy atrocities in modern music: distorted voice, cheesy keyboard effects, squealing guitar riffs. It was horrible. I was guessing it sounded hip now but ten years later in sober retrospect, I was sure that it would be seen for the ghastly musical creation that it was.

"The Mountain Warriors! Dun dun dun dun!" Scott obnoxiously sang along with the theme song as the screen showed a compilation of different people in the tribe fighting, hugging, and living the life on the edge.

I didn't hear the lyrics. I was too busy glancing over my shoulder. Bryan was shattered. The Mountain Warriors title was his baby. At one time he had run a fun week-long camping trip to hone survival, woodsman, and martial arts skills. It was a week of escape from the overbearing reality of modern life. Now it *was* life. The Mountain Warriors title was what the survivors of the camp now called themselves. Tommy had turned it into a cheesy jingle to a TV show that mocked the lives of Bryan's family and friends. It turned everything that Bryan loved into a silly thirty minute episodic reality show.

I felt that same anger burning in me. I nudged my way past Robert and fast-forwarded through the episode. I was on trial. I had to take control. I buzzed over parts as I realized Tommy's production crew had rearranged the order of what was shot. I was shocked at what was left out and how things were edited to create drama that wasn't there. They made it look at times like Critter was staring longingly towards Anna.

I recognized lines lifted from a conversation days before and then edited into a later conversation for even more drama. Discussions were changed so that when one person actually answered with a, "yes,' a, "no," from an unrelated conversation was spliced in.

The men saw through the deception. None of their anger was directed at each other but rather at who they saw as the deceiver who made the show possible, me.

I could almost sense the men tense up around me and I guess we were approaching what set Bryan off the most. We watched a scene I filmed of Bryan and Anna walking off into the woods together holding hands. To respect their privacy, I had cut off the bodycam footage when I realized what was going on. However the drone footage took over where I left off. I distantly heard Scott swear something that involved an intimate relationship between a grizzly bear and a rattlesnake.

The drone footage continued to show Bryan and Anna passionately kissing. Their hands roved over each other's bodies.

That was too much. Bryan's fist crashed through the table and he slammed the laptop shut as his wife's breasts were about to be exposed. He glared at me with a savage fury that told me he wished to hit me next with that same fist.

After the crashing echoes from the destroyed computer died down, I felt everyone's eyes on me again. As far as they were concerned, the evidence of my betrayal was laid out plain on stark video. I could think of nothing to say. I was as shocked as they were and still dizzy from getting choked out.

All I could do was plead my innocence beneath their stoney faces. I wasn't stupid. I knew exactly what had happened, now.

"Guys," I pleaded. "I didn't know the drones could pick up sound and conversations. When I was exiled, it was reported that they only had video recording abilities, not audio."

Bryan looked like a bomb set to detonate on me at any moment. Instead of a ticking clock, it was the color rising on his face. Critter placed a calming hand on Bryan's shoulder but pierced me with an executioner's stare.

"How did your buddy Tommy get your personal footage?" Critter demanded. Critter seemed to take control as Bryan quietly tried to regain his dominance over his stoked, fiery rage.

"He's not my buddy anymore," I replied.

"That's not what I asked," Critter shot right back.

"I think they get it on the live stream. Tommy told me that he would send a drone to pick up the chip with my footage. I was told that they had no access over the internet to my video." I shook my head sadly.

"Why did you assume that?" demanded Bryan.

"Because they have no access to the internet in the Forbidden Zone," I said.

"Are you that stupid?" Bryan screamed as the others held him back again. "How do you think they get access to the drones? Those in power obviously have their own connections to the internet. Dexter obviously has access!"

"Guys, please. This banishment happened so fast. I never had time to soberly consider everything." I was very close to breaking down as Bryan and his fifteen warriors stared at me with a homicidal fury that was seconds, or one stupid reply from me away from disaster.

I continued, "Everything I was told is a lie. Even worse, I repeated those lies to you believing they were the truth. I don't fault you for anything you do to me." I looked Bryan in the eyes and said, "Bryan, all of you, you've been like brothers to me. I'm sorry. I honestly didn't know. I feel like a jackass. I should have guessed what was going on. I should have known."

"So Tommy is probably seeing all this too?" asked Scott.

I looked at him confused. "I guess so."

Robert looked up from a computer screen. He had my vest with the hidden cameras embedded slung over his shoulder. He said, "Hell yeah he can. Even Dexter was tapped in. Check this out."

We could clearly see the room we were in on the computer's screen from my point of view.

"Damn it! It's this cap!" I swore. I threw it to the ground.

Just as I was about to stomp on the camera in the cap, Robert said, "Wait, place it back on your head."

I did so.

We gathered around the computer and gasped as we looked at the screen. I saw my POV on the computer screen. As I stepped back, the screen showed everyone's angry faces glaring at me.

"You're still secretly filming us!" Bryan accused.

Critter said, "We know that, Bryan. Let Eric finish."

"No! I didn't secretly film! You guys gave me permission to film! You knew I was filming!" I shot right back, standing my ground. If I showed these men weakness, I was sure that I was dead.

"But you have hidden body cams!" he shouted in my face.

I shouted right back, "Hell! Everyone has them these days! Don't be so naive! They were doing this even before you all were quarantined! Police had them for decades, journalists like me, people on the streets, car dash cams, everyone, everything has those damn cameras!"

I was waiting for Bryan to pounce on me with cat-like speed, but Scott pushed forward.

Scott said with his lopsided, smartassed grin, "So ole Tommy is seeing all this right now?" He looked at my hat searching for the imbedded cameras.

"We've already established that, Scott." I said.

"Of course the son of a bitch can!" Bryan shouted.

Scott laughed out loud, gave me the finger and yelled, "Hey Tommy, suck my toe fungus, asshole!" He gave my ball cap the finger. "Because," then he sang, "I'm a Mountain Warrior! Dun dun dun dun." He finished with an air guitar solo and a rockstar lead guitarist's pose.

I angrily took off the cap and held it in a tight fist like I was strangling Tommy.

Some of the men laughed at Scott.

I however was distraught and looked back to another computer screen. I had to occupy myself for fear that I would break down crying in front of them. I was betrayed, and in my stupidity, I betrayed others.

I watched Robert scroll down the videos. I gently nudged him aside and said, "I want to watch that one."

We watched an awards ceremony. Tommy walked on a stage offering a hand to Jennifer, my girlfriend, as she was in a fancy gown and helped her mount the stairs. I watched in dumb silence.

Jennifer stood beside Tommy looking so stunning, definitely an arm trophy. She gave a speech about how I was like a brother to her and how, despite my exile for my crimes, she hoped my debt to society could be repaid by my work in bringing the story of the survivors to life.

I sank into a chair and buried my face in my hands.

"Dagum she's cute," said Scott. "That your sister?"

I glared at him not knowing if he was being serious or still in smart ass mode. "My girlfriend." I said as Tommy and Jennifer exchanged a look that only people who are intimate exchange. His arm slid like a serpent around her slim waist.

Scott replied, "Eric. Well... I don't know how to break this to ya, but you're getting cuckolded, son."

I had been about to break down crying from the weight of despair and knowledge that I was a chump, but something in me exploded when Scott spoke. I shot to my feet and glared at him, "Well no kidding, jack!" I swore and kicked a desk, denting it. My foot hurt like hell, but I was too pissed off to show anything but rage. Everything in my life was a lie. Everything!

The men backed up. Including Bryan who had a touch of fear in his eyes. They reacted the same way they'd react when Bryan was in a rage. Looking back, I realize that I enjoyed the temporary power that I felt.

"Hey, calm down," said Bryan.

"Calm down? Go to hell! You tried to strangle me before you even heard my damn story." My rage propelled me toward him and Bryan actually stepped back.

It looked like Bryan was surprised by my rage. He opened his mouth and by the look in his eyes, I anticipated an apology from him, but suddenly the power went out in the house. The lights flashed out, but the computer screens stayed alight.

Krristie, the flame haired sniper who was stationed as a guard on the second floor balcony, called from upstairs at us, "Guys. The zombots are attempting to breach the building."

I saw a platoon of zombie bots march past the window. A solenoid clicked and the front door opened.

I turned and saw a line of zombies entering the back door as well as the front. I guessed that Dexter must have remotely opened them. I shouted a warning as they poured in running to catch us, their prey.

Then revulsion hit me as I watched a zombie crawl out of the pipe where Dexter had escaped through and disappeared in his roll. The way it inexorably headed towards me crawling from the darkness and then stood, followed by another and another was something from an abysmally deep, dark nightmare.

We were completely surrounded and inundated by the numbers. Just the sheer weight of them would crush us as they pushed in the room on us. We were too packed together to fight.

"Up the stairs," Bryan ordered.

We rushed back up the stairs. The man in front of me fell to the floor. Critter and I lifted him up and we made it to the landing with the monsters right behind us. I heard the screams of one of the men in our group getting devoured. The screams were deep in the mob of zombies and far from any chance at any rescue attempt. Sad to say, it was an everyman for himself in a headlong rush, but there was no choice.

We rushed up the stairs into the second story room where Critter and I had entered from the balcony, but the door wouldn't close behind us. It was electronically controlled from wherever Dexter was hiding.

Scott smashed through the drywall with a high stomp kick, and Robert disabled an electrical box inside the wall. Three men pushed on the heavy steel door, muscles bunching in their backs and arms. We all rushed into the room as the door closed. The zombies rushed up to the top of the stairs with mere inches behind us. A zombie's arm shot through the closing five inch opening as Scott shouldered into the door slamming it on the beast, crushing the arm. Bryan's sword descended in a flash, amputating the zombie's arm. The door slammed shut with finality as the stump was withdrawn and the severed arm thunked on the floor. The hand kept opening and closing in a fist.

"We're screwed," a wiry youth complained as he kicked the severed arm. He then carefully picked up the amputation by the sleeve and tossed it off the balcony. The zombies below rushed it with snapping teeth, but then ignored it when they smelled that it was rotted meat. They liked fresh living tissue.

"No, we're not screwed. Because," Scott said seriously. He paused until he had everyone's attention, and then he sang, "We're The Mountain Warriors, dun dun dun dun dun dun!" He continued on some long air guitar riff.

Most of us actually laughed. It was either laugh or cry and crying wasn't an option in this group.

"Who did we lose?" Bryan asked.

"Nick," someone who I didn't know well answered and all the silliness instantly ceased. "He fell and I-- I" the man stammered, "couldn't grab him in time. It was hopeless."

The room became somber. I didn't know Nick very well, but he had always been nice to me. I felt guilty because I had to struggle to remember what his face looked like. It was sad to think of how fleeting life could be.

"No time to dwell on that or we'll soon join him," Bryan yelled. "Get a barricade against the door, now!"

Two bookshelves and a heavy metal desk were moved to barricade the door as we moved with a sense of urgency. The zombies on the other side, pounded, clawed and howled at the door.

We were crowded in and trapped in the upstairs room that was about two times the size of a large master bedroom. It acted as a storage room for whatever wasn't working in the laboratory. It was mostly junk, but I saw Scott, Robert, and Tomas rummaging through the stuff looking for anything that might be of any help for escape. Tomas was hoping to find some sort of controller to possibly reign in the remote controlled zombies or even the drones that were wired with explosives. No one held out much hope. It was mostly pieces of burnt up electronic leftovers that anyone but a neurotic hoarder would throw away.

Scott yelled excitedly to all of us, "Hey, I got a way out of here!" He held up a self inflatable raft.

"Yeah, we can float away on your bullshit," Tomas said without any humor. That made it actually funny especially when Scott threw the deflated raft at him, but any chuckles that followed died quickly.

The outlook was grim. We were trapped up here. Our ammo was also low and we would lose people, friends and family, if we fought our way out. Having traveled light, we had just enough bullets for a quick firefight, nothing prolonged. Although all of us were in relatively great fighting shape, many, especially some of the older warriors or those with injuries, couldn't make a run for it as quickly. We didn't wish to go head to head with a zombie army, for fear of not just losing a member or two, but we also weren't one hundred percent sure of how much contact could result in succumbing to the zombie virus. Because of that, we preferred to avoid any contact with zombies even if we were sure that we could win the fight without any casualties.

The zombie bots, on the other hand, had time on their side. With the power out we no longer had running water. We had little food. The zombies were already dead and could wait us out indefinitely. Sitting in the bowl of the valley we worried about a sniper setting up and easily taking us out one by one over a few days without fear of reprisal.

I stood next to Critter and Bryan as they stayed in the recess of the balcony that overlooked the front to avoid potential sniper fire as they peeked out the sliding glass door. I had quickly realized that it was wise to stand wherever they instinctively stood and duck if they showed any inkling of making such a move. They usually had a reason for anything that they did.

I had taken off my hat with the recording equipment. I noticed that Robert brought up the vest with the cameras. The kid was interested in anything in electronics and actually studied it as a major in college before everything went to hell. He brought the vest with him up the stairs. Whether it was out of curiosity or it was just in his hand and came along for the ride, I didn't know. Tommy had given both the vest and the cap to me. The clothing had a total of five cameras that combined with instant computer editing to give a steady coherent stream no matter how bouncy. If I got out of this fortress alive, I vowed to burn the recording equipment and rely only on the old fashioned written word in my notebooks. I admit that I came here for fame, to make a name for myself. Now I just pursued the truth.

Bryan compressed his lips as he looked over the crowd of zombies beneath the balcony waiting for us to move out or a command from Dexter to try to storm the upstairs of the building. His eyes lit up as a drone flew low over the undead.

"I'll get us out of this mess," Bryan said with a wolfish grin.

He brought his AR-15 from his strap and placed the butt against his shoulder. I smiled as I knew that he would shoot out the drone. The drones were wired to explode if captured or shot. It would take out a big enough chunk of the zombies for us to jump off the balcony and rush through. We had escaped a few tight spots in the past with this technique. I knew it would work again, but as Bryan lifted his rifle to aim, the drone suddenly zipped upward and then zig zagged away.

Bryan cursed.

Robert said, "It looks like they're programmed to recognize when a firearm is trained on them."

"Baloney," Bryan said. He aimed again, but before his sites could lock on the drone, it took the same evasive measures. He tried a few more times, but it seemed that Robert was correct.

He cursed and raised his rifle to throw it against the floor, but stopped. He was too smart to ruin his rifle in a tantrum, but to see that the idea to smash his rifle even crossed his mind bespoke his anger and frustration. I was sure he'd kill a person before damaging his weapon. Especially a person who he viewed as a betrayer, such as myself.

"If we could just get word to the camp to send the rest of our fighters with the ammunition..." He let the words hang.

"Send me," said Critter. "Just fire enough rounds to blow a hole big enough through the zombie horde for me to slice my way through. You, Eric, Tomas, and I are the fastest men here. I can bring reinforcements in less than a few hours. Maybe less than that if they're still at the place where we left them."

"No," said Bryan. "You saved my neck from the rooftop. I'll return the favor. Also, as second in command, Adam will relent to my request for more ammo and warriors."

Critter nodded.

"I'll also bring Eric," said Bryan.

I did a double take with surprise. Not only for his requesting me, but also I worried about whether I was back in his good graces, or if he was going to kill me when we were alone in the forest.

"Don't look shocked," Bryan said. "You kept up with us on the run from the Lowboys and the vamps."

I shook my head. "I almost died."

"But you kept going. You sell yourself short. You are even stronger now."

I quickly swallowed my doubt.

"OK. I'm ready," I said grimly as I patted my swords, the handgun at my hip and Winchester rifle that I had strapped across my back.

"No, you're not," Bryan said sternly.

"What?" I asked not sure of what he was getting at. I had all my weapons and raw determination.

"Get your camera vest," he said. "They constantly film us with drones. They know our moves already."

"What?" I asked again. I guessed my explosive burst of rage had convinced him that I was honest and that I had been as duped as they were, but him telling me to wear my camera vest should have relaxed me, but it had the opposite effect and unsettled me even more.

"Just do what I say!" he ordered.

I did so, but I worried that he was taking me into the woods to kill me as a message to Tommy. If that was the case, that would give me a better chance, because he didn't have the rest of the tribe backing him up. Whether he completely forgave me or if he was simply pretending forgiveness to kill me on this adventure, I prepared myself for either one.

Bryan then looked at Robert. "Hold up," he said to the wiry teen. "You told me that you could disable the transmission from the cameras to Tommy."

"Yeah," Robert said as he looked over the vest. He grabbed his multitool clipped to his front pocket, opening a phillip's head screwdriver. He undid a small plastic plate that was hidden in a pocket and rubbed his chin and made a thoughtful, "hmmm," sound. He then worked with some of the wiring and then screwed the plate back on. He handed me the vest.

Robert looked at me and said, "I turned off the transmitter Eric. You'll record, but it won't go to your 'friend' Tommy anymore."

I nodded my thanks. Despite the backstabbing from Tommy, I realized that these guys were my true friends. My mission to record the truth was still intact.

As I was thinking that, a cell phone rang in a pile of junk. Everyone looked at it with trepidation except for Scott.

Scott picked it up and answered, "Vinny's Pizza delivery service. Would you like pepperoni or my sausage on your pie?"

As he listened his smart assed grin disappeared and he made an odd serious face. Then he looked at me speechless for a moment before saying, "It's for you, Eric."

"What the hell?" I said. I took the cell phone from him apprehensively, expecting some trap or at least one of Scott's quirky punchlines. The bright sounding voice on the phone shocked me to my core.

| 8 |

"Hey buddy. It's me Tommy!"

I was too stunned to say anything other than, "What?"

"Eric. Yeah. It's me, I need you to have that kid turn back on that transmission. We need your footage," he said.

I paused, speechless for a second before screaming, "Go screw yourself, you son of a bitch!"

"Now, Eric, I know you're mad, but-- "

"No shit, Watson!" I screamed our inside joke at him. I was sure that I gripped the phone with enough pressing force to crush it.

"Listen, we have a great thing going," he said in a salesman's pitch, seemingly oblivious to my raging mood.

"No, you have a great thing going! I'm screwed here, you son of a bitch!"

"Eric, listen. The public loves you and your tribe. You guys are becoming national celebrities. I'm working on getting you a reprieve. We may get you out of the Forbidden Zone in a short amount of time."

That caught my attention for a moment until I caught the eyes of my tribe mates. The phone's volume was all the way up and they could hear Tommy. They grimly watched me and I realized that I was still on trial.

"I am not leaving without the entire Mountain Warrior tribe, and I can't see you pulling that off," I shouted.

The warriors crowded tighter around me to ensure that they didn't miss anything.

"Trust me," he said.

"Ha!" I screamed more than laughed.

"We're working on it." There was a pause as my silence told him that I knew he was full of it. He again said, "Trust me."

I laughed bitterly as the Mountain Warriors stared at me curiously. "You stole my girlfriend," I said.

"Dude, you knew we had a thing for each other before she even met you."

"You're scum."

"Listen, I saved your life," Tommy said the absurdity in a reasonable tone.

I gasped at his audacity, "You ended my life!"

"You were wasting away in a bottle. I've seen what you've been writing for your documentation. Your life when I sent you into the Forbidden Zone was hopeless. Reread your description early on about, 'the cheap plastic decor in the bar aging faster than a bar hag's face' said it all. You were a male bar hag. You were killing yourself, becoming a wastoid. I gave you a reason to live. You always kick ass when the chips are down and you're kicking ass now, my friend, thanks to me."

"Bullshit! You've always been jealous of my connections, especially through my uncle."

"Yes," he agreed.

I thought what I delivered was an underhanded blow to him, but when he agreed with me, I was left speechless as he continued to happily talk in a thankful sounding voice. As he spoke I shifted nervously under the curious glares of the Mountain Warriors.

Tommy continued in my silence, "I admit I was jealous in the past, but I made it to where I am, because your uncle left some doors open for me that I, I," he emphasized, "powered through. On the other hand, he tried to drive you through those doors in a stretch limo, but you blew it because of your pride. You could have had twice the success that I have had, but you didn't want help. You acted like a spoiled brat. You had disdain for your connections. Well, now you have the challenge. Everything you have gained has been through your own sweat, your own muscle, your own brains. Before this, mediocrity was too lofty of a goal. Now, you are amazing, my friend."

I sighed. Despite the provocative backhands, Tommy had me pegged and I knew it, and he knew that I knew it, but it didn't excuse my banishment into the Forbidden Zone.

After a moment without me saying anything he said, "Listen man. I'm sorry about everything that's happened, but if you want to live, I suggest you kill that vampire chick next time you see her."

"Abigail?" I asked. The few Mountain Warriors who were looking in other directions immediately focused their attention back on me when I mentioned the vampire's name. I wished that I could turn down the volume. Tommy had gotten too personal and now he mentioned the vampiress who terrified even the toughest in the tribe.

"Yes. I've been resisting the science department's efforts to turn you."

"Turn me into what?"

I saw Bryan roll his eyes at my question. I looked away, wishing that I could walk to a more private space.

Tommy sighed like I was as big of an idiot as I felt. "Into a vampire," he said. "When I thought the Mountain Warriors were going to kill you, I thought that turning you was the only way that you could survive. I gave the final permission, not that they needed it. I acted rash."

"No kidding, jack!"

"That son of a bitch," the usually quiet Critter boomed. The others shifted around edgy for battle. Unfortunately, the phone was the only visible opposition.

I covered the phone and stepped away for more privacy. I shot the crowd around me a serious glare and they honored my desires. I didn't have any more privacy, but at least they weren't looking at me, nor did they follow me on my two step retreat.

Tommy continued, "I found out that if she doesn't turn you soon, they'll kill her. Currently she's resisting those orders, but in the end she will choose her own life."

"How do you know? She has a good heart," I said, feeling naive.

"Maybe, but she will eventually save herself. Even if it is an undead existence, it's still an existence. You need to kill her. She stalks your tent at night. You know it's true. You saw the video."

"No," I said.

"You'll come to your senses, but in the meantime, I need you to do me a quick favor."

"What's that," I asked hesitantly.

"Have that kid turn the transmissions on your body cams back on. I need--"

I had no hesitation when I yelled, "Go to hell, Tommy!" I realized the whole conversation was just to soften me up so I would turn the transmissions for the camera vest back on.

I threw the phone against the wall with all my strength. After the shattered pieces quit rocking and spinning on the floor, I looked at Bryan and said, "Let's go get the rest of the tribe."

***

From the balcony, Critter simultaneously pulled the cord and threw the self inflatable raft into the pack of zombies below us. It exploded with air and was fully inflated as it floated down and landed on the horde of undead below. A split second later Bryan and I flew off the balcony and landed on the raft causing the zombies beneath to collapse. The raft quickly started to deflate with a hiss of air as a zombie's sword penetrated the bottom of the raft. The sword slid up my leg and ripped my pants. My calf bled a little, but I had no time to dwell on that. I felt another long blade penetrate the raft but stopped at the steel shank of my boot.

With the loss of air, the raft was hard to keep balanced. Bryan and I jumped off the boat as the surrounding zombies started to close in.

Ahead, a wall of zombies stood armed in front of us. The zombie wall instantly began to collapse as Critter and the other warriors above opened with a barrage of gunfire from the balcony. I could hear the bullets whistling angrily just inches over my head. I prayed that their aim was steady.

Bryan and I charged the zombies slashing at them as the gunfire ceased. The gunfire didn't eliminate those directly in front of me but that's what our swords were for. Although armed with long blades, the zombies simply fought at an atavistic level and had no skill as they hacked.

I charged right behind Bryan. Without breaking stride he ran through four of them with his two blades swinging with deadly speed and accuracy, slicing through two necks at a time. I had to duck as a severed head flew at me. Following Bryan, I slashed two zombies myself, and then we were past them running at full speed for the hill. The horde started to follow, but although they could move fast, Bryan and I were much quicker.

Immediately after running out of the gate from the walled complex, a bullet kicked up dirt between Bryan and me. It was a lone distant shot. Our friends had ceased their fire. This was a sniper somewhere in the mountains above us.

A few more gunshots exploded in the distance. The impacts of the bullets into the ground around us seemed louder than the far away shots. In fact, I heard the impact a split second before I heard the distant discharge. This was because the bullets traveled faster than sound and the lead arrived ahead of the sound waves.

"Keep running, Eric! We're almost to the cover of the gulch." Bryan screamed over his shoulder. I followed as Bryan powered through the distance.

Another bullet smacked the dirt behind us, but a hell of a lot closer to me than the first, almost hitting the heel of my boot. I could feel the earth tremble beneath my sole from the impact. The shooter was quickly zeroing in on the range. We continued to run but would suddenly switch directions in a zigzag pattern. We heard the distance shots but had no idea where they were coming from. It's hard to pinpoint a distant sniper, especially when running for your life.

A few more shots slammed into the rutted and partially eroded dirt and gravel road around me.

We ran down a decline into a gulch and Bryan slowed to a jog. We were both breathing hard, totally winded, but resisted bending over in fatigue. We had sprinted uphill for almost a quarter of a mile.

"I'm about ninety percent sure where that bastard is shooting from," Bryan said in a ragged breath. "He's way out of range for my rifle," he said as he slapped the butt of his gun.

I nodded.

We continued at a light jog until we caught our wind and breathed much easier. He was pretty confident that the gulch gave us cover but we both instinctively kept our heads down.

"Let's go," he said.

He left the trail and kept some cover between us and where he suspected the sniper to be. We picked up the pace to a fast jog, and after about fifteen minutes, we reached the top of the ridge much quicker than I had expected.

Once we were on the relatively level ridgeline, we ran faster. We retraced the old buffalo/fire road back to where we had separated from our camp.

With the road leveling out, I caught my breath and went over what Tommy had said in the phone conversation. It annoyed me that he was correct. I had been wallowing in hopelessness and self-defeating, self-pity. Although I knew him exiling me here wasn't due to a bout of altruism on his part. However I had to agree that I had never felt more alive than I had in this last week in the Forbidden Zone. I had always felt under the weight of my Uncle's help and expectations. To be thrust in a situation where I lived solely, moment by moment on my wits and by my sword was truly enlivening.

I then thought of Abigail. I thought about our encounters when she took control of my mind in person. Seeing the video of her as a dark phantom lurking in the hills above our camp and stalking my tent, I feared that Tommy was correct that I would have to kill her. A part of me didn't want to. She had helped me and my friends in the past. We had a connection through her psionic abilities that she said was unique in its power. Her biting and infecting me was supposed to be a science experiment to see if the vampiric virus would intensify those psionic abilities through her viral variant.

But I never wanted to hide from the sun, or from humanity, only to seek camaradship with the abominations of the underworld and seek nutrients from the blood of the living. She had said that she would die before doing that to me, but would she? In the video I had seen her pause beside my tent. Did she consider biting me? Did she just want to talk? Even on the green and grainy night vision videos I could see confusion, a war waging in the depths of her eyes and soul.

If she was facing death if she didn't turn me, she could not simply defect to humanity. My tribe, for one, would never accept a vampiress among its members. No tribe would. The vampires were the most feared creatures in the Forbidden Zone. If I welcomed her into the camp, I would be exiled from the tribe in a land where I was already an exile. I could not see traveling in the Forbidden Zone with a vampiress as my only companion. She had even warned me not to approach her alone, especially at night.

I didn't fully make up my mind about how I would deal with her, but I steeled my nerves to be ready to kill her on our next encounter if necessary. I may have felt that I owed her my life, but a life as a vampire was not in the cards. I could never trust her completely. I didn't trust myself under her hypnotic power. If I didn't want to become a bloodsucker, I would have to kill her, I resolved.

| 9 |

Bryan expected our tribe to be long gone from the temporary camp on the ridgeline, and we were expecting to have to run another couple of miles to catch up with them.

However I was relieved when we arrived at the point where we defeated the first zombie army, where Bryan had led our separate team to the scientist's laboratory. We went off the road to avoid the decaying zombie bodies.

Looking ahead, I was surprised that there were still people there tending the fires and the meals. I felt a sense of relaxation and desired to slow to a walk with our goal in sight. However, despite our exhaustion, Bryan picked up the speed due to his sense of duty, and I found myself starting to fall behind, but I stayed close enough.

I entered the camp right behind Bryan. My vision blurred from exhaustion and sweat dripping from my brow. I couldn't see the faces of the people clearly, but I saw them stand up with a sudden sense of urgency and aggression towards us.

I heard someone curse savagely and proclaim. "That's Bryan!"

I wiped my brow and looked around the camp. It was only as we reached the center of the camp where I shared the omelet with Critter just a few hours before that we realized our deadly mistake. We now saw what was actually there rather than what we had expected to see. The camp was totally occupied by the tribe that we had soundly defeated this morning. The rest of our tribe was long gone. Our enemies surrounded us. Enemies who had their family members killed by Bryan himself just this morning.

"What the hell? It *is* Bryan!" someone yelled in confirmation.

The warriors of the Rat Man's army reached for their firearms and swords ready to fight. They were reenergized by the hatred from their humiliation and the meager food that we had left them.

The armed fighters around us swore in anger and disbelief. They clenched their fists as many repeated Bryan's name as if it was a curse. As much as they burned silently for revenge, I could see that no one suspected that the opposing warchief would stand before them in the middle of their camp so suddenly. The momentary shock was the sole reason we still breathed. In the silence, I could almost swear that I heard their fingers tightening around their swords and guns. Leather holsters creaked, knuckles cracked, and swords clanked and scuffed in scabbards during this calm before the certain storm.

Oddly, Bryan stood tall acting like everything went according to plan. I knew he controlled his breathing so as not to look exhausted. He confidently looked each person dead in the eyes. He nodded approvingly as if he expected to end up in their camp. I could almost hear him yelling at me to be confident, not to fake it, but to feel it. Indeed the people in the camp around us looked unsure of how to respond to Bryan's sudden appearance. I forced myself to stand erect and slowed my own breathing as well.

Bryan said with arrogance, "It's good to see you all here! I wasn't sure if you'd be strong enough to make it up the mountain. But I'm wondering why you losers would abandon the camp that we so graciously left you."

Inwardly I cringed as he insulted them. I saw the Rat Man stand with something that resembled confidence now that his tribe had the advantage. However, I could see some insecurity as he responded to Bryan. The Rat's shoulders haunched defensively as he tried to take control of the situation.

"Of course we left! When the snow melted, we discovered those rock walls weren't rock walls. They were dead zombies! As soon as the sun hit them they started to stink something fierce," the Rat Man said. "You didn't leave us any food and we were afraid that the gunfire from earlier would attract more zombies."

Bryan walked up to the communal fire and looked in the pot that was simmering some thick and sickly grayish brown gruel. He dipped the tip of his calloused finger into the mix and tasted it showing no sign of pain from the hot acorn porridge. He made a sour face and spat it out in disgust "This is chicken food! What kind of men feed this crap to their families? Your kids will grow to be as weak as you are."

The men of the camp had their faces slightly downcast, but at the last insult, their eyes blazed as they turned up and glared at Bryan angrily under stormy brows.

I stood strong beside him, but deep inside, I wondered what in the hell was Bryan doing going into the middle of a group he soundly defeated in battle just that morning and insulting them. He executed their leader, and now he boldly insulted their manhood. I wouldn't have taken such a tactic even if I had my own tribe standing protectively behind me. My instinct was to run away after mistakenly entering bad company, not to stir up more anger.

The people of the camp glared at him with growing resentment. Bryan and I were seconds from getting slashed to shreds. We were outnumbered fifty to one and the desire for vengeance now burned brighter in their eyes.

Bryan eyed the gruel with disgust and stepped to a nearby tent that was constructed with some of our discarded tarps and kept upright with a few saplings. It was shoddily put together. He lightly toed a support and it fell over. "Is this what you've become! A defeated tribe who runs from zombies and feeds off of our refuse and lives in discarded hovels of your conquerors?" Bryan spat again. It looked like he was trying to commit suicide and take me with him.

The Rat Man stepped angrily toward us and stopped ten feet away. He grabbed the handle of his machete at his hip but didn't draw it yet, "Are you insane? You come into a tribe that hates you and you insult us?" he stuttered with the shock of it all.

"No, no, no," said Bryan with a booming laugh. His chest expanded and he planted his hands on his hips, "I don't offer insults."

"What do you offer?" the Rat Man sounded as mystified as me.

"Redemption." Somehow that word caught their attention. After a pause Bryan continued. "You lost your leader this morning."

"Thanks to you!" the Rat Man challenged drawing his machete and pointed it at Bryan.

Bryan drew his sword as well but pointed it at the sky. He was vastly outnumbered and I was sure that a fight would be kept to swords. Gunfire would only draw more zombies and this tribe was running on fumes. They had no desire to run again at this moment.

"And you gained a better leader in me," Bryan proclaimed. "I defeated him fairly in one on one combat."

"You're not our leader! You're the enemy!" said the Rat.

"Have you picked a new leader yet, Rat Man? Since I killed your last leader, technically I still rule. Do you want to challenge me, Rat Man?" Bryan asked as he slowly advanced towards the Rat Man with a confident step. The tip of his sword suddenly pointed at the Rat's pinched face. The rest of the tribe stepped out of Bryan's way. So brazen was Bryan's movement and so thoroughly did he defeat them that morning, that no one took him up with his challenge, yet. Yes, they outnumbered us, but they all knew that Bryan would take out a few of them. No one wanted to be the first to fall before Bryan's sword, and right now his sword focused on only one man. The rest of the tribe seemed content with that.

"You're the enemy," The Rat said again as he nervously looked around to his tribe for support, but no one returned his eye contact.

"No. We, the living, are all brothers and sisters. Those undead are our mutual enemies, and together we can defeat them. Do you still challenge my leadership?"

Everyone looked down except Bryan, me, and the Rat Man.

After a moment the Rat Man backed up into a group of people. When he saw that no one would come to his aid, he slid his machete back into his scabbard with a hiss of steel on leather. "No, I don't."

Some other men stood up. Their hands on their yet undrawn swords. "What do you mean by redemption, Bryan?" someone asked from the crowd.

The tribe eyed us, weighing the odds, but still no one had any desire to be the first to meet their maker. They knew that no one in the tribe was anywhere near as good as their dead leader, Randall, who Bryan easily defeated, and we knew that too.

I didn't draw my sword, but I had my hand on the hilt and stood confidently at the ready. For all they knew, I was Bryan's equal. Personally, I considered myself average by the standards of the Forbidden Zone after a week of intense training and some of my training before entering, but in the moment, confidence and show was what was really winning the day.

Bryan smiled and nodded his head. I knew a lot was an act, but I knew Bryan well enough to know that this was the outcome he had hoped for. He announced boldly, "I come to offer you a supply of food that will last your tribe until the end of the winter and a chance to defeat the people who created the zombie army that drove you from your home, but you must submit to my rule, and I will lead you to live free, where your children will grow strong." Bryan's voice quieted in a way that everyone in the camp hung on his every word.

"Where is this place?" someone asked.

Bryan confidently replied as if in a riddle, "It is the place where I shall lead you. Are you interested? Do you want food? Do you want a safe place for your families to live?"

The warriors in the camp stood still and looked at each other for guidance, but they were all equally confused. They liked the promises that Bryan delivered but they were still wary.

"Well, don't look at each other. You have led each other to defeat so far. Will you follow me to victory?" Bryan shouted as he dramatically raised his sword toward the heavens.

The warriors of the camp nodded their heads. A few answered affirmatively.

I watched in amazement. I wouldn't call Bryan's action bold but rather brazen. I didn't believe that Bryan truly cared for this group. I was grateful that he plucked the two of us out of the frying pan, but I could not look at these people and pretend to want to save them. It was another reason why I wanted to leave the Mountain Warriors, but as far as the barbarous Forbidden Zone went, the Mountain Warriors were one of the more merciful and civil, but that wasn't saying much. And where did I have to go if I left?

"Are you sure you'll follow me to victory?" Bryan asked louder.

More people answered aloud or nodded their heads.

Having the Rat Man's tribe on a hook, Bryan finished reeling them in as he shouted in a voice that boomed across the hills. "Bullshit! I can't hear you."

"Yes, Bryan!" the men called out as they stood straighter.

"Louder! And raise your swords up high!" Bryan demanded with an energy that sparked an explosion in the crowd around him.

"Yes!" they shouted even louder, raising their swords with their voices.

"Then let's go. Leave the weaker behind, we shall return victorious by nightfall." Bryan said it with such fire and full faith that the whole tribe, including the noncombatants, were on their feet ready to storm the gates of hell at his lead if necessary. Hell, even I almost believed him.

If these people believed Bryan now, this area was ready to follow any tyrant who claimed to be the "One," that the Mountain Warriors joked about.

***

We retraced the trail along the ridge top as Bryan's new army followed us. He and I marched ahead a few paces. It took me about a mile of marching for my nerves to calm. I had yet to believe that we had survived going into the heart of the enemy's camp. Bryan however seemed unfazed by how close we came to getting shredded by their swords. In fact, he looked quite pleased with himself.

In the Rat Man's group, there were three times as many fighting men and women than with the remainder of our tribe who were probably at the destination, setting up their tents. So it worked out great. We were bringing back more fighters than expected, and as a bonus, no one in our tribe would have to risk their lives in the rescue attempt. Bryan had been worried that Adam wouldn't part with any more fighters. His realistic expectation was to get a few hundred rounds of bullets which would have been a heavy load to carry back. Also, Bryan was sure it would've been another few hours wasted to catch up with our tribe, and we probably wouldn't have returned to Dexter's fortress until the next day. Bryan tended to hate putting off a fight, especially leaving his friends to the terrors of the night if Abigail was correct that Dexter's work was under the protection of the vampires who ruled the night.

In the long term the plan would work out well. Any men the conquered tribe lost in the coming battle would be less who could attack us in the future, and Bryan was confident with the larger tribe that they could completely wipe out the zombie bot force. Another bonus would be if the Rat Man's tribe decided to stay in the valley of the mad scientist, there would be less chance of them wandering into our new territory.

"What if there's no food like you promised?" I asked Bryan in a whisper after looking behind to see if we were far enough ahead so as not to be overheard.

"There has to be plenty of food socked away somewhere. That crazy scientist has everything to survive a zombie apocalypse, even zombies," he added with an ironic smile. "He has to have a cache somewhere. If not, we'll slip out while the Rat Man's crew tries to find it, but I'm sure it's there. I'm also hoping to walk away with a few cases of MREs for our tribe as well. If there isn't a stockpile of food, we'll just change plans like I did when I came across this tribe instead of our own. There's always opportunity if the mind is sharp enough and fluid enough to see it. Only make a molehill into a mountain if it works to your advantage," Bryan said. He walked with a bit of a swagger. I guessed that if we weren't trying to maintain a degree of silence he would most likely have been whistling a carefree tune.

I had to admire him despite the fact that I thought our dealings with the Rat Man's army was less than honest. Bryan could maintain his confidence even in the worst situations. Where I was faking it, I thoroughly believe that he felt his own power. I vowed to master that one day, while keeping my integrity.

He turned to me and said, "I was impressed how you maintained your cool when we arrived in the camp. You had no idea what my strategy was until we were in the thick of it, and you played along well."

"I had no choice," I said. "What would you have done if they attacked us? We were surrounded."

"I would have had to kick as much ass as possible until they were pacified," he shrugged as if it were no sweat.

"But they had both of us surrounded," I pointed out the obvious.

"You had my back."

"Me?" I laughed.

"Yes, you. You discount yourself too quickly. Other than the leader I killed earlier this morning, I would put you up against any man in that group. I would even put you up against two or more at once."

His confidence in me was shocking. I protested, "But I've only been training for a week. They've been carrying swords and machetes for two years."

"Exactly. The key words are training versus carrying. You had training before coming into the Forbidden Zone and have been training about twelve hours a day and have some actual fights under your belt. Most of the Rat Man's tribe has been carrying a sword and gun like a talisman that will magically appear in their hands and defend them when needed. They wouldn't know what to do with a sword anymore than a six year old boy knows what his cock is for. Besides, you do have one of the best teachers in the Forbidden Zone, if I do say so myself."

He could see my doubt in myself. He continued, "I bet you were a clumsy teenager. You participated in athletics but never excelled. You busted your ass more than others, but never were as good as those natural athletes who never worked that hard. Everything you did achieve was paid for by sweat."

I nodded.

"You're a late bloomer. Your body has finally figured itself out. I've seen you doing things you never thought were possible, and you have light years left to travel." He patted me on the shoulder. "This is your time to shine. You're an ass kicker. Be it, brother! I didn't feel comfortable in my body until a few years ago. Once you master yourself, mastering a tribe is easy."

It dawned on me that Tommy and I were a lot alike. I had to struggle athletically against people with natural skill, but that was paying off now. Tommy on the other hand was a bit socially awkward when he was younger. Where I could have had a good career almost handed to me, I took my uncle's help for granted and even despised it. Now Tommy's hard work was paying off. I digested this for a while, as we quick-marched back, and I determined never to quit in any endeavor I started. There is always a payday if you live long enough to see it.

I thought about what Bryan had said, "Once you master yourself, mastering a tribe is easy." That was a common thread whether in religion or philosophy.

Bryan saw the firm resolve in my eyes, nodded and went back to quietly leading the march. A quiet song whistled upon his lips. For the first time in my life I could see myself leading like Bryan, in the distant future, of course. He had mastered his calm when he came upon the other tribe and was subsequently able to master them. This dream of self mastery wasn't a dream that I would run from once it took shape in reality, but I actually saw my path ahead as clear as the path that we threaded upon now in the warm winter thaw.

I looked behind me and saw the ragged army trailing us. They looked away, avoiding my eye contact. I wasn't arrogant enough to believe that it was purely me who intimidated them, but I was associated with a tribe of warriors, yes the Mountain Warriors, who despite our small numbers ruled them. Despite the cheesy jingle of Tommy's show, yes, I was proud of my tribe and my place in it. Still, I wasn't sure how long I could stay. They, Bryan in particular, almost killed me earlier today. I needed not to forget that.

To think that Bryan thought I could lead also set my mind in motion that he probably didn't anticipate. I might have to plan on surviving without them. I vowed to put all my energy into learning, because I would not tolerate anyone placing their hands on me again like Bryan had earlier. I would either fight or just walk away. I just hoped when I left, it was on friendly terms and not a life and death struggle.

***

We arrived at the top of the ridgeline overlooking the valley and gazed down from the same spot where Critter and I had originally split up from the group to sneak up from behind the fortress earlier that day.

The Mountain Warriors had stashed some backpacks to lighten the load before the potential combat at the mad scientist's fortress. Bryan recovered some of those packs and fed the warriors some of the food we had. This ranged from old emergency protein bars to leftover eggs and meat that had been scrambled or grilled at our brunch. The other tribe gobbled the food up quickly. Although it was food for our warriors, Bryan reasoned that the Rat Man's army would fight better for us with a full belly.

I could see gratitude in their eyes. It was obvious that it was the first meat and eggs most of them had had in a few days.

As they ate, Bryan gave me a rundown to all of what he saw in our new followers. By combining forces, man per zombie we were pretty much matched one man per five undead. That would have been a blowout for us with trained and healthy troops, but the new recruits lacked the training of the Mountain Warriors. They were hungry, and although they were motivated by the promise of food, the quick march over a short distance had nearly exhausted many of them. Still, I could see life returning to their eyes as they ate.

Bryan looked over the situation below with his binoculars. Seeing that Critter and crew were still trapped but secured on the top floor, we had some time to let the new recruits regain their stamina. Bryan had the men rest for another fifteen minutes at the top of the hill after they ate. The whole time he gave an encouraging peptalk of how to defeat the zombies.

Bryan took me aside and asked, "Do you remember when we discussed being late bloomers and how this is our time?"

I nodded, suddenly nervous about what he was getting at.

"Think of how awkward you were when you were sixteen, when you were nineteen, when you were twenty-five. Think of how much you've matured not just with knowledge and skill, but wisdom."

"OK?" I said, trying to figure out where he was going.

"When Alexander the Great was only a teenager, a mere kid, he led a legendary and victorious cavalry charge that broke the enemy's line."

The Battle of Chaeronea," I said.

Bryan smiled and nodded his head and continued, "At the age of nineteen, he became the Macedon king. As the emperor he could have sat back and sent others to their death, but he still led charges into the heart of the enemy ranks. His troops would have followed him just about anywhere and they pretty much did because he wouldn't send his men to do anything he wouldn't do himself. At twenty-nine, he attacked the walled city of Malli of the Punjab. He was the first over the wall and the rest of his men were repelled. He fought alone against a city for five minutes until his men could enter the city and rescue their king. Even then he was younger than you."

"But he was Alexander the Great. Not Eric the Journalist," I said with a wry smile.

"He was only the Great because he had a chance to prove it. I've always wondered what would be worse, to be a king with no ambition and watch your kingdom crumble due to your indecisiveness, or to be a slave with ambition to wrest a kingdom. You aren't called Eric the Great by others simply because you were never given a chance to lead a cavalry charge at the age of sixteen and be heir to the throne, but you're no different from Alexander. He was only a man, the same as you, the same as me."

I felt my blood run cold as I figured out where he was going. So I asked him, "Why can't you lead these men down there to attack the fortress? Why me?"

"For one," he explained, "You're the only one on this hill I trust, but more importantly, you're ready."

I didn't like this. Yes, I could see leading, in a few years. I felt like I was Bryan's last choice and that he was hoping to get someone more reliable from our tribe, but was stuck with me in this situation.

"Why can't you lead them?" I persisted

He pointed to that rock formation that caught his attention earlier in the day. "Because I'm going there to attack the head of the snake. I paid attention to the time it took for the power to go out in the fortress and the zombies to become militarized. It was about the same time it would take for that mad Professor Poindexter to run up to that place. I also believe that the sniper bullets that rained down on us were fired from that vantage point. He'll be able to take this crew out one by one from that vantage point. I may be able to turn off the zombie army with his controls and our tribe can just walk away without a fight."

"You think there might be more people up there besides Dext? You might need some backup. I could go with you."

Bryan looked into the distance as if considering. "Aside from his zombie army, I think Poindexter is a one man show. He's too eccentric to be loveable. Also his love for his pet zombies seems to be his only outlet for affection. Dexter looked pretty broken up that we killed his zombie bots." Bryan then looked at me and said seriously at first and then a smile slowly broke his face, "I'm confident that I can handle him. If there are more people up there, I'll just have to kick more ass, so quit trying to get out of leading your army. Remember, confidence is your key. This is Your Army. Your Army! Own it!" he said as he confidently slapped me on the shoulder.

"You got it, man," I said. "I'll act--"

"No, you won't act. You will be confident. Because you got this, my brother!" he said and we firmly shook hands as his left hand firmly grasped my shoulder.

"I got this," I stated with well acted confidence. I was getting tired of Bryan's motivational speaker type lectures, but I withheld my gripe.

Bryan divided the Rat Man's army into three squads and then called a few of the men he thought looked the most influential over the group and assigned them as leaders over the squads. He picked the leaders by who the others treated with respect and who could maintain eye contact with him. Bryan explained the plan by drawing it out in the dirt. It was a simple three pronged attack. Two of the squads would perform a full frontal assault. I would lead that.

The third squad would slip down a trail on the creek and flank the zombie army. The lay of the land hid this route from Dexter, if he was indeed sheltered in the rock formation above.

Bryan was confident that if Critter saw the attack coming he would lead an assault on the rear of the zombie formation. It should be like cutting grass with a scythe if the zombies stayed programmed in formation to attack straight ahead. Due to their stupidity and remote programming, the zombies would ignore their backs especially if Bryan could take out Dexter. Bryan finished telling me his plan and then he stood tall and turned away from me, facing Rat Man's army.

"Alright," Bryan announced to the three squads with a finality of the deal. From the tone of his voice, they were compelled to stand to receive his message. "I will go to attack the head of the snake. I now leave you in the capable hands of Eric Hildebrande, the son of the Governor. Take charge, Eric."

Bryan stepped aside letting me address the group.

"OK, warriors," I said in a loud and deep voice holding my sword at my side, "Let's avenge the usurpation of your town." I didn't know if usurpation was the correct word for getting chased from a Boy Scout camp by automated zombies, but it felt right in the speech. "Let us also win food to feed our families for the rest of the winter. May our children grow strong. Let's move out!" I raised my sword in a salute.

I felt the surge, a rush of energizing strength shoot through me as the men and women raised their swords, saluting me in return, and cheered. Some even shouted my name.

I pointed my sword down the trail and started to lead.

"Move out!" I commanded.

Bryan smiled and nodded his approval at me. Then he turned and sprinted into the woods on his mission. I was now alone with these people.

My army was alive, fresh with a motivating speech in their heads, fresh food in their belly, and the warmth in their hearts of knowing their families would be fed through the winter. Gravity was also on our side and the march was down hill and didn't tire us at all.

In fact, the march happened too fast for my liking. I wasn't exactly nervous. I was just worrying about everything that could go wrong. I worried that I would freeze and not follow through with the charge that I was to lead. I vowed to press forward at all costs.

I also worried about the people I was leading. Although they were my enemies earlier today, I now felt a responsibility towards them. I didn't see these people as mere tools to be used. They placed their trust in me. I felt I owed them something back. The least that I could give them would be my courage.

I scolded myself for overthinking the situation. I found myself doing that on a lot of the long treks I had been on in the Forbidden Zone. I told myself to focus on keeping my head. All I had to do was position the two squads, wait for the third squad to get into place to flank the zombies and then lead with passion into the heart of the zombie ranks.

When we arrived at the gulch that had earlier shielded Bryan and me from the sniper fire, I paused and directed the squads to go to their respective positions. I waited until they were in place.

The troops spread out and I saw fear on their faces as they looked upon the superior numbers of the zombies in formation just inside the gate.

I caught my breath as doubt, not only in myself, but those who I commanded, flooded my mind. I stood on a slight knob where I had a vantage point and watched the men spread out off the trail. In the heart of winter I had no problem seeing into the leafless forest. I briefly wondered how I would command a group in the summer when the thick deciduous foliage hid troop movement, both ally and enemy. That was why bugles and drums were so important to direct battles in ancient times. I smiled as I remembered Bryan telling me in training to yell like I had a pair. I guessed I'd have to both listen and speak loudly in such a situation.

I looked at the mini fortress and wished I could send a message to Critter. I wondered if I could order an opening barrage of gunfire from Rat Man's ranks. I decided that the charge itself would be a signal to Critter. From the safety of the gulch, I was thinking that we could easily take out half of the zombies before we ran out of ammunition. Having the Rat Man's army run out of ammo would be a good thing when they finally met the Mountain Warriors. At present we were united against the zombies, but when the zombie bots were killed, the Rat Man's army may turn their overwhelming numbers against us. However, because Bryan didn't specifically tell me to use firearms, I finally decided to stick with only swords and machetes.

As I was getting ready to issue the order to charge, I heard some of my men from the conquered tribe screaming to my right. I looked and saw a handful of zombies attacking our flank. They were the typical disorganized lot of zombies, not in formation. I didn't think they belonged to Dexter's army. However it was time to attack. I assumed my position and prepared to give the command, hoping that my voice would not crack with fear as I looked at the ranks of zombie bots guarding the fortress.

| 10 |

I stood on the knob and raised my sword. The men nervously watched me and the zombie hordes ahead. We would have to cross a two hundred meter field to the open gate. I was hoping that Bryan had taken out whoever was sniping at us earlier. Then we would have another hundred yards to fight through an army of armed zombie bots between the wall and the house where the Mountain Warriors were trapped.

"Attention!" I yelled louder than the men on the flank who were screaming as they were just finishing their battle with the handful of zombies. They were done with the fight but unknown to me at the time, they were in complete disarray because they were hidden in the forest and the hilly land. I thought we were ready to attack. At least, I was ready.

"Alright warriors! Let's go!" I yelled forcing my voice into a deep masculine tone. I then screamed with all my soul, "Charge!" I pointed my blade dramatically towards the zombie formation two hundred yards away in the compound.

I heard the men around me scream as they followed my running charge. I yelled incoherently as I led them. It was supposed to have a psychological effect on the enemy and boost the courage of the attackers. However, I wasn't sure if zombies were vulnerable to the psychological warfare of a screaming charge, but I felt my fear melt as the adrenaline surged through my veins. I transformed into an unstoppable juggernaut. Bryan and Critter always reminded me to keep my peripheral vision, but at that moment the tunnel vision of battle took control of me.

The Rat Man's army charged right behind me. I could hear their bootfalls and warcries. I saw a man fall to my left as I heard the crack of the sniper's rifle. I screamed louder and charged harder. I charged through the open gate and felt the surge of an adrenalin rush as I led my men.

I wiped sweat from my brow, one last time before I smashed into the formation of the zombie bots with my sword and felt myself taken over by a berserker type rage. I told myself to charge and not freeze. I slashed through six or seven zombies and continued fighting in my fog of war. I lost all sense of time and the number of zombies I had slain. My only thought was to smash the line and push forward clearing as many of these zombie bots as possible. After totally losing myself to the combat rage, I soon found myself at the stairs to the two story fortress house. I slashed through three or four more zombie bots and mounted the top of the front porch and cleared the space before the front door.

I realized I was exhausted and breathing hard, but gung ho and motivated to fight on. I did not expect to make it to the steps so quickly. It was an adrenalized three hundred yard sprint with fighting, never mind the run to the camp and back. It took a toll and I was foolish to burn myself out so quickly, but there wasn't time to rest. I cleared the rest of the zombies off the porch with mighty swings of the sword.

As I felt victory massaging my ego, I turned to face my warriors to see how they were fairing and swore bitterly. They were one hundred yards behind me still battling the first ranks of the zombies at the gate. Many had not left the gulch from where the charge began, especially the group that had been attacked by the straggler zombies. I had been the only one to smash my way through. I was now surrounded by hundreds of zombies who advanced at me mindlessly but ferociously swinging their blades.

I looked for the third squad on my right flank that was to launch a surprise attack from the side and saw that they were just now making a weak charge far beyond the walls of the compound. They then stopped and a few men fought at the front as they battled a few zombies at the vanguard. The rest of the squad stood idly behind them watching the battle unfold.

I had recklessly got caught up in the moment. I was screwed and beyond the reach of any rescue. I had to fight and save myself.

"Your new found zeal will be your death," I muttered out loud to myself as I hacked off the hand of a reaching zombie and followed with a slash at the monster's throat. I launched an attack as some zombies stumbled up the stairs to the porch. It was easy for a moment attacking from the height advantage. I killed many by hacking into their heads beneath me on the porch, but the sheer mass was pressing me back. I would kill one and the others kept coming inadvertently using the dead as a shield.

I slashed at the advancing horde as I heard Scott's thick accent yelling at me above the din of combat, "What in the unholy hell of the Forbidden Zone are you doing, son? You realize you're in the middle of a zombie horde?"

I looked up and saw Scott peeking over the balcony like a scolding rooster.

"No kidding, Sherlock! Come down and help," I screamed through gritted teeth as I continuously hacked at the seemingly endless, growling horde.

"Sorry kid, I can't jump my old ass down there. Come inside and we'll fight our way down to you. There are less zombies inside than out."

"You got it," I said as I fought a retreat towards the front door.

I opened the big oaken door into a wall of zombies. I slashed through two zombies who pushed their way out the door and quickly stepped aside. A few more pushed out onto the porch leaving me a space to fight my way inside. I charged into that space.

Once inside, I realized that I was totally screwed. It was packed like a standing room only concert. A hell of a mosh pit, I muttered to myself as I continued to fight. There had to be close to one hundred zombie bots crammed in that large room. Scott was full of crap. It was far worse inside than out, but as Scott would say, "The bullet had done already left the barrel." You have to accept where it hits and move on to the next target.

I began to fight for my life. These zombies were unarmed. Whether they were from the start or Dexter had them drop the weapons due to the sheer press of the crowd inside, I didn't know, but it was no easier fighting them. Their noses twitched with my scent and their eyes widened in bloody desire. I realized I acquired a minor cut in the melee and in the confined space of the room, the scent of my fresh blood drove them crazy.

I saw Critter and Scott burst through the door above, but the sheer mass of the zombies on the stairs kept them confined to a small space on the second floor landing. The few that they killed piled up forming a barrier at the top of the stairs as other zombies kept fighting to reach the swinging bloodied blades of the Mountain Warriors.

"Hang in there kid!" Scott yelled as he whacked a few zombies at the top of the stairs with his wooden bat, crunching skulls.

The zombies crowded around me. Even in my panic fight, I almost gagged on the smell of rotted death. I tripped on something and saw that it was the gnawed up skeleton that I guessed to be Nick.

I had a temporary space in the approaching mass and replaced my longer vampire's sword into its sheath at my belt with one hand and drew the wakizashi with a one armed slash with the other hand, but the zombies packed in tighter so that I couldn't even wield that shorter sword. Standing at jaw level, I was at a danger of being bitten as they pressed in snapping their hideous teeth at me. They glared into my eyes as their jaws kept biting, but I wasn't bitten yet.

As a last ditch effort, I quickly threw the short sword into the writhing mass, withdrew my handgun, and opened fire in rapid succession. I snap aimed at the heads. I just pointed it into the mass ahead of me and kept pulling the trigger until it clicked empty.

A small space opened before me from the gun blasts. A mouth snapped at me from the side. It's death scented cheek brushed my own cheek. I smashed the butt of my handgun into its skull. In panic, I threw the empty gun at a vampire hitting him in the face. I ducked a zombie's bite and another snapped at me. I dove through the narrow space formed by the bullets and hit the floor in a roll. I bounced off the legs of a few zombies and kept crawling and rolling as they scrambled after me, but I lost them in the mass. I crawled a few feet for my goal and had my hands stepped on by a few of those things. I then rolled toward what I originally feared the most, the dark hole where Dexter had escaped through. I heard Critter and Scott scream for me. They had no idea where I was in the roiling sea of wrecked humanity.

I rolled under the table, and dove head first. I actually held my breath as I shot into the black hole of the pipe where Dexter had escaped and a bunch of zombies had crawled out of. At first I felt the mild dread of the unknown as the blackness engulfed me and then sheer terror as I shot down a slide at an insane speed.

| 11 |

From high up on a cliff, Bryan cursed as he watched Eric lead the charge. He had hoped to have made it to Dexter's perch before Eric launched the attack into the fortress. Although Bryan had run fast, he had hit a dead end when he ran up a ravine and found a rock wall with a waterfall that was a hundred feet high within a steep sided gorge. Too stubborn to retrace his steps, he pressed onward and began to climb. Halfway up he realized it would have been quicker and far easier to have back tracked and found another way, but it was too late. With muscles aching, he pushed himself up the rock wall.

He made it to the top having wasted fifteen minutes to cover a few hundred feet and began to run again. Another fifteen minutes passed before he stopped and looked ahead. He squatted a few hundred feet above the suspicious rock outcropping. Peering down, it was indeed a shelter and a lookout and it was much larger close up than it appeared from down in the valley. It looked like it was made of a clay like material that was cleverly molded into a round rock shape figure. Although its main purpose was camouflage, it did remind Bryan of a multi roomed Hobbit style house that was two stories high. Despite Dexter being a royal jackass, Bryan grudgingly appreciated the mad scientist's flare for style.

From here Bryan could see Eric leading the attack. He couldn't see distinct faces from the great distance, but he knew Eric well enough to recognize his fighting style. Hearing the sniper firing from the structure, Bryan hastened to take out the scientist.

He carefully made his way down the mountain toward the large hobbit style house with the barrel of his AR-15 leading the way like a bloodhound's nose. He covered the distance quickly as he kept an eye both on the battle at the fortress and his target ahead. He quickened his pace as he watched Eric heedlessly disappear into the zombie horde while foolishly leaving his troops behind in his passion.

Bryan reached the lookout post and noticed that the windows were in niches recessed back far enough to remain unseen to a casual observer. They looked like small caves that would draw the attention of only a raccoon or an opossum. The windows themselves had that plastic like look that made him suspect bullet proof glass. They were locked as he suspected.

He made his way to a larger recessed area and was correct when he assumed that it was a doorway. A camera was mounted above it but he hoped that Dexter was too busy monitoring the fight down below as he had heard a few more explosive shots fired from the sniper rifle. He cautiously touched the doorknob, expecting it to be electrified or booby trapped in some other way, but he had no time to dwell on that. He tested it with a light touch and sighed with relief when he wasn't shocked but disappointingly the knob was stuck. He wrenched it, but cursed under his breath when he realized that it was locked.

He cautiously stepped back, aware of the camera's eye and scanned until he saw what he was looking for, an aperture in the rock on the second story. It was a few meters above his reaching finger tips. Bryan jumped and dug his fingers into the small grooves in the rock façade. For a moment he thought it would be an impossible task, but he pushed on. Many people would have thought the wall was unclimbable, but in his twenties, rock climbing was among his many hobbies, one that he gave up with marriage and kids. When the zombie apocalypse calmed, he looked forward to his kiddos being old enough for him to teach them his skills as an excuse to get back into the sport. His fingers held onto the most seemingly insignificant cracks, grooves, and indentations as he relentlessly pulled himself upward.

His climb was rewarded. He saw what he had hoped for. The small window was opened for Dexter to take a sniper shot at the fortress below. No one was by the window now. Bryan guessed that Dexter was too busy controlling his zombie army on a computer. This was risky as hell climbing in an open window occupied by a semi-active shooter, but he had to take out Dexter now. His friends below depended on him.

Bryan took his eyes off the window that served as a gunport and scanned the valley but couldn't see Eric anywhere. The zombies were actually driving the Rat Man's army back toward the gulch and hacking at their backs with swords and machetes as they ran away in retreat. Bryan ruefully shook his head. That group was way over their heads in the Forbidden Zone, he thought. Bryan had no idea how they survived as long as they had other than the stark isolation from the horrors that Bryan's people faced on a daily basis.

As he was thinking that, a storm of people blasted out the front door in the fortress in the valley. He saw Critter's figure launch off the front porch with a sword in each hand whirling like a windmill in a hurricane. Scott followed with his Louisville slugger, "Whackin' the bastards," as he put it. The man had little grace, seemingly no skill, and was goofy as hell to just look at, but he was terrifying when unleashed. The rest of the crew rushed out and began to cut their way to meet up with the Rat Man's army.

Bryan was tempted to abandon his quest to neutralize Dexter and just get his people out of the valley, but he didn't relish the idea of having the crazy little genius as his neighbor. He surveyed the valley one more time. It brought back memories of a writer's retreat that he had attended with his wife just a few years before it all ended. Bryan thought with regret how the beauty and inspirational scenery of the area was wasted on the creation of an army of horror.

With his handgun leading the way, Bryan squeezed in through the window and was met with a barrel of an ancient looking sniper rifle chopping his gun out of his hands and then aiming his face.

Dexter smiled at him over the barrel and gloated, "Ah Bryan, second in command of the," then he sang, "The Mountain Warriors, dun dun dun dun!" His face stiffened with deadly seriousness and quit singing. He instructed, "Get in here and drop your weapons."

Byran dropped-crawled in through the window and placed his two swords, a rifle, and another handgun on a computer desk at his side. He took his time putting the weapons down so as not to damage his weaponry by dropping them to the floor. He planned to use them again shortly. He looked around the room for any possible weapons or escape. Maybe even a large pipe under a table for him to roll into.

He couldn't help but marvel at the craftsmanship of the place. It reminded him of a well designed cob style house. The room was molded into a circular shape. There weren't any corners. Even the oaken door and doorway were circular archways. Beyond that door lay a hallway. He guessed there were probably five rooms upstairs. It had a definite fantastical feel.

"Just shoot me already, weirdo," Bryan said, feigning resignation.

Dexter laughed, "Not here. I would rather not get your pea-sized brains all over my beautiful cabin."

"A Mosin Nagant? Our best sniper, Kristy, prefers that as her gun." Bryan asked about the trusted Russian sniper rifle that Dexter aimed at his heart. "With your flare, I was expecting a laser gun or something more..," he paused thinking of the right word and settled on, "more you."

Professor Dexter said with scorn, "Because I care so little for the opinions of idiots. I will say that your Kristy has great taste in guns." Then he added with overbearing pride, "I like cutting edge modern and reliable relics of history. I'm an admitted eclectic eccentric."

"'Eclectic eccentric.' Interesting appellation, but not quite the words I'd use to describe you, but you have the gun trained on me, so whatever you say," Bryan said with a shrug.

Dexter laughed long and loud. Bryan wasn't sure if it was real insanity or an act. He guessed it was a combo. Dexter knew how he appeared to others and didn't attempt to dissuade anyone. He seemed to revel in the mad scientist routine, the way a big biker with the personality of a teddy bear will enjoy the way his spikes and leather cause discomfort in a yuppie.

"We'll let's go outside so you can shoot me." Bryan looked at his wrist as if pressed for time. "I have a full day ahead."

Dexter pointed out the room and down the hall, "Get moving. It's a shame. I'd rather not do away with you. I rather like your show."

"Then why not call a truce?" Bryan asked as he walked out of the room.

"You killed my babies," Dexter whined.

Bryan stopped walking and felt the rifle barrel jab into his back. Bryan snapped angrily, "They were zombies. They eat babies. No hyperbole. Literally. They eat fricken babies."

Dexter jammed his back again, harder this time. The barrel painfully speared the ridge of Bryan's boney spine. The scientist ordered, "Get moving."

Bryan turned and faced Dexter, acting as if suddenly enraged by the circumstances and the sudden pain. Dexter jabbed Bryan in the belly and ordered, "I said get moving."

"No. Not until you realize how insane this is. You sent an army of zombies to kill my people and you're mad that I defended my loved ones?"

Dexter shot right back, "You encroached on my territory."

"'Your territory!'" Bryan stated incredulously. "You should have no trespassing signs up if you find having neighbors so offensive."

"Are you crazy? No trespassing signs would give away my presence," Dexter whined.

"The fricking zombie army gave away your position, dumbass!" Bryan paused and then provoked, "And no, you are the crazy one! And not very bright!"

Dexter was about to jab Bryan again, but saw that Bryan was waiting for the thrust of the rifle as a way to get in and disarm the scientist. Dexter laughed heartily.

"Oh no. Get moving, I've seen enough of your moves from your TV show to know not to trust you. 'The Mountain Warriors, dun dun dun dun!'" he sang. "Get moving!" Dexter ordered with a knowing smile, but his eyes behind the glasses were deadly serious.

Bryan knew that ploy was up. He turned and walked down the hall. As he came to a room he was able to look out a window and caught a glimpse of the battle below. He stopped and watched as Critter and crew charged into the zombie horde. At first, he was relieved to see that they were winning. Then he saw that two armies of zombies, hidden from Critter's view, were marching from either side of the steel walls that surrounded the house, and would surround his tribe. Critter and crew were far outnumbered and stood no chance once surrounded. Trapped in the middle in the walled yard, they'd be wiped out from the sheer press of the bodies.

The zombies, armed with machetes and swords, seemed to be marching in formation on a pre-planned program. The two zombie formations were hidden by the walls and knowing Dexter's flare for the unexpected, Bryan could tell the walls would collapse as the zombies touched them and Critter and crew would be overwhelmed in a nanosecond.

Bryan had to make a move now or all would be lost.

"Take a right, and go down the stairs," Dexter ordered.

It wasn't optimal, but Critter and crew needed him now. Bryan turned the corner and made his move against Dexter. Dexter fired the rifle.

| 12 |

The great speed through the darkness of the tunnel terrified me. I could see nothing around me as I slid down the pipe. I felt like an explosive rocket blindly flying through dark space at light speed. I expected impact and detonation every second of the breakneck decline.

I slid on what felt like a giant playground slide, but this was not designed for kids. With the steep slope, I acquired a speed that would give most mothers a heart attack. I gritted my teeth as I feared a plethora of dangers: Sharp blades at neck height to decapitate, to land in a nest of zombies, or just to slam into a brick wall at sixty plus miles an hour. I lay flat to avoid anything above that could decapitate me, but the aerodynamics crazily increased the speed. I felt that this ride would never end, at least not in this life.

However the slope shallowed and I slowed and came to a rest against what I thought were pillows but were actually stuffed animals. Anime dolls actually. I discovered that as the lights flashed on, powered by motion detectors.

I leapt off the slide to the floor three feet below, and stood in a great room. Contrary to the Spartan designs in the house above, this was a party room. From the disco ball above lit by colored lights, to the hip abstract paintings on the wall, to the comfortable couches, to the sound system, to the thick plush carpet and fancy pillows and stuffed animals everywhere. The Professor had set himself up a nice party pad. Unfortunately I guessed that he had no living persons to entertain. A Dead Man's Party, I thought of the song.

I guessed that I was sixty feet deep in the bedrock beneath the fortress, but the walls were wood framed. Windows, with realistic videos of the New York City skyline, ringed the room giving the real sensation of being in a penthouse. The only violation was the slide poking through the wall. The slide came through an open fanged mouth reminiscent of a fun house. Across the room by the leopard skin sofas was another slide. If I was correct with my sense of direction, that slide led to the curious rock formation that Bryan was off investigating. I wondered if Dexter would be coming down there anytime soon.

I also noticed several bookcases around the room. I suspected them of being doors to secret passages, but that would have been too obvious. From what I knew about Dexter, it was best to expect the unexpected.

As I got my bearing, six zombies approached from a side hall and surrounded me with a slow relaxed shuffle. They were surprisingly dressed in clean clothes and had relatively clean skin, a greenish gray under a coat of caked on makeup, but no gashes nor sores. The clothes ranged from a butler's tuxedo to a quirky school girl's skirt.

I drew my sword in a panic and scrambled to a corner so as not to be flanked. I backed up, bumping into the slide. I looked at the platform and then jumped back up on the slide a few feet above them to get a bit of high ground to my advantage. I braced for an attack, but prepared to leap from their reaching grasp and slavering jaws if I needed to.

However, they just stared stupidly at me, seemingly unconcerned about the danger of my drawn blade or the feral look that I probably had in my eyes. I wiped at the blood on my forearm that I acquired in the previous combat above ground. The scent didn't seem to set off any atavistic urges in them. As I was thinking about finding a bandage for my small wound, one of them shocked the hell out of me. He spoke.

"Yes, master," the butler zombie croaked in a disjointed voice as if from a throat that hadn't spoken in a century. It was a middle aged man with a nice haircut, a buttoned up shirt, bow tie, and khaki pants. He looked like a businessman and wore wire rimmed glasses.

No body parts were rotting or falling off. Even better, they didn't smell like the grave. One of them was a gorgeous woman in her teens, or she would have been pretty if she was still human. I could never get past the dull zombie look in the eyes that could suddenly blaze with hunger.

I caught the aroma of a hint of human waste masked by a sickening chemical sweet floral disinfectant and colognes. One of the zombies stepped closer and I could tell from the bulge in his pants and the worsening smell that they all probably wore adult diapers.

Despite my horror and confusion, something in my brain worked. I was so overwhelmed by the friendly approach of well dressed zombies that it took a few synapses of my brain firing to register that one of them had talked coherently to me. As they stared blankly at me, I suddenly realized that they were waiting for directions.

"What?" I asked.

"Yes master." the butler said again, and then added, "What can I do for you?"

After a moment, I ordered with confidence, "Get me some food." Why did I order food? I don't know. I was too stressed to eat but that was the only thing that I could think of ordering from a man dressed as a butler. If it had been a zombie dressed as a nurse, I would have ordered a bandage.

I looked them over for a moment and noticed that these zombies didn't just have an incision in their head for a remote control, they had a black box a little bigger than the average cell phone fastened to their neck. Wires disappeared into their skulls. There was much more electronics on them than on those battle zombie bots in the formations. These zombie servants had a more intricate programming, I guessed.

After I overcame my initial apprehension, I actually jumped down from the slide, walked up and studied one of the female zombies as she blankly looked ahead. Wires disappeared into her blouse. I looked over her outfit. She wore a school girl's plaid mini skirt and fishnet stockings. The fetish clothes mixed with her being an undead horror agitated my stomach. I was also unsettled by the fact that she looked to be too young for a man to legally and morally look at with lust, yet Dexter dressed her in this manner.

The businessman/butler zombie interrupted my inspection.

"Kind?" he asked.

"What?" I asked slightly confused, thinking he meant "kind" as a pleasant disposition.

"Kind? Food?" he clarified.

It was weird communicating with the zombie. It spoke words, but his eyes weren't engaged like a person. They stared past me dumbly, almost as if it were communicating with distant spirits.

I hesitated and decided to try something. "MRE," I said. Bryan was hoping to find a stash of MREs, (the military's Meals Ready to Eat) in this labyrinth. MREs were worth their weight in gold in the Forbidden Zone. They nearly lasted forever, they self heated, they were light, but could supply a person with a full day's supply of calories. I didn't know if the zombies would recognize the word MRE, but the day was full of surprises.

They stared at me stupidly and then the butler said, "Yes, master."

"Anything else, master?" a nerdy but sexy looking middle aged female zombie asked. She wore a business style power suit with a cute skirt. She held a pen over a small notepad as if ready to diligently write down my every command.

I walked past them and began to look the place over better as they stared blankly past me.

The nerdy female zombie asked again, "Anything else, master?" There was no inflection of a question in her voice. It was like a robot's tone from a zombie's mouth. She continued to look past me like a goldfish will look mindlessly out of its fishbowl.

I wanted to follow the businessman/butler zombie to see if there was indeed a large stash of MREs but the other five zombies stood in front of me. I didn't want to push my way through because despite their clean appearance, I didn't want to touch them even with my sword. I saw no obvious bite marks. No sign of skin lacerations from living in the wild. I worried that these were purposely infected by Dexter to be his special zombie slaves.

"Master?" she asked again. "May I help you."

"Yeah," I answered. I mostly wanted them to go away as I considered the full ramifications of what was going on in Dexter's secret realm. I absentmindedly said, "Yeah. Blow me."

I was horrified as the pretty young zombie and an androgynously handsome young male zombie walked toward me, reaching zombie-like for my crotch and then when close enough, they immediately dropped to their knees to perform my obscene and not intended request.

Both kept saying, "Yes, master," as they chased me on their knees as I backed away in terror.

I bumped into the wall and stifled a curse as I was cornered. I quickly jumped back up on the slide a few feet above them, my sword at the ready. The young man and woman stood back up and pursued me with a slow staggered gait, always reaching stiff-armed for my crotch. The horror of a zombie attempting a sex act on me was far worse than if they tried to kill me.

"Stop!" I ordered. I bit my tongue before I swore an oath. Who knows how they would have tried to fulfill my withheld profanity if they interpreted it as a request. I stared at them from my perch on the slide.

The young zombies stopped and stared at me with dull eyes, waiting for new orders. I kept my mouth shut in fear and wondered what all the crazy professor had trained his minions to do. Hell, I couldn't think of any worse venereal disease than—I forced that from my mind as I fought against dry heaving from my knotted stomach.

"Anything else, master," the nerdy middle aged chick asked again as she wrote on her pad like a professional personal secretary. From my vantage point on the slide, I looked down at her notepad as she held the pen above it. The pen left nothing but scrawled nonsense on the notepad.

"Yes," I said carefully. I still stood on the slide fearing to come down. I ordered them, "All of you guys, go over there and have a seat on that couch. Rest."

"Yes master," they chanted together and complied.

I then looked towards the hallway where the butler zombie disappeared. I was about to follow him down that passage when he reappeared with a single MRE wrapped in a plastic bag of the dullest brown.

"Your MRE, master. Enjoy sir," he said as he extended his hand with the bag of survival food.

I winced a little, wanting no contact with him despite his professional and clean appearance. I jumped off the slide and pointed to where I had just stood, "Place it there, Jeeves."

"Master?" he asked and I realized that I couldn't nickname these idiots.

"Place the MRE on the slide." I said.

The zombie butler bent over and set it down. He stood back up and looked at me asking, "Yes master?"

"Get me some food." I ordered with the desire to see where the cache of food was hidden.

"Kind?"

"MRE."

"Yes master," he replied as if I hadn't asked for an MRE just a minute ago.

The zombie butler shuffled off. I followed this time. As I followed him past the five zombies sitting on the sofas, I cringed slightly. They harmlessly stared off into space but I was aware of the horror they could unleash if not controlled by Dexter's technology.

They looked like people stoned on hoopla. Hoopla was a type of designer drug that swept the nation recently in the Safe Zone. Contrary to its exciting name, the person would simply blackout for a few hours and sit still, staring into space like a zombie. I didn't get the point of it, but I guess for some people they liked to just completely numb themselves to their issues for a while. There were quite a few viral videos outside of the Forbidden Zone of hoopla parties but that video fad was quickly fading. They were quite boring. Usually it involved a sober person drawing obscene pictures on the stoned person's face as they sat there with their eyes open and staring into oblivion. To blank out that badly in the Forbidden Zone could result in death from a number of things

I had seen some people "partying" with it at get-togethers that I had attended, but it just wasn't my thing. After seeing these zombies, the thought of getting "high" in such a manner really turned me off even more.

I followed the zombie butler out of the party room and down a hall. The lights flicked on automatically as we entered a new area. Despite being about sixty feet beneath the surface of the Earth, I felt like I was walking down the hallway of a first story suburban home. The drywall and the lighting gave the feeling that there was sunlight streaming in through the windows of another room.

The Butler led me into a storage room. Contrary to the rest of the underground facility, this place looked like a basement or really a bunker. The ceilings and walls were structured with the coldest gray concrete you could imagine. The lighting was strictly sterile fluorescent.

I swore reverently when I saw the mountainous stack of MREs. There were hundreds of boxes, each box held twelve meals that held a day's worth of calories and that you could fit in a cargo pocket. They also came with a means of heating the main dish. This was a gold mine. If I could get Bryan and

Critter down here, they would be indebted to me. I relished that because I really did owe them my life a few times over.

I watched the butler zombie shuffle to grab a fresh MRE bag from an opened box. He picked it up without regard, and I felt sorry for him. He cut himself on the box leaving a sliver of his flesh and a very slight smear of zombie goo on the cardboard, but he continued on his mission with no sign of pain or concern for his well being.

I thought of how governments would love such people in their military. I shuddered as I was sure it had already been considered long before, probably before the zombie apocalypse even happened. I pushed it from my mind. Not out of denial, but conspiracy theories ran rampant from my former home in DC to campfires all across the Forbidden Zone. I knew there were some nefarious things going on, however, everybody had their own beliefs and preached them like they were the truth. I had seen fist fights start between two people arguing two different conspiracy beliefs on what, why, and how the zombie apocalypse happened. Neither with any proof, and the worse thing was everyone believed that ultimately the goal of The Powers That Be was to divide all the little guys against each other. Yet we did that well enough on our own without their help, and the help they did give turned people against each other even fiercer.

The butler turned and without surprise when he saw me standing behind him, offered me the bag. "Your MRE, master."

"Thank you," I said.

"You're welcome, master," the butler replied. I noticed his reply was slightly different from the first time he offered me an MRE. Maybe he recognized the thanks that I felt.

After a pause, he said, "I am at your service, master," and stared off into the distance.

I took the plastic wrapped MRE, careful not to touch any of the plastic that touched his hands. There was a very small dab of zombie goo on the bag from his recent cut. I smelled it and dry heaved. It smelled worse than a three day old road kill in the hot summer sun.

I studied the zombie butler for a moment. He didn't hear me follow him, yet he showed no startle or surprise when he turned and saw me behind him. He simply responded to any stimuli that was presented to him.

"I am at your service, master," He repeated again.

I felt a surge of compassion despite my revulsion. I was more repulsed by the disease than the man himself. Looking him over, I could see he was in good shape in middle age. He was probably a bit of a health nut in his prior life. Despite his age he was sturdy and well maintained other than the zombification, of course. He was probably quite smart before this happened to him. His face was not ravaged by stupid decisions from the destruction from drug abuse to scars from bar fights. Yet here he stood, simply programmed to serve me or whoever ordered him. If he was transferred suddenly to the moon from sixty feet under the ground it wouldn't register to him. Probably if his leg was cut off he'd simply propel himself with his other leg and arms.

I guess my true compassion was for the man's soul, if it was anywhere witnessing what had happened to his body.

"I am at your service, master," he repeated again as if for the first time.

"Go have a seat with the others and rest, my friend," I said.

It may have been my imagination but I swore that I saw a moment of confusion, maybe humanity at the understanding of being told to rest. He hesitated for a split second and said, "Yes master. Thank you."

I felt totally relaxed by his domesticated demeanor and in a lapse of reasoning, I led the way back to the party room. The zombie butler slowly shuffled behind me.

Suddenly I was overwhelmed with a mind full of Abigail. I always got these when she was either warning me or I was about to see her. I worried that I was losing my mind. She had no idea where I was and I didn't know if her mental waves—if that's the correct term—could reach me sixty feet under the Earth. Hell, I still doubted whether I was receiving mental waves from her or if I had simply gone mad. Going mad was definitely an option. That was not a hard thing to do in the Forbidden Zone and very common. I had met a few madmen and those right on the frayed edges of sanity in my short time here. The difference between fools, prophets, madmen and sages was sometimes hard to decipher.

I tried to go into a different compartment of my brain to shut off her influence (or my madness) when I distinctly heard Dexter scream, "Servants! Attack all outsiders." He repeated that a few more times and each time his voice seemed to be getting closer. Stupidly, I wondered if Dexter was sliding down another slide instead of thinking about the butler zombie bot walking behind me.

The butler savagely growled and launched himself, knocking me over. His teeth snapped continuously, biting and grabbing hold of my jacket with his teeth. He shook his head like a pit bull. His bite tore my jacket. Inexorably, his mouth reached at my throat even grazing the skin over my trachea with his teeth. I fought back as a wave of panic inundated me. I was sure I had been bitten.

| 13 |

Back, just before Eric slid down the slide, Critter stood on the second floor landing above the chaos. He watched as the zombies surrounded and pressed in on Eric as he drew his handgun and emptied the magazine into the bodies that reached for him. However he didn't see Eric dive, but rather he thought Eric was taken down inundated by the mob and devoured like Nick.

Critter roared in fury and opened fire with his MAK-90, a civilian model of the AK-47. He pumped the thirty rounds of his magazine into the zombies on the landing, stairs and the room below. Scott and a few others joined into the fusillade.

A gory path opened. Critter rushed down through the opening and hurtled over bodies down the stairs. The dead zombies were haphazardly stacked on the stairs where they fell two or three bodies deep. All the warriors made it to the lowerlanding, except Kristy who Critter ordered to keep an eye above them. As the sharpest of the sharpshooters, she watched over the tribe from above with her sniper's rifle taking out anything that got through their defenses..

After making it to the bottom of the stairs, Critter sighed as he quickly assessed his ammunition. He had only one more thirty round magazine for his AK-47 variant and a few more bullets randomly placed in his hidden pockets. He slung the rifle over his back. He drew both of his swords as more zombies converged on him. He immediately attacked with a flurry of swings from both of his savage swords, followed by his men as they sliced through the horde.

After not finding Eric on the first floor, the Mountain Warriors pressed out the door and flew at the zombie formation that attacked the Rat Man's army.

The counter attack continued to go well. Critter took a zombie out with every single swing of each of his two swords. However his arms were starting to feel like lead from the constant sword work. The only thing that kept him going was that he was starting to see the end of the battle. As he saw that it was turning into a cleanup, a new gusto for battle returned, but as the feeling of victory burned in his chest he paused for a moment. He sensed something was wrong, deadly wrong.

As a man who spent many days alone in the woods with silence as his only companion and savage instincts guiding him, Critter learned to hear and listen to that inner voice that most people drowned out with constant electronic and interpersonal distractions. He swore an oath as he looked around, trying to locate whatever triggered his well honed instincts.

It was something that reached him above the gunfire and screams of combat.

"Keep your senses open!" Critter barked to his already embattled warriors. "Something's not right."

Whether it was the rank smell that was added by the hundreds of extra zombies marching in the formation, the sound of the marching boot falls that were in lockstep, hearing the distant scream of Bryan on the mountain above him, or something mystical, Critter wasn't surprised when he saw the three meter high steel walls collapse with an ominous thud and the hundreds of zombies armed with swords march towards him and his men. He only felt hopelessness, but he had no time to dwell on it.

He cursed louder as he watched the Rat Man's mob run away at the sight of the new zombies. Critter was about to shout an order to his men to follow them in the chaotic retreat, but before the words left his mouth, the electronic gate slammed shut like a coffin's lid and the walls that had collapsed snapped back upright into place. He and his twelve remaining warriors were trapped, surrounded inside the compound with the disciplined, armed zombie horde. Two columns numbering in the hundreds approached from either side in the walled in yard.

There was nowhere to run. Instead of ordering a retreat into the packed house where more zombies staggered from, Critter screamed a savage curse into the air, and ordered his men into formation to prepare for battle in the open. He could easily hurdle the wall to escape, but Scott and a few others couldn't due to injuries or age. Probably only he and the teenager, Robert, could escape by jumping the wall.

He pointed with his sword at the wall, "Go! Get out of here, Robert!"

"No! I'm with my tribe 'til the end." Robert declared without hesitation.

"Very well. Formation!" Critter bellowed in a booming bark.

The men and women formed two lines together, back to back, facing outward. There was nothing left to do but to kill as many as they could. They were well aware that most, if not all, of them would die. At this point it was to meet death as free men with their brothers and sisters rather than cowards, and hope that they could somehow carve out an escape.

A ray of hope shot through Critter as he heard the whir of a drone. He watched it fly low over one of the zombie formations. Maybe if he could snap off a quick shot, he could set off its explosives before it could zip away and clear a path through the zombies. The Mountain Warriors had escaped many tight spots in the past with this simple trick. Critter shouldered his MAK-90. He had watched one drone escape Bryan's rifle, but he wanted to test it himself. Critter was better at snap firing where Bryan tended to take longer to aim.

"Prepare to duck, men!" Critter shouted as he raised the gun and drew a bead on the drone. It was at the perfect height to level scores of zombies. His finger tightened on the trigger as he swung the big rifle toward the drone.

However the drone abruptly flew away. He followed the drone a few times with his barrel and every time he got close, it buzzed away in an erratic zig zag pattern that was impossible to follow.

"Shoot the damn thing," Scott roared as he smashed a zombie's skull in with his bat.

"I can't. I think The Powers That Be are on to us. It keeps flying away." Critter said.

"Basically, it would be relatively simple for them to electronically reprogram the whole swarm of drones," Robert said with the tone of an expert.

Critter almost snapped something in anger and frustration at the kid but restrained himself.

Critter tried a very quick snapshot without taking time to aim down the iron sites, but the drone finally flew away, before the bullet even thundered out of the barrel. The drone hovered a few hundred meters harmlessly above them and then disappeared behind a ridge.

Critter turned his attention back to the approaching zombies. "Guns!" Critter bellowed. "Fire!"

They opened fire and ripped through the zombie ranks. The Mountain Warriors were disciplined well enough in lanes of fire to ensure that they didn't shoot a zombie more than it needed to be shot. It was satisfying to Critter to watch the effects of the firearms as the enemy fell, but within seconds, the last gun clicked on empty. Critter laid his rifle on the ground. Empty, the AK-47 was a great club for bashing a skull, but from here on out, it was a sword fight.

Words of encouragement were passed between the tribe as they set their grim determination on the horde. The remaining zombie bots stepped over their shot fellows and kept up the relentless approach on both sides of the Mountain Warriors.

"This may be it, but I am proud to stand with all of you right here, right now," Critter said bravely to his warriors.

They shouted their agreement.

"No offense," said Scott. "but I would rather be safely hanging out in a gay bar right now than getting to be part of a zombie smorgasbord."

"You'd rather be in a gay bar, any day," said Tomas with a grim smile.

"Hey man, I'm straight as an arrow," Scott retorted, "but I would make an exception for you."

"Hey, not that there's anything wrong with that," said Tomas. "You can be you."

"Come on Scott. Embrace it!" chided Critter with a wry smile, eyes grim on the approaching horde. His fatalistic smile slowly spread across his face.

"If we survive, remind me to kick y'alls asses," Scott said.

"You got it, brother," Tomas said with the steely affection only brothers in combative arms will know.

Critter's attention was fully on the horde now. A toothy smile fully cracked his usually dour face and lit his eyes as the zombies were within feet of his sword slash. His eyes blazed with the fire of his life's blood as he opened his mouth to issue a final order, but stopped.

"What the hell?" Critter muttered thoroughly perplexed. He tightly gripped both of his swords, but didn't swing the mighty blades as the zombie horde approached.

| 14 |

Dexter nudged Bryan with the long sniper rifle at his back.

"Turn left and go down the stairs," Dexter ordered with a prod of the barrel.

As Bryan rounded the corner, he twisted his body and went against the wall near the corner. Dexter wasn't able to keep the long rifle barrel pressed against Bryan's back. As Bryan turned he used the motion to grab the barrel in one hand and slam his palm under Dexter's jaw. Bryan heard the sickening crash of the teeth of the lower jaw slamming against the teeth of the upper jaw as the gun fired smashing into the opposite wall. The blow lifted Dexter off the ground.

Bryan caught the rifle as Dexter's grip loosened. Bryan was about to slam the rifle butt into Dexter's head but he could see the lights were already out for the mad scientist. Dexter lay on the ground with his head propped slightly on a small stack of scientific journals piled in the hall. A trickle of blood flowed from his mouth, staining his white lab coat. A few white specks of shattered and blood-streaked teeth lay around Dexter.

Bryan grabbed the small but deadly man by the scruff of his jacket and dragged him back into the room where he was originally caught attempting to sneak in the window. Bryan then went to the desk, picked up his weaponry, and organized the guns and knives on his body. When he was satisfied and ready for war, he looked out the window as he double checked the ease of drawing from the holsters and scabbards.

He swore savagely as he looked out the window and saw the two zombie formations march toward his friends. He watched Critter rally his warriors as they stood boldly to make their final stand. He knew a few of them were praying and he offered his own with theirs.

He found the computer that Dexter had been using. He swore again as he tried to figure out what he was looking at. The computer was open. The password was already typed and the file was running. Dexter had entered the codes already. Bryan found that he could simply use a joystick to command the zombies like a video game.

With a sense of urgency he looked over the controls with his peripheral vision seeing the zombies were about to inundate his friends Critter's legs and sword arms were coiled like springs, ready to slay..

Bryan's work with the joysticks was successful and he watched the zombies turn away from his friends. It was simple. Give the formation a command and they executed it and only stopped when given another command. Then he saw a sword avatar. He clicked it hoping that they would attack whatever he pointed at.

"Please work," he muttered.

***

Down at the fortress, Critter's small but brave force readied for battle as the zombies approached from both sides. The Rat Man's army was unseen on the other side of the three meter high steel wall.

Critter coiled his muscles to unleash his swords as the formation marched within slashing distance, but just before he unleashed the fury of his blades, the zombie bot opponents suddenly executed a sharp column left.

Critter watched with shock as the formation marched past him towards the fortress-like house. Both his jaw and his swords lowered. The formation continued past him and he watched them crash into the fortress. The zombies behind piled up on top of each other and kept piling as they were programmed to simply march forward.

Critter looked behind him and saw that the zombie formation on the other side of the Mountain Warriors' ranks did the same thing. He laughed as he realized that someone had taken control of the bots. Critter raised his sword to the hills above in a salute to his friend. "Bryan!" he roared.

The rest of his men and women echoed the cry and the sword salute.

The two groups of zombies stood back up and then marched into each other and hacked each other to pieces. Critter watched for a minute. When the zombies had slain most of each other, the Mountain Warriors rushed in to kill any that remained. It was quick but brutal work as the Mountain Warriors attacked the zombies from behind. No one felt a sense that these stabs and slashes to the back were unethical. They just wanted the job completed expeditiously.

Critter took a satisfying deep breath once the clean-up work was accomplished. He then turned and walked to the gate across the yard.

"See if you can open the gate, Robert," Critter requested the whiz-kid.

Panting, Robert nodded his head without verbalizing and ran to the tracker's side, and after a quick look over the electronic controls, he opened the massive gate for Rat Man's army.

Critter muttered to Robert, "Play along."

"You got it, boss," the kid said as he watched the gates open smoothly with the quiet whine of high end electric motors.

The Rat Man's army stood in shocked amazement just in front of the gate. It was clear by their wide eyes and raised swords that they expected to see a zombie formation greet them. They lowered their swords as just Critter and Robert stood before them. The other Mountain Warriors stood behind them surrounded by the bodies of hundreds of slain zombie bots.

With zombie goo dripping from his blades, gore covering his clothes, and a wild look on his blood splashed face, Critter scolded them, "Cowards! Had you helped, we'd've slaughtered these bastards in half the time!"

Scott laughed in the background instantly joining in Critter's ruse, "You dumbasses owe us. You missed out on a hell of a party."

The Rat Man stepped forward. "How did you kill all these--?" He couldn't finish. He stared in disbelief at the piles of slain undead. There were easily several hundred bodies. Then the Rat Man and his mob stared at Critter and his crew of twelve men and women in disbelief and awe. The Mountain Warriors stood proudly and surprisingly still full of strength. The Rat Man's army looked at them as if they were seeing an immortal army from hell. Critter was sure that they would have dropped to their knees in worship if he ordered them to.

"Get in here!" Critter ordered the much larger group of people with the confidence that he would be obeyed. He understood how he was perceived at that moment.

Although Rat Man's army vastly outnumbered Critter's crew over four to one, they fearfully obeyed his order.

When the ragged crew stood before Critter, he ordered them, "You men!" he pointed to five men, "Quickly clear the dead so that there's a path from the gate to the fortress." As they stood staring at the hundreds of bodies laying over the yard, he bellowed, "Now!" and smacked one of them on the head for emphasis.

They instantly obeyed.

He turned to the others, "Half of you start clearing them out of this walled area and place the dead in the woods. The rest start digging holes out there for a mass burial. I want this completed before nightfall before they start stinking even worse."

The members of Rat Man's army stood for a moment. Critter clapped his hands together again, resounding like a gunshot. "Move!" he ordered in a booming voice.

They jumped to it. They ran helter skelter. The fear blazing in their eyes showed their worry that Critter would turn his terrible blades against them.

Critter yelled at them some more as he watched them gingerly touching the bodies. It reminded Critter of Scott gingerly drinking a large mug of ale with his pinkie out just for laughs. "Just grab them and move them. I want this done today. You're going to be filthy anyways, you might as well get it over with." Critter nudged the Rat Man toward a body.

"Hold up," said Tomas as he jumped down the steps of the front porch. He had a box of latex gloves tucked under his arm. "These gloves that Dexter kept will help."

Critter stepped back as the people gathered around and donned the blue gloves, thanking Tomas profusely. They quickly got to work.

"Now where the hell are you, Bryan?" Critter asked, looking up and scanning the surrounding mountains.

He ordered some of the Rat Man's army to clean the bodies from the inside of the fortress. There was a lot to yet explore, both in researching Dexter's computer files and pillaging the fortress of anything that they could use. As he thought of the potential hoard of MREs, his stomach growled loud enough for Scott to hear.

"I heard that," said Scott. "How 'bout we find something to eat and then I'll kick your ass later for what you said just before the fight."

"You got it, brother."

Both men laughed as they headed back inside the fortress-like house.

***

Bryan straightened up from the computer and smiled after the zombie formation easily defeated itself. When Critter raised a sword in salute to him, Bryan raised his fist in a salute back even though he knew that Critter couldn't see him.

As he sighed with a feeling that all was accomplished, he heard a noise of a shoe scuffing the floor and then he heard a scream. Bryan instinctively fell out of his chair and ducked as he rolled on the floor.

Bryan spun as he lowered himself into a combat crouch, legs ready to spring. Something whistled above him where his head had been a split second earlier. Turning, Bryan saw that a sword slice had just missed him as Dexter yanked at it where it was embedded in a wooden bookshelf. His eyes ablaze with crazed bloodlust.

Once the sword jerked free, Dexter smiled a bloody jagged toothed grin as he wound up for another swing. He charged, crazed by his madness and slashed down. Bryan stepped to the side as the sword bit deep into the wooden desk. As Dexter yanked to free the sword, Bryan shoved him savagely in the chest, knocking the smaller man out through the door into the hallway. Bryan drew his own handgun and snap fired, but Dexter had rounded a corner and the bullet smacked harmlessly into the clay wall. Bryan gave chase as Dexter ran from him through the hallway of the rounded hobbit-like house.

The scientist pushed his way through a door and Bryan followed him into a room. Again the little guy dove, tucked into a roll, and disappeared under a table.

Bryan kicked the table out of the way and swore. It was another pipe. Bryan took a deep breath not wanting to go, but he wanted a definite finality to this cursed chapter. Instinctively he placed his gun on safety, and kept his thumb on the safe button to take it off when he was ready to shoot. He blew the breath out and took another one as if diving into a cold pool of water. He launched himself into the pipe and bumped his head on what he guessed was a low hanging support board. This caused him to drop his handgun. He couldn't catch it as he found himself on a sliding board going almost at freefall speed, cutting through pitch darkness. He heard his gun bouncing and scraping on the metal slide ahead of him. Bryan began planning how to face Dexter unarmed at the bottom of the slide.

***

An odd sensation ran through Bryan's body and mind. Never had he been on such a long slide at such a great speed and especially in total darkness. Bryan guessed that he was in an underground tunnel heading towards the fortress far down in the valley below him. He tried to relax and steel himself for a fight against Dexter at the bottom of the slide, but the free-fall speed through the dark was terrifying. He kept expecting to slam into a brick wall any second. He forced himself to listen to the sound of the handgun sliding ahead of him. If it stopped or made a different sound, it could warn him of a change in slope or obstacles, but it continued on a seemingly endless journey ahead of him.

Because of the length of the chute, his mind had time to wander between one terrifying thought after another. Oddly, one thought was that this would be a lot of fun under different circumstances.

He was tempted to draw his sword, but in the complete darkness, he didn't dare move for fear of getting snagged on something protruding from the wall or ceiling. He guessed he was plummeting at at least seventy miles per hour. If he hit anything at his current speed he would not just lose his sword but possibly his arm.

Ahead, he heard Dexter's scream echo above the sound of his handgun rattling on the metal slide. The scientist yelled, "Servants! Attack all intruders," multiple times. The effects of the tunnel made it sound like the man was right in front of him, but Bryan knew that wasn't the case due to the sound of his handgun still rattling on the long fall between the two men.

Bryan then heard the scientist giggle insanely, and soon after, he literally saw the light at the end of the tunnel, and he approached it fast. Everything that happened next happened in a brief moment, but time seemed to slow as he helplessly watched it unfold at the bottom of the slide.

He saw his pistol slam into a bunch of stuffed animals at the bottom as Dexter jumped off the slide. Bryan could see enough of the tunnel to know that it was a smooth pipe that was about three feet in diameter. It reminded him of a water slide he had been on as a kid. The lifeguard at the top made him and his friends go down feet first on their backs, but Bryan and his mischievous buddies found that they could sit up and the wind resistance would slow them enough so that they could switch over and lay on their bellies. When the lifeguard at the bottom yelled at them, they would claim the lifeguard at the top allowed them to go face first on their bellies. After a few more incidents, Bryan and his buddies got kicked out of the pool for the day.

Now, Bryan sat up hoping that he wouldn't hit a crossbeam and slowed his descent enough to lie on his belly. His goal was to grab the handgun in a head first slide. Unfortunately, Dexter read his strategy as Bryan reached for the handgun. Bryan realized that his time was probably up. He watched as Dexter extended a sword so that Bryan's own weight and velocity would impale himself.

There was nothing Bryan could do. He reached his hand forward like he was placing everything on getting the handgun. Dexter giggled.

As the sword was about to pierce Bryan's mouth, which was opened in a war-cry, and impale him, Bryan twisted his body and was able to roll off the slide where he slammed onto the concrete floor three feet below the end of the slide. Pain shot up his arm and he was uncertain whether he broke his forearm or not.

Before he could worry about the arm, he looked up and saw Dexter standing above him with the sword raised above his head. Surprisingly the scientist backed up a step and giggled, "Don't worry, Bryan. I will not kill you nor let my servants kill you. I want you in my army. Now, you will hold still and let them bite you, and you will rest quietly until you fully turn."

Bryan looked to his side and saw five well dressed, well groomed zombies approach him. As they lumbered towards Bryan, he rolled from his prone position into a combative squat.

Dexter took a step to the slide and said, "Lie face down or I will shoot your leg off." He grabbed Bryan's handgun off the slide. Dexter aimed it at Bryan's knee cap as he placed down his sword with his other hand.

Bryan glowered at Dexter refusing to move. The zombies halted a step away as if waiting for the order to bite.

"This is your last warning! Get on your face now, tough guy. I don't want you or my servants getting maimed, but I will blow your knee cap off if I must."

"Go to hell," Bryan growled as he tightened his crouch to spring at Dexter, who had the trigger half pulled.

"Sic him," the scientist ordered

The zombies launched themselves with savage growls. Bryan was buried beneath them as they attacked.

| 15 |

I raced around the corner from the hallway as I heard the commotion from the other slide that led to the room. My sword dripped with the zombie goo from the butler zombiebot. His bite at my throat didn't penetrate my skin.

Bryan made eye contact with me as the scientist yelled, "sic him." As the zombies attacked, Bryan faked a lunge at the scientist but at the last minute rolled to the side. The five zombies crashed into each other. The sound of their heads smashing into each other was almost comical. They pulled themselves back to attention, shook their heads, and chased Bryan to the wall. I ran and slashed at the zombies. Two quick swipes resulted in two of them crashing dead to the ground.

Dexter screamed in horror at the loss of his babies and leveled Bryan's handgun at me. I placed myself on the opposite side of the remaining three zombies. I backed up as the three slowly advanced on me. It was a temporary reprieve.

Bryan rolled again into a crouch and launched himself straight at Dexter as the scientist aimed the gun at him.

"Are you mad?" I screamed at Bryan as he streaked at the gun aimed at his head. I flinched as I expected his brains to fly out of his skull.

The gun jerked in Dexter's hand from his panicked pull of the trigger, but otherwise, nothing happened.

The heel of Bryan's palm crashed into Dexter's face, and the scientist fell to the ground. Bryan deftly caught the gun as it dropped from the scientist's grasp. He flipped the safety switch on the gun and aimed it at Dext. "Hey genius," he said with sarcasm. "A firearm doesn't go boom with the safety on, jackass. It'll work just fine now. Get on your stomach."

Dexter obeyed as he commanded the zombies, "Servants rest." They immediately stopped their attack. Then he said to Bryan, "Relax, man, relax."

Bryan shot back, "I'll relax when your ass is on the floor with your hands on your head."

Without a word but a regretful look on his face, Dexter complied.

While Bryan placed a knee on Dexter's back to handcuff him, I had killed two other zombies with two quick flicks of my sword. Their heads rolled on the floor before the bodies collapsed. Only the pretty young child-like female zombie in the plaid skirt remained. Killing the other zombies set something off in her and she came at me with eyes blazingly lit up for my flesh.

Bryan handcuffed the man with the same set that Don had restrained me a week ago when this mad adventure began. Dexter glared at us with his hands cuffed behind his back.

Dexter screamed, "Carla! Stop!"

The zombie quit her approach and stood in place, resuming the hoopla type stare. I had my sword ready for a decapitating slash, but withheld it. I just couldn't. Zombie or not, I just couldn't kill something that wasn't attacking me.

Bryan and I watched in slight amazement as the scientist struggled to sit up and call her over. She obeyed. "Kiss me baby," the scientist commanded.

Bryan gagged slightly as she knelt beside Dexter and kissed him on the cheek. Bryan looked at me and grimaced.

I nodded back and said through clenched teeth, "You ain't seen the half of it, brother."

A sudden anger clouded his eyes like the sweeping force of a summer storm. I kept my teeth and fists clenched trying to restrain myself as well.

Bryan kicked the scientist away from the pretty zombie girl, sprawling him on the floor. Carla stared into space waiting for a command. Bryan violently thrust his gun in his holster and his sword flicked out of the scabbard like a snake's tongue.

In the quick action, he severed the wires at the black box at the base of Carla's neck. She stood for a moment as if in shock and then, without electronic control, reverted to her true nature. She suddenly launched herself at Bryan with a savage snarl. Even though he expected it, the savagery of the sudden attack almost caught Bryan by surprise. His next hasty slash cut off her hand at the wrist and went through her abdomen; rotted guts splashed into the plush shaggy carpeted floor. I guessed that the cut severed her spinal column because she dropped like a lead weight. Despite her outside skin of feminine beauty mostly enhanced by a thick layer of cosmetics, the stench of deathly decay bled out with her zombie goo and guts. The foul odor was almost too much for me to bear. My boots made sucking sounds as I stepped in the gore that seeped into the plush carpet as I stumbled around for somewhere clean to stand.

Carla demonstrated no pain, only the desire to feed on one of us. Once her zombie brain processed that she couldn't walk, she began to crawl toward us, eyes afire. She left a disgustingly thick trail of zombie goo in her wake. The carpet would need a hell of a steam cleaning.

Dexter hobbled over on his knees screaming her name and issuing orders to her. A mad foaming spittle tinged red from his shattered teeth flew from his panicked lips.

She struggled to bite him as he came to her. Her snapping teeth were inches from his face when Bryan pulled him away with one hand and sliced off her head with the other.

Dexter collapsed in sobbing defeat. "She was a great woman."

"Hell, my wife is a good woman too, but she would never turn on me like that," Bryan then said with an ironic grin. "Don't worry. There are more programmable zombies in the sea."

"She was like a child," Dexter whined.

Having seen the way Carla attempted to go down on me earlier, I was overwhelmed with a sense of disgust. What Dexter did was a mix of rape and necrophilia. Him referring to her as a child did something to me. Carla should have been buried respectfully long ago, not used as a sex slave.

I charged him screaming, "You raped that dead child, you son of a bitch!"

I savagely kicked him in the stomach repeatedly. As I wound up for the third kick, Bryan grabbed my shoulder. "Get a grip, Eric. There are a few things we need to ask the professor."

I stopped, panting like I had kicked him over well one hundred times rather than only twice. My emotions threatened to hurl me into the pit of madness.

Bryan stared at me in confusion. "What's wrong with you, Eric? Control yourself."

"That zombie-- That dead girl was programmed-- Tried to give me a fucking blow job. That sick son of a bitch." I couldn't say anything more.

Bryan's face was neutral and it pissed me off that he calmly took in the knowledge of what Dexter had done. Bryan had only heard about it, but I had had those zombies coming after me, trying to have sex with me. I really wanted to see him get disgusted. I wanted to see Bryan unleash on Dexter what he had unleashed on me earlier when he thought I had given Tommy the video. This was a far worse crime, in my opinion. I had been duped. Dexter was genuine evil.

Dexter sat up moaning with his hands cuffed behind his back and staring at the dead zombie chick, mumbling Carla's name over and over.

Bryan grabbed the scientist by the front of the collar and slapped him in the face. "Wake up, Poindexter!"

His eyes narrowed from a blank stare to a piercing stare of hatred at Bryan.

Bryan slapped him again. "Get a grip. Everyone." Bryan said as he slung the scientist to his belly. "Eric, put your sword to his back and keep your emotions under control. I don't want him dead, yet."

I was under control at this point, however I think he wanted Dexter to worry I would run him through and it was only Bryan's tenuously calm demeanor that was stopping me.

"You got it," I said. "Just make it quick before I lose control again," I added, playing along.

With Dexter facing the floor, Bryan grinned and nodded at me. He placed a knee on Dexter's back and then undid the handcuffs on both hands and ordered him to put his hands above his head. Dexter complied and Bryan placed the cuffs back on both hands so that his hands were cuffed in front of him rather than behind his back.

"Hey, Bryan?" I said.

"Yeah?"

"Next time you do this," I explained, "you don't have to undo the cuffs on both wrists. You can just undo one."

"Why are you telling me this?" he asked with slight irritation in his voice.

"It will save time," I replied.

Bryan swore and said, "Don't you go getting all Poindexter on me now. No one likes a know it all."

Bryan hauled Dexter to his feet roughly, seemingly irritated from my know it all suggestion. Bryan pushed Dexter to a desk with three computers. The man seemed to have three to five computers in every single room.

Bryan shoved him into a chair with his gun at his back, well aware of how the scientist had flipped him into a wall and escaped earlier and said, "I want to see some security cameras."

Dexter replied to Bryan as if he were an idiot, "I can't show you the actual cameras from the computers. I can only show you what they film."

Bryan smacked him on the back of the head, "One more know-it-all remark from anyone and that person loses a head," Bryan said with an exasperated chuckle.

The threat may have been funny had I not seen a few decapitations already today.

"OK, OK, I got the point," Dexter said with an eye roll as he went to work on the computer.

Even with handcuffs, he worked the keyboard with the masterful flare of a concert pianist. Bryan watched the touch screen and butted in to choose which video feed to look at. He chose the screens with his left hand while he kept Dexter's restrained hands pinned with his stronger right. I kept my sword poking into Dexter's back.

Bryan clicked on a few videos and saw different vantage points of the fortress. He watched Critter and his men directing the Rat Man's crew. Even though Rat Man's crew were all armed they gave deference to all of the Mountain Warriors. I wondered what had happened up there.

Bryan tapped different views. Some showed nothing but wooded mountainsides. I was tempted to make a smartass remark about him taking a liesurely virtual nature hike but refrained after thinking about his last threat to Dexter and me.

Bryan grabbed Dexter's hair firmly. Not enough to cause pain, but enough to let him know not to trifle with him and asked Dexter, "Where are the rest of your zombie armies? Don't lie," he added, giving Dexter's head a shake.

"You idiots wiped them out," he yelled a few bloody flecks of foam landing on the computer screen. From his genuine anger, we believed him.

Bryan ignored him and leaned in reading something on the screen. He asked, "You got access to government drones?" Bryan clicked on a few options and then was looking through the eye of the flying drones.

"Of course I have access! You clowns don't know who you're messing with."

Bryan retorted, "And you don't know who you're messing with. "

"Yes I do," Dexter said.

Bryan looked at him curiously.

Dexter started off seriously saying, "I know who you are. You are," then he sang, "The Mountain Warriors, dun dun dun dun," he ended by laughing maniacally, eyes still ablaze with hatred.

Bryan smacked him on the back of the head.

Dexter reached and rubbed the back of his head with both shackled hands. "Sorry. I thought you would be proud of your fame. The show looks cool. I mean you guys kick ass and all, but the title…"

"What about it?" Bryan asked.

Dexter didn't notice the dangerous tone in Bryan's voice as he replied, "I mean 'Mountain Warriors?' I don't know. I mean it just sounds cheesy as hell for a TV show? Who came up with that name?"

Bryan clenched a fist trying to control his impulse to not just smack the scientist but to smash his face in and take his head off with a punch. "Just shut up," Bryan muttered. Then he glared at me, "You too, Eric."

"What?" I asked.

"That smile," he said. "I know what you're thinking."

I bit my lip and shrugged, becoming very serious.

He finally chuckled lightly and said, "Aw hell," out his usually serious character. I think the stress was getting to him and it was either laugh or cry.

He looked at me as if he was trying to figure out the expression on my face.

Bryan asked, "You OK, man."

"Of course I am. Because," then I sang, "I'm a 'Mountain Warrior dun dun dun dun dun!'" I knew that I was pushing it, but I took a gamble to lighten the mood.

Bryan glared at me for a second and then we shared a laugh. When Dext giggled, Bryan smacked him lightly upside the head and said, "What the hell you laughing at?"

Dexter just gave him the evil eye.

As the laughter died down, I realized that I had to relieve myself. "Excuse me, Dexter, do you have a bathroom down here?"

"Of course," he said in an annoyed voice as if I implied that he was too uncivilized to have such amenities. He pointed with his chin towards a doorway. "Through the master bedroom."

"Thanks," I said.

"Don't touch anything," Dexter ordered

Bryan smacked him on the head again, "You don't tell anyone what to do," Bryan admonished. Then he looked at me and said, "Don't touch anything. It could be booby trapped."

"Don't worry," I said.

"Don't ever tell me that!"

"What?"

"Don't ever tell me not to worry. That tells me that you're not worried and you're not paying attention."

I was annoyed. He always told me to quit worrying over fate. "You tell me to be stoic and not to worry—"

"Knock it off and just go to the bathroom and don't touch anything. He may have a zombie horde in his closet."

"Yes sir," I said with heavy sarcasm and a rigid salute as I turned to the bedroom. It had to be getting late in the day. We were all getting punchy and irritable.

Bryan didn't reply but I could feel his glare on my back. Dexter warned Bryan that he had help coming within moments. I heard Bryan smack Dexter's head again. Usually Bryan kept control of his passions even in the worst of times, but I always felt like a storm was raging beneath ready to let loose, and today he seemed pretty rattled.

I entered the darkened bedroom. I could still hear Bryan and Dexter talking through the open door. As my eyes adjusted to the dim light, I first noticed a mirror on the ceiling reflecting the light that trickled in from outside the room. There was a heart shaped bed with some frilly crimson satin sheets that were heavily stained.

I said, "Yeah Bryan, you don't have to worry about me touching anything."

"What?" he asked from the other room.

"Nevermind," I called back.

I walked in the bathroom and left the door open for the light that trickled in from the living room. I didn't even want to touch the light switch. Enough light bled in that I could see well enough to do my duty. I was vaguely aware of photos taped to the walls, but ignored them as my mind was over-maxed with reality.

I used the toilet, flushed it with my foot, and then used my elbow to turn on a faucet to wash my hands. I washed my face, enjoying the simple luxury of running water. I caught a slight whiff of an unpleasant scent. My eyes had gradually adjusted to the gloom. I now could see clearly in the unlit bathroom. Maybe it was the lavish shock of running water that brought me to my clear-headedness, but I could now see that the walls were covered in photos of Dexter in pornographic poses with his zombie minions. The contrast of his eyes drowning in erotic passion and the dull disinterested eyes of the zombies simply following orders took its toll on my soul's sanity. I then saw the source of the unpleasant smell. A medium sized trash can overflowed with used prophylactics. I heaved violently over the sink as it seemed every aspect of me revolted against such abominations. I felt it in my physical body, logical mind, and the morals of my soul, and they all revolted all at once. I desired full ablutions.

Until this point, I wondered if man had a soul. It was only in feeling the ravages of the human mind that I came to feel the soul and believe. To see a person so twisted and devoid of an internal spirit demonstrated that Dexter once had a soul to lose.

"You OK?" Bryan shouted from outside of the room.

"Yeah, yeah," I said. I spat out some drooling, bile tasting saliva into the sink. The dry heaves had been violent, but I had nothing in my belly to expel.

"I'll be right out," I promised.

I looked at the sink and had no desire to wash my mouth or face again. I was even disgusted by Dexter's water from the spring beneath this accursed place. I was about to run out to the party/computer room when I felt myself bend over almost like I was pushed. I heard her scream loudly in my head, "Eric!"

"Abigail," I muttered.

"What did you say?" Bryan yelled from the other room.

"Nothing," I said as I rushed to the door. I knew that we were in trouble.

***

Abigail took her mind off of Eric and tried to anticipate their mission. It was daylight outside the Caverns of the Vampires. Vampires, although the greatest terror in the Forbidden

Zone at night, most were far less powerful during the day. She guessed that the Mountain Warriors must have breached the fortress and were inside the compound from the agitation of The Specter.

Destroying the zombie bots and Dexter was a good thing in her opinion, but to even show that she thought that would result in the death penalty from The Specter. Even Richard, her vampiric father, would have to order it.

Even if she and the Mountain Warriors killed The Specter and her coven, she would be marked for death by the powers that ruled the Forbidden Zone and she could not seek refuge with the survivors. People instinctively hated her kind. Even if she was accepted by the Mountain Warriors, the Governor, Daniel Hildebrande, who was Eric's uncle, would send helicopters and weaponized drones to kill every man, woman, and child who stood in their way to kill her.

She lived in a nihilistic state at this moment. As much as she loved the gift of life, she was not just a vampire, she was a coven member. There was no way they would let her leave alive to follow her morality. She was beginning to look for the most honorable death to die. As dismal as that was, Death seemed to be her only way out of vampirism and the organization.

She had to put that out of her mind and carry on with the present mission. Led by The Specter through the caverns, the vampires delved deeper into the mountain and arrived at their destination. A series of crystal doors stood before them. These led to numerous places throughout the Forbidden Zone. To walk through a portal could take you miles away in mere seconds. None of the vampires understood the ancient technology that was rumored to be antediluvian in origin. Supposedly, The Specter and Richard alone held the keys and the knowledge of where they all went. Abigail was figuring them out on her own and hoped to steal one of the crystal keys that were kept in The Specter's and Richard's pockets.

Although no one knew who the creators of the doorways were, a part of Abigail prayed that whoever or whatever created them would return and defeat The Specter. A part of her also feared that whatever made them would be worse.

Mysterious creatures lurked beneath the vampires' lair. Whatever they were in the dark passages below, those creatures killed wayward vampires who wandered deeper into the earth. Maybe meeting them would be the best way to either gain a powerful ally or to depart this life. It was a gamble that she was considering more and more.

The Specter walked into another crystal wall and it seemed to wrap around him as he disappeared like mist. Abigail and the other five vampires followed. They were now in a bedrock passage. Abigail sensed Eric was near. The Specter growled, breaking her compounded reverie.

"Get your swords ready. We should take them by surprise. Kill everyone in sight, except Dexter. If Eric is there, Abigail, you must turn him whether he wants it or not." The Specter ordered as he drew his sword.

"Eric!" Abigail sent the thought to Eric with intention. They walked toward the doorway to Dexter's party room. It was within a hundred meters at the end of the passage.

| 16 |

In my head, I heard Abigail scream my name again with greater urgency. I had a picture in my head of the party room and what she wanted me to see. It was the view of the bookcase by the sofa, but I didn't understand.

"Bryan!" I screamed as I rushed out into the party room.

"What's the matter with you?" Bryan demanded. He tended to get irritated if someone abandoned what he considered a manly stoicism.

"Get your gun out," I yelled. When he hesitated, I ordered in an urgent voice, "Just do it. Your gun. No swords."

He nodded and complied, bringing his battered, but trustworthy and deadly AR-15 off of his shoulder strap and to the ready. Bryan of all people understood gut reactions and this was the strongest I had ever displayed other than when I burned Tomas's zombie bite to disinfect it and ultimately save him.

Bryan grabbed Dexter and flung him from the chair to the floor and unlocked one handcuff and re-braced his hands behind his back. Bryan rested a foot on the back of the prone man's head.

I had my Winchester 30-30 in my hands. I pointed it at a bookcase. "Aim there, at the center of the bookcase."

He raised a curious eyebrow, but nodded and aimed his AR-15 where I had instructed.

Nothing happened. The more time that passed, the more antsy that I became. Bryan and Dexter were now giving me sideways glances. Their stares told me plainly that they doubted my sanity. Dexter, however, seemed worried about something. I guessed that he knew that I knew something was behind the bookcase.

"Dexter. Don't lie. That bookcase is a doorway, right," I asked.

"You are freaking coo-coo for Froot Loops man!" Dexter proclaimed.

I ignored the reference to the wrong cereal.

Bryan's eyes narrowed with suspicion. "Where does that passage lead?" he asked Dexter.

"You both have lost your minds!" Dexter said louder.

"It leads to Shining Rock," I said confidently, aiming at the bookcase. The gun held firmly in my sweating grasp.

"What! No way!" The high-pitch tone in Dexter's denial told me that I was correct.

"The lair of the Vampires," I said.

Bryan looked at me like I was crazy. He was about to say something, but Dexter spoke first.

"How in the hell did you know that?" Dexter blurted, visibly scared.

Bryan kicked him, "We told you not to lie." Then Bryan looked at me with wide eyes. "Shining Rock is far away. That's gotta be a long ass tunnel. It's over a day's march from here."

"I warned you that you didn't know who you were messing with," Dexter said.

"Everybody, shh," I shushed them with my finger over my lips. My right hand firmly gripped my rifle.

We waited. I heard Bryan sigh and even I doubted my sanity, when, as if by its own volition, a book leaned out slightly, causing a solenoid to click, and then after a pause that seemed to last forever the door that was the bookcase slowly began to open.

Most people would have missed it, but behind Bryan's grim set face, I saw terror welling up in his eyes as we waited for the creatures behind the door to expose themselves.

The bookcase doorway opened, and Richard, the lead vampire, guiding five others including Abigail, appeared. They were followed by The Specter. All of them, except Abigail, looked surprised to see us. Their swords were ready, but they had their rifles slung on their shoulders and pistols holstered at their hips. As they stared at our rifles in shock, their swords hung limply in their grasps.

"Stop!" Bryan barked as The Specter started to reach for his gun.

The Specter stopped and a tense moment of silence followed.

Bryan smiled and taunted, "Bringing blades to a gunfight, dumbass freaks."

"It won't happen again," growled The Specter.

"Got that right," said Bryan. "You may not live that long." I could almost hear Bryan's finger creaking on the trigger.

The Specter glared at me with supreme hatred that curdled my blood. The last time we met, I had knocked him out with a butt of my handgun. Admittedly, I basically sucker punched him. I knew he was the most dangerous enemy to provoke in all The Forbidden Zone. I wanted to shoot him immediately. However, remembering Tommy's warning, I aimed my rifle at Abigail's heart as my finger tightened on the trigger. For a moment her eyes blazed with fear and maybe anger at the betrayal and then softened to hurt as she sighed.

I had originally commanded the use of rifles, but I let Bryan have control of when the lead would fly, and wondered if he withheld bullets out of a sense of fairplay or if the vampires had enough mind control over him to cause him to withhold the bullets. The last time we met the coven, it was at night when they had full psychic strength. They had us almost completely under their power. Only Abigail had saved us.

Although safe from the daylight in the basement, these weren't the same creatures that we had met during the night. During the daylight, their powers were greatly weakened. Indeed, they looked more like harmless pasty faced weirdos, rather than the terrors of the Forbidden Zone. The fact that they would attempt to rescue Dexter in this weakened state confirmed Dexter's importance to their diabolical plans.

"You led us into a trap, you fool!" The Specter excoriated Dexter who lay on the floor beneath Bryan's firm boot. The Specter had a deep gravelly supernatural sounding voice. It had scared me the first few times that I had met him, but now I was beginning to believe that it was all kabuki. However he had a very tall, solidly built frame beneath his skull mask and spiked, black leather clothes and hooded cloak. He also commanded an army of vampires who obeyed him. All the short hairs on the back of my neck were fully erect.

Dexter screamed back. "Not if you had gotten here earlier to save my babies. These jackasses destroyed all of my—all of ours, our work!" he sputtered.

"All of you drop your weapons," Bryan growled. I could see him sweat. I knew he was judging his own mental capacity trying to determine if they were attempting mind control. Abigail had taught me how to put up a mental wall against them. I had taught that in turn to Bryan and Critter, but we had yet to test it against the mental powers of the vampires.

"You can't threaten immortals," The Specter growled back.

"I knocked you out last time. I can do it again." I said with my own growl. It wasn't a taunt. I wanted him to know that I didn't fear him. I don't think I succeeded. He just glared back through the eyeholes of his skull mask almost through my soul.

The Specter started to reply but Bryan cut him off, "I have never seen a ghost wear combat boots and carry an assault rifle. Now drop it all before I prove that you are indeed mortal," Bryan said as he flicked his AR-15 to safety and then back to fire just to emphasize his order with the click of steel. I can attest that when a gun is aimed at you, any metallic noise causes any sane man to flinch.

The Specter didn't flinch, but he was the first to place his weapons down. He did so slowly, with his eyes glaring at me the whole time rather than Bryan. There was no fear of my gun on his masked face. Just a promise that he would kill me when given a chance. The others followed except Lucius, the youngest vampire who was in his early twenties at the most. He stared at us as if trying to project something from his eyes. It was almost laughable. The way they were bugging out and the way he thrusted his chest as if physically trying to channel psychic power. He then raised and pointed a clawed hand at us to assist. The fingers extending and clenching with his effort.

"Knock it off, punk. It's daylight. You're harmless as a kitten," I scolded the young vamp. I knew not to underestimate them even in daylight, but I couldn't resist the taunt, "and drop the weapons."

Richard squinted hatred at me and said, "He's immune to us, except for maybe Abigail." He cast an evil grin at her. "It seems that Eric has helped Bryan out as well. I sense a mental wall against me."

Abigail looked a little worried that Richard suspected her of something. She delicately bit her crimson lower lip.

Lucius widened his eyes one more time, trying with one last burst, but threw his sword and rifle down when I simply laughed.

"Specter, get down on your belly," Bryan ordered.

The monster deliberately took his time to lay down, eyes never leaving me.

"You lay across Spec on your belly, Richard." Bryan instructed the vampire patriarch, and then he ordered each vamp to lay on the one before him or her. They were laying crisscross across each others' upper backs, facing away from the hidden passage. They braced for balance with their feet and hands on the plush carpet.

When he lastly ordered Abigail, she hesitated and I grabbed her by the hair and pulled her to the pile as I said, "Get down, you blood sucking witch."

She screamed, "Ouch!"

I had been told that no one could cast the evil eye like a woman scorned, but mortal women have nothing on a vampire woman scorned. I returned her eye contact and shrugged and told her telepathically that I had to treat her rough so Richard wouldn't suspect anything between us.

I heard her tell me, "OK," in my mind and she physically nodded slightly, but that anger of betrayal burning in her eyes did not fade in the slightest.

Bryan then uncuffed Dexter, pocketed the cuffs and had him lie on top of Abigail. It was an awkward pile that came just above my standing belt-line. To keep the stack from tipping over, the vampires had their feet on the ground for stability. I had never seen anything like this before, but I couldn't see these monsters launching an attack against us. They would have to get off each other one at a time. This was preferable to them laying next to each other where they could attack all at once.

As Dexter laid on top of Abigail, she glared at us and then yelled, "Stop it!" at Dexter.

Dexter removed his hands from her bottom, acting like he slipped and had reached out for the first thing within reach for balance. He finished laying down on top of Abigail. He smiled and said, "Sorry, babe," in a sweet and slimy voice.

"It was an accident," Bryan said in his reasonable tone to calm the situation.

"Damn it!" Abigail snarled, still glaring at me. "The sick bastard is aroused!"

I punched Dexter's head and body a few times as I commanded, "Get your junk off of her, you freaking pervert!"

Dexter moved his hips off of Abigail, but her eyes blazed without gratitude.

Bryan shook his head, "You are out of your mind, Dexter. That's playing with fire. Vampires are no joke."

Abigail opened her mouth to say something when The Specter whined, "I can't breathe under here."

That was Bryan's point to disable them as much as possible without outright shooting them, especially since we didn't have handcuffs for all of them.

I actually laughed at The Specter. I had never seen him display any weakness and I suspected it to be a ruse to get some people off so he could have a chance to escape or attack.

Bryan laughed as well at him and said, "Shut up. I know you're faking. Anyway, you're immortal right. Why would an immortal need to breathe?"

"He doesn't look immortal," I taunted.

Bryan shook his head at me and I realized he didn't want to antagonize The Specter too much. In fact, I suspected that if it was Dexter complaining, Bryan might have smacked him, but he left The Specter alone to a degree. I didn't blame Bryan. Even with two guns trained on him and a pile of vampires above him, the man or monster that was The Specter still scared the hell out of me.

Bryan said, "OK, you ladies and gents are going to wait here. I'm getting some friends. Poindexter owes us a few MREs for our troubles. After that you can party, have an orgy with the undead, or whatever you freaks do for fun. However, in the meantime, Eric will have his gun on you and will shoot anyone who takes their eyes off the floor and makes eye contact with him."

Bryan looked at me and said, "If you feel woozy or weird in any way like they're screwing with your head, shoot all these freaks. I mean that rifle needs to blaze until you run out of bullets and the barrel turns red, and then reload, and keep blasting until we get back down here to help you with our own rifles. Got it?"

"I got it," I said.

Dexter pleaded in a panicked voice, "Don't shoot me! Please. I can't do that mind stuff. I—"

"Quiet, human!" The Specter rumbled in his inhuman voice.

Bryan said sarcastically, "If you can shut that pain in the ass up, Specter, you have my undying friendship."

"Bryan. Please, take me with you," Dexter begged. "Don't leave me with these monsters. You don't know what they do to men who displease them. Please."

Bryan looked at the pathetic man in amazement who moments ago tried to molest a vampiress. "You tried to turn me into one of those things," Bryan said. "The only mercy you can expect from me is a bullet in your brainpan rather than torture."

"Please! Don't leave me down here with these things!" Dexter pleaded.

"Quiet, human!" The Specter bellowed with no struggle to get breath to power his vocal cords.

Bryan lost his temper. He took a couple steps forward and kicked The Specter on the same side of the temple where I had cold cocked him with my handgun's barrel the week before. A trickle of blood leaked through the skull mask onto the floor to let us know that the wound that I gave him was reopened.

It only angered The Specter as he glowered at Bryan.

"Shut up! All of you!" Bryan said. "If any of them talks, especially Poindexter here, blast away," Bryan's eyes were filled with a fire I had not seen before. Any fear of the supernatural was temporarily consumed with anger. "And you, Specter! You bled once when Eric hit you. I am curious to see how much you would bleed if you were shot by a gun. Don't tempt me. I am sick of this illusion."

Bryan observed the bookcase where the vampire crew had entered. He then went to another bookcase by the slide that I had slid down. He pulled a book that looked similar to the book that had moved when the vamps door opened. The bookcase swung open on a well oiled pivot. He took off bounding up the stairs to the fortress above us.

"Abigail," I thought.

She looked at me and shook her head and said in my mind, "Don't! I think he may pick up things between us."

I knew she meant Richard, but dared not to even think his name for fear of alerting him. I felt myself start to sweat.

| 17 |

Bryan raced to the top of the stairs inside the bookcase opening. The long climb winded him after a hard day. His path dead ended at a solid concrete wall. He felt around, shining a small flashlight around the corners. The light was weak, batteries near death. After two years in a primitive life, fully charged batteries were a rarity in the Forbidden Zone. He felt around some more and pushed the wall in a few places where he thought an unlocking mechanism might be. He swore. It shouldn't be that hard to find the means to open it. Anyone on this side of the wall should already know that they were in a secret passage. He finally gave up and snarled, launching his shoulder against it. The wall pivoted on the center and spun easily. He fell through, rolled to his feet, ready to fight. Bryan immediately realized that he was in the room on the second floor. It was empty except the junk hoarded by Dexter, minus the inflatable raft.

Bryan looked toward the sliding glass door to the balcony and realized they only had a couple hours of daylight left.

He had to get moving before the vampires were at their full strength.

Bryan heard people moving and speaking on the lower floor. Some of the talk was rough curses and grunting as people moved the dead zombies. He walked onto the landing. Although he had seen it on the security cameras, Bryan was not prepared for the carnage and some of it had been cleared out already. The Rat Man's army was doing the work of dragging the dead outside the building as Bryan's people supervised. Critter was one of his men who was still inside the fortress.

"Hey Critter," Bryan said casually from the upper landing.

Critter whirled around in unnatural panic, unnatural at least for him. It was so rare to sneak up on the woodsman that it made him doubt his reality for a moment. "How the-- How the hell did you get up there?"

"You need to do better with your guards and your own alertness," Bryan said with a half-smirk. "I walked in the front door right past you."

"Baloney, man, how the--?" He left the question unasked and then ran up the stairs and gave Bryan a spontaneous hug. "I, we, owe you a thanks, brother. I know that was you behind the—" He let the rest of the comment hang as he looked downstairs and whispered, "Rat Man's people think we slaughtered them ourselves. They've even been embellishing the story as the afternoon wore on. We're damn near mythical in their eyes."

Bryan smiled with the knowledge that one set of enemies, Rat Man's army, were pacified. However the true enemies were about to be on their home turf as night approached. Although they were monsters, he didn't like the idea of shooting anyone who was disarmed, including The Specter and the Vampires piled on top of him. Besides that, The Specter could call helicopters in to attack his village. Bryan walked a razor thin line between keeping his humanity versus coldblooded killing monsters who would set up to attack the tribe when they weren't prepared.

Bryan said, "Speaking of the afternoon wearing on, we need to get out of here before night. We've less than two hours."

"Yeah," Critter agreed. Then his somberness returned as he related what he thought to be bad news, "We lost Eric."

"Naw, he's guarding our MREs," Bryan said. "Our mountain of MREs, I might add."

Critter looked at Bryan as if he had lost his mind.

"Get our men up here. Don't say anything to the Rat Man's Brigade. Keep them working. I'll explain more when we're well out of earshot. We're also dealing with the vampires, again."

Fear briefly glossed across Critter's eyes.

Bryan reassured him, "They don't seem to have their full mental powers during the day, but even though they're disarmed, we're probably best off killing them while they are relatively helpless."

Critter nodded and called the men and women. They bounded up the stairs two and three at a time and hugged and smacked their leader on the back and shoulders thanking him for the earlier rescue.

"Let's talk somewhere else," Bryan said.

He led the way to a secluded room. Once they were all in the room, they looked at the bookcase that Bryan had left open.

"Holy secret passages, Batman," Scott exclaimed, not caring that the dated remark went over the heads of the younger warriors. People were used to him talking nonsense anyway.

Bryan said quickly, "This leads to where Dexter escaped when he rolled under the table, but we caught him. There are enough MREs to keep our camp fed for the year, but just take two cases. The Specter and six vampires are detained downstairs, but let's move fast. We need to be long gone before the sun even thinks about setting." Bryan turned and ran down the stairs through the bookcase door. Without looking behind he waved for them to follow and said, "Let's go."

***

I heard footsteps coming back down the stairs through the bookcase opening from the above fortress. I gripped my rifle and watched the stack of vampires, not daring to take my eyes off of them.

I feared for a second who might be coming down the stairs, but was happy to see the Mountain Warriors rush inside the room.

Critter swore, "What the hell, Eric? Are you a ghost?"

He punched me hard enough in the shoulder for me to elicit an, "Ow! Yes! I'm here enough to feel that, jackass." We both laughed.

"You'll have to tell me the story. It looked like you were eaten by the zombies," Critter said.

The other warriors greeted me with kinder but still rough signs of affection.

I started to explain my escape when Bryan said urgently, "Another time for story hour! Let's go!"

"Hold up," Critter said.

He walked over to the pile of people, vampires, monsters, or whatever you want to call them and squatted down.

He looked The Specter and Richard square in the eyes and said, "I owe all of you a sword thrust through the hearts if you clowns still have such organs."

The Specter showed no sign that he was having trouble breathing. He simply glared at Critter from under the pile. His eyes said every murderous thought in his heart.

Bryan snapped his fingers and ordered, "Come on. Let's grab some MREs. Two boxes per man. We have a long run back to our new campsite!"

I kept my gun trained on the vampires, Dexter, and The Specter. Mostly I pointed it at either Richard's or The Specter's face. I was pretty sure that we were going to execute them. These enemies were too powerful to let go, and I could see their desire for revenge in their eyes. They would hunt us down at night. I must have been getting jaded because regardless of them being disarmed, I really did want to see The

Specter, and Richard die. They had no purpose being on the Earth. They were pure evil.

I could feel someone, probably Richard, probing into my mind. I felt like I was putting his probing in a compartment in my mind and walling him off from the rest of me. I looked at him and told him to stop. He gave me a patronizingly innocent look. I had to kill them. Preferably now. Cold blooded or not, I had to do the deed. They could kill each of us on their own time once it was night.

I instinctively looked at Abigail and quickly, purposefully looked away. I didn't know if she was sensing my thoughts even though I felt like they were in a separate compartment of my mind that she couldn't read. Could I kill her? She had helped me in the past, but why? Even if I let her go and killed the others, how would she respond? I looked at the back of her head as she stared at the floor. She was so beautiful. I thought of life with such a beautiful and mysterious woman. It was all so swimmingly fanciful. I shook my head and glared at Richard and the Specter at the bottom of the stack.

One of the vampires was playing with my mind and stirred my fancy for her. It was not Abigail doing this. She seemed to focus her annoyance on Dexter. I knew they all had different types of mental powers. I suspected Richard was messing with my erotic thoughts for Abigail, because a tense situation usually has the opposite of an aphrodisiac effect on me. It felt like something was shutting down my reason and clouding it with carnal fantasies.

I forced my rational mind to think logically. I told myself that Abigail was undead. Not as bad as Carla, Dexter's zombie sex slave, but undead none-the-less. Was a relationship with a vampiress any less of an abomination than Dexter's relationship with Carla? Surely not. It wouldn't be as bad. Abigail's mind is sharp. She is beautiful. She had a good heart. She is beautiful. She is all I need. She is beautiful. She is beautiful. She is beautiful. I kept finding my mind drawn to that phrase and it repeated itself in my head like a mantra.

This was madness. I should not be dwelling on lustful thoughts while I held vampires at gunpoint!

While the erotic thoughts flittered though my head, I also kept sensing the thought, "Kill her. Kill her. Kill her."

But I quickly realized that the conflicting feelings of love and desire for death weren't from my own heart or mind. If it wasn't insanity, at least two of the vampires were screwing with my head, I determined. I could feel the battle. One of these vampires wanted me to fall for her, so that she could bite me. The other wanted me to kill her for... For what?

"I won't kill her!" I blurted out.

Lucius looked up immediately with a guilty look.

Richard then shot me a worried glance. There was dissension in the vampire ranks. No wonder Abigail was disillusioned. One of the vampires wanted her dead. But whatever was going on, my sanity would not be a casualty in their war.

"Stop it! Next time, I will shoot you. All of you." I shouted out loud to all of them.

Abigail's glare snapped up at me, but I wasn't talking to her. Where Abigail and I could communicate, Richard's power seemed to be limited to making me passionately feel whatever emotion that he instilled in my head. Lucian (if it was indeed him telling me to kill her) simply fired my savage instincts to kill. In some ways Richard and Lucian were more powerful than Abigail. She could communicate on an intellectual level where these guys by-passed that and simply fired up my passions and base instincts.

Just a week ago, I thought these psionic abilities weren't real. The rational side of me assured me that these powers were non-existent and I was simply losing my mind, but it was too real. I was a hair trigger from acting against them.

I growled at the pile, "Stop screwing with my mind! All of you! I will start shooting now!"

Richard snarled at me baring his fangs when he realized that I caught his mental meddling. He didn't like failure. I lashed out and kicked him in the face. He snapped his jaw and tried to bite my foot. His two inch fangs scraped my leather boots. I kicked him again, breaking one of his fangs. I was about to open up on the monsters with my 30-30. I aimed between Richard's eyes. My finger shakily squeezed the trigger, but stopped.

"Don't, Eric," Abigail said out loud.

She had a definite power over me. I hated it! I wanted to scream! I wanted to kill. To kill something to get whatever was foreign from my mind! I needed to kill her first if I was to kill the others. She stared at me in shock and horror. She knew my current thoughts.

I shook those thoughts from my mind with a physical shake of my head like a dog wringing water from its hide. I looked away from the vampires.

The warriors of my tribe came out from the storage room with two boxes of MREs a piece. They were overjoyed. Each man had enough food for almost a month. The warriors immediately ran up the stairs with their treasure. There were also candies for the kids in the MREs, I heard a father in our group mention.

"And candy for Scott too," Scott jovially added.

Also, and maybe more importantly depending upon who you asked, there were packs of instant coffee. As much as I normally hated instant coffee, these were a blessing from the gods out here. The thought of instant coffee brought a smile to my face.

I realized that as I thought calmly of the coffee, how scattered and violently changing my thoughts were becoming. One second, I was considering cold blooded murder (if shooting a monster that wants to drain you of your blood is murder) and the next second I was thinking of coffee. I felt like I was going mad. I decided that when I got back to camp I would speak to Shelley, the camp herbalist and healer. She always had good words of wisdom and concoctions for healing troubled minds and bodies.

Bryan told me to go get my boxes of MREs from the other room, and then he sent the rest of the warriors up the stairs.

Critter took over the duty of guarding the vamps and The Specter. He pointed his AK at Specter. I should have warned Critter of the psychic warfare that the vamps were reeking on me, but my base instinct just wanted to leave. However, I didn't have a chance to run back to the storage room.

"Stop it, you pervert!" Abigail screamed as her elbow slammed into Dexter's ribs. She glared over her shoulder at the scientist. Dexter's hands were inappropriately placed on the vampiress' breasts.

"Ouch," he screamed and removed his hands from her to his suddenly sore chest.

"Specter! Your vampiress assaulted me! I am irreplaceable," he screamed, sounding like an oversized child.

"Abigail, keep your hands off my scientist," The Specter commanded.

"This is crazy!" she shouted with frustration.

I suddenly wanted to kill Dexter. Abigail looked at me and I wondered if the impulse came from her and not totally from me. No, that was my own impulse. I wanted to kill him from the moment that I realized that he was responsible for the zombie bots. What he was doing to Abigail was the final straw.

"Alright, come here you weirdo." I pulled him up by his hair with one hand and aimed the firearm at his heart through his upper back with my other. My finger was firmly placed over the trigger. I remembered that he had good fighting skills from the first time he escaped from us. Any bump and he'd be dead. I didn't care, and I could see in his eyes that he knew that.

"Ow," he whined. "Go easy."

"No," I said back.

Abigail looked grateful to have the scientist off of her.

Bryan didn't question my taking command. Instead he kept his weapon trained on Dexter.

"Go Eric. Get your MREs. We'll deal with these things," Bryan ordered as I stood there trying to sort out my own thoughts from the probings of Abigail, Richard, Lucian, and who knows who else.

Bryan led Dexter back to a computer.

I sprinted to the back storage area to get away from the craziness and grabbed two boxes by the plastic binding straps, immediately aware of how heavy they would weigh on my arms after running up the ridge for a few hours.

I looked at the mountain of storable food. We didn't even make a dent in it. I hoped we could get more, but I wasn't looking forward to coming back either. This stack would keep us fed for a year, easily.

I walked back out of the storage room. All that was left of the Mountain Warriors in the basement was Bryan, Critter and Scott. Scott and Bryan looked over the computers with Dexter explaining things while Critter stared blankly into space near the vampires and the Specter. His rifle pointed at the ground instead of at the monsters.

I realized that one of them had a hold of his mind. Even though it was daylight and the vamps couldn't incapacitate me, the vamps still had enough power to mess with my mind.

Critter had proven to be a lot more susceptible to their wiles in our last confrontation with the vamps.

"Critter," I screamed as I dropped my boxes. The vampires made their move to escape with The Specter throwing them off of his back and rising to his full height. Critter could only stare dumbly into space.

***

Before The Specter launched his escape and Eric was still guarding them, Abigail glared at Eric from atop of the pile and felt a rage coming on that was partly compounded and stoked by the vampiric infection and bloodlust. She had not fed all day and the hunger for blood burned in her heart. The origin of the rage originally was inspired by her frustration at attempting to do the right thing. She had been trying to save Eric and the Mountain Warriors as she had in the past, and yet Eric pointed his rifle straight at her heart. He was battling with his intentions to either kill or rescue her. She saw it in his eyes and felt it in his mind. She also knew that someone from outside the Forbidden Zone had told him that he must kill her or be turned. She could not dig deep enough in Eric's mind to determine who. A part of her couldn't blame him. However, her lips tightened at the irony of the phrase heart break. A bullet through the chest into the heart from someone she had come to care about and had helped at the risk of her own life would be the ultimate example. Decapitation and piercing the heart were the two ways to kill a vampire. She had given Eric that knowledge.

On top of her, Dexter's hands were nowhere inappropriate but then she felt them creep up her back like starving cobras hunting prey. His hands found the tension in her shoulders and began an attempt to massage her. They felt like deck nails digging into her as her muscles roiled back in repulsion and rebellion against his touch.

"Your muscles feel like snakes coiling and uncoiling beneath your skin, my sweet darling," he said.

"Quit touching me!" she said in a low growl. Eric didn't seem to hear her. He seemed preoccupied. She guessed that Richard was doing something to him. She usually tried to protect him from psionic attacks from other vampires, but now he seemed dead set to kill her. Presently Abigail's goal was to get out of this situation of having a gun pointed at her and get the pervert off of her back. Do your thing, Richard, if it gets us out of here, she thought.

"I can help you relax, my dear," Dexter said.

"I can't relax with your hands on my shoulders," she retorted.

"Is there another body part of yours that I should touch instead?" he cooed in a tone that made her want to vomit the blood she drank last night.

"I will kill you if you don't get your hands off of me," she shot right back.

"You aren't allowed to harm me, baby. I am protected," he purred back to her, his mouth too close to her ear. His breath tickled her in a way that added to her nauseated stomach. "By the way, I have always wanted a vampire chick."

"Shut up," she said.

Eric raised his voice at them. "Stop it! Next time, I will shoot you!"

She glared at Eric thinking that he threatened her. She realized that something intense was happening between Eric and Richard. Maybe Lucian was in on it. Lucian held a grudge against her for killing his female partner before she was turned into a vampire.

Eric was on edge about something and leveled his rifle at Richard. The intent to kill him was clear. "Don't Eric," Abigail said out loud.

He glared at her with confused eyes. Richard really was getting to him, but Eric didn't know that Richard was getting disillusioned with working for The Specter. Abigail couldn't let Eric kill the head vampire. Although it was a long shot, she was hopeful that he would be a potential ally when she launched a rebellion, even if at the moment he seemed to be full in with The Specter.

She watched Eric as he shook his head to clear it.

She squirmed as Dexter buried his face in her hair at her neck. Then instinctively, her arm shot back and elbowed him in the ribs before her conscious mind registered that his hands were on her breasts.

She was grateful when Eric yanked him off of her and she began to scheme on how she could escape once Eric was released from his duties to get MREs. Critter stepped in front of them. His AK was leveled at The Specter. He looked formidable and she had seen him in action. She knew that he could ventilate all of them with his AK before they could even think about moving against him, especially piled up as they were. That is if Critter was in peak condition, but he suffered the most from the psychic assaults the last time that he faced the vampires.

Abigail sensed Richard's psionic work on the tracker. She joined him. Although it was daylight when their powers were diminished and they were in an awkward position in the pile, she saw Critter's quickly eyes cloud over. He stared blankly at the wall above them. She could feel a pause, a stillness in the vampires beneath her as they were aware that they would soon spring into action.

The barrel of Critter's rifle drooped and aimed just in front of his feet. She felt an impulse from the base of the stack. Immediately she sprang to her feet as did the rest of the vampires and The Specter. They ran toward the passageway past the bookcase. She was the first one through and she pressed a button that slammed the bookcase shut as the last vamp ran past. They rounded a bend for cover of the rocky wall. They could hear the concussion of the bullets smacking through the bookcase, scream past them and then heard the soft lead splat against the crystal walls.

Everyone crammed in tight together in a small alcove, waiting for the hail of lead storm to quit thundering. Richard stood next to Abigail and she could feel the bulge of the crystal key in his pocket. She moved closer to him.

The Spector glared at the bookcase and said, "We need to go back and rescue Dexter. He can have another zombie bot army up and ready in a week or so, and then this time, we will wipe out the so-called Mountain Warriors."

As The Specter said this, Abigail threw herself into Richard's arms and buried her head into his chest. Richard's arms warmly wrapped around her.

"Father," she cried.

Richard's arms held her tighter. She knew that this would get him. This was the first time his favored offspring from the bite called him by his paternal title. "Yes, my dear. Is everything alright?" he asked as he softly ran the back of his hand down her cheek. His other hand lovingly cupped the back of her head, massaging her scalp and ran through her hair.

Abigail sobbed. "No, you and Specter were right." She sobbed again, "The way Eric looked at me and pointed the gun at me. He wanted to kill me. The humans will never accept us. You are my only family."

Richard smiled and nodded to The Specter as he continued to caress her head and neck, letting his finger comb through her long silky hair. She rested her forehead on his chest.

Richard consoled her, "It will work out, my dear."

"I know," she said with hidden firmness behind her crying, but she kept her head down so he wouldn't see that her sobbing generated no tears, her eyes full of resolve instead. "I will do what must be done."

The gunfire had stopped.

The Specter walked to the bookshelf door and cautiously peered through a bullet hole. "They're gone," he said. "Get ready. We must pursue them. Darkness will dawn soon."

Lucian stood straight and said with forced authority, "The night is ours! Get any weapons ready! We must win even if we fight to the death," but his voice was hollow with self-doubt.

The Specter rolled his eyes at the youthful vampire and growled, "Let's go."

Abigail and Richard released each other. As they did so, Abigail's hand left Richard's pocket and deposited the crystal key into her own cloak. Now she had access through the different doorways and the ability to enact her plan.

Abigail slowly stepped back as The Specter and the other vampires walked to the bookcase door. She watched them draw hidden knives. They also pulled small handguns from holsters concealed in the ankle, small of the back and other areas. The Mountain Warriors had no desire to touch the vampires anywhere for a pat down over a fear of infection. Once armed, they stood rigid as they anticipated the opening of the bookcase. Richard and the Specter peered through the bullet holes.

"The room is empty. Let's go," The Specter said as he pushed the button to open the bookcase doorway. It slowly moved outward. Once it was fully opened, The Specter held a small handgun out as if trying to probe the space ahead, but didn't move yet as he took in the sights and sounds.

The Specter grumbled, "They took our weaponry and Dexter as well. Let's move out slowly."

The vampires followed The Specter into Dexter's party room, walking softly on the plush carpet soaked in Carla's zombie goo.

Abigail watched them as she backtracked away, backed into the passage. As they focused on the room she had the perfect opportunity to go off on her own.

From the stairs, she heard the thundering of many boots on the steps. Scores of human warriors raced down the stairway. Gunfire erupted from both sides.

Abigail used Richard's key and slipped out through a crystal doorway and manifested a short distance away just outside the fortress. The vampiress would have her vengeance.

***

The Specter had just escaped from us. He had bided his time for when our guns were off of him, exploded upward and threw the vampires off of his back as if they were only wisps of smoke. The Specter and the vampires didn't have time to grab their weapons as they got up and ran past the bookcase back into the black mouth of the tunnel. Abigail gave me one last evil glare, and then the bookcase seemed to magically close behind them. We opened fire, pumping many rounds through the bookcase. Paper and wood exploded, but I wasn't sure if we hit any of the vampires.

None of us had the desire to chase those things back into their lair. Who knows what weapons and creatures lurked behind the bookcase.

My ears were ringing from the gunfire in the enclosed space.

We were staring at the bookcase that had just closed as the other warriors from our tribe ran back down the stairs to join us.

"What the hell happened?" Bryan demanded as he walked up to look into Critter's face.

"They-- They did something to my mind. I'm fine now," said Critter.

"No kidding. You know what they're capable of," Bryan scolded. "Why didn't you do something or ask for help?"

"Back off!" Critter said, returning the stare.

"Guys, argue later. We need to go now," I said. Part of my butting in was due to guilt from not warning Critter about the mental attacks that I had suffered from the vampires.

Bryan and Critter nodded, but I could see they were still irritated with each other. They gathered up weapons left from The Specter and the vampires. Both Critter and Bryan were happy to get their hands on some of the vampire's swords. I knew deep inside they resented that a newbie like me got my hands on one before they did. Both men put one of the scabbarded vampiric swords into their belts.

Bryan also picked up The Specter's rifle. It was dangerous looking. It was shorter than Bryan's AR-15, but looked very similar to me. I learned it was called a carbine, an M4. I wasn't quite the gun expert as the Mountain Warriors, but Bryan looked it over and nodded his approval.

"Hey, Eric," Bryan handed me his AR-15. "This is yours if you want it."

"Thanks!" I said. I was elated. Although I was quickly learning, I didn't know much about guns, but I knew that he seemed more accurate with his rifle than me with my 30-30 and he could shoot thirty times without reloading or pulling a lever. It was a definite advantage. You never heard anyone in the Forbidden Zone making an argument for the unnecessity of shooting thirty times without reloading.

I knew some of the guys in our group might get jealous that Bryan bequeathed his favored weapon to me, but I was too excited to worry about that at the present.

Bryan pushed Dexter toward the stairs, and the rest of us headed up the stairway to the passage back above to the main house.

"Get going, freak," Bryan ordered Dexter.

"Can't I just go?" Dexter asked, pointing to the bookcase where Specter and the vampires had exited.

"I thought you were afraid of them?" Bryan asked, looking at the bookcase doorway with horror.

"No," Dexter answered. "I just said that because I thought you were going to shoot us all, and I was hoping that you wouldn't see me as a monster like those guys. They really aren't so bad," he added with a gapped tooth grin.

Bryan looked perplexed about Dexter's honest words about his dishonest words. His face suddenly turned stoney, "Get your ass up the stairs," he barked the order, leveling his new M4 at Dexter's face.

We ran to the bookcase that led upstairs to the house. As our bookcase was closing behind us, the bookcase where the vampires and The Specter had disappeared began to reopen. We sprinted faster. No one wanted to wait to see what emerged.

"Move," Bryan yelled. "We may have company."

All of us raced up the dark stairs and entered the second floor room. The weight of the MRE packages, while manageable, was a burden and I realized that it was going to be a long walk back with the extra weight.

We gathered on the second floor landing. Critter called the Rat Man and a few of his men to join us. They bounded up the stairs to the second floor and hungrily eyed the boxes of MREs in each man's hands.

"Holy cow!" the Rat Man exclaimed as he looked between our faces and our boxes. "Where did you get that? Are there any more?"

"Oh, yes," said Bryan. "There is a mountain of them, and they are all yours for the taking in the labyrinth below."

"How do we get them? Is it hard to find?" asked the Rat Man.

Critter gave him a wolfish grin. He still resented them for attacking us this morning and then retreating and abandoning us to fight against the zombies. Although Bryan's intercession saved them, Critter still looked down upon their cowardice and treachery. Critter said, "It's easy to find. Just go down the stairs. When you get there, ask the nice vampires where to go."

The Rat Man and his people laughed and looked for a sign that Critter was joking.

Their jaws dropped as they realized that he might not be joking and that something may indeed be lurking down there.

Bryan advised, "I would take your full crew and your guns, of course. That's if you're hungry enough."

The Rat Man gathered his forces and headed down the stairs with their firearms at the ready.

Bryan said, "Let's go," to the rest of us.

As we were walking towards the door, Scott said to me with his goofy grin, "It was with great regret that I found out that you survived. I thought I had a new gun." He handed me the handgun that I had thrown at the zombies when I ran out of ammo just before rolling in the pipe.

It wasn't that funny, but I could only laugh in reply.

The smile left Scott's face. "I am glad you made it, kid."

"Thanks. So am I," I said, "but I am out of ammo."

"No problem," Scott said. "I shook down one of Rat Man's people. You have a full magazine. They won't need it. They can't fight worth a damn anyway." Scott started laughing, "Hell you should have seen the look on their faces when they thought we slew all those tens of thousands of zombies, barely a dozen of us, I tell you, surrounded by thousands," Scott exaggerated the story already. He then did a comical impersonation of how the Rat Man must have looked shocked when the gate was thrown open. "Hell, we owe our victory to Bryan but those numb knucklers don't—"

Scott's words were cut off as gunfire ripped and echoed up the stairwell from the party room far below us.

Bryan stopped and looked guiltily towards the entrance to the stairs to the basement. I started to head down the stairs. There was nothing psychic drawing me down. Deep inside, I wanted to make sure that Abigail wasn't killed in the barrage.

"Hell no," said Critter. "I am not saving them. They abandoned us. They can handle themselves."

"Yeah," agreed Scott. "It's a whole army of them against a few pasty assed, wingless mosquitoes and some freak in a skull mask. A little skirmish like that will build character, and Lord knows they need character."

Bryan nodded. "Then let's move. You too, Eric," he ordered me as I stood looking down the stairs and then we all took off at a trot.

Before I left, I shot one more look at the doorway, hoping that Abigail would be safe.

We left the building and were soon walking up the steep incline, leaving the beautiful but accursed valley behind.

***

As the fighting raged in the basement, Abigail slipped through the crystal doorway with Richard's key. She had seen a map of the crystal passages on Richard's computer and memorized as much as she could. With two confident strides she left a cave and stepped out high up on a mountainside deep in a forest facing the rapidly setting sun. She scowled and lowered her head protecting herself from the brutality of the sun's rays, but in minutes she would be in her element. With her black cloak unfurling behind her like a pirate's flag in a stiff sea breeze, she ran down the slope to get in the shade of the mountain.

It was now dark enough in the shade for her to feel comfortable, although most vampires would still find it intolerable for the next thirty minutes. She wanted to start hunting her prey long before the other vampires and The Specter could pick up his trail. She did not want to share.

She saw a spire-like rock formation on a distant ridge line and knew exactly where she was. She ran a half mile through the forest and climbed a great rocky knob that overlooked the trail that snaked up from the fortress. She reached the top that had just acquired shade from the setting sun. She crouched down and observed the mountains like a lioness observing her Serengeti. A smile crossed her face as she watched the caravan of Mountain Warriors trekking up the steep path far below her. The path wound around her as darkness settled. Her smile broadened. All she had to do was wait for night when darkness had fallen and her vision was superior to theirs. She just needed a ten-foot wide space between them to get to her prey easily. With her stealth and psionic abilities, she could take out any night blinded man. Either that or wait until her target was alone, even for a few seconds, in the remaining daylight.

She kept her eyes on them from her rocky perch. A grimness settled over her face as she watched her target separate from the group.

She leapt from her rocky perch, feeling a thrill like flying as she plummeted from a height well over four times higher than she would have dared as a human. Her knees protested slightly as she crouched in the landing, but as a vampire, any damage to the cartilage would quickly be healed. Yes, tonight she loved being a vampire. Usually she consumed animals, but this night she would get her fill of human blood from a hated enemy. The rush of excitement from the hunt, revenge, and the hunger drove her as she raced toward her target. Human blood was a genetic match. Easy to be turned into energy. Animal blood sustained a vampire, but human blood was an intoxicant better than alcohol, and in her mind, no human deserved death more than her target.

***

We were loaded with weapons, backpacks of light survival gear for winter, and of course each man carried two boxes of MREs. Each MRE box weighed over twenty one pounds and there was only a small plastic strap to carry them that seemed to cut through the calloused skin of our hands. Under the weight and urgency, we struggled up the path that wound back up the mountain.

The only one unburdened with weapons and a backpack was Dexter. In our rush to leave, Bryan seemed to have left his rational mind behind. He should have loaded up the prisoner with most of the weight and drove him up the mountain like we had done after defeating the Rat Man's army.

Instead Dexter just carried two boxes of MREs like the rest of us and nothing else. As we rounded a bend, where he was unseen by most, he simply dropped his two boxes, sucker punched Robert who was guarding him, and sprinted into the woods. I tried to draw a bead on him with my newly acquired rifle that still smelled like the wood smoke of Bryan's buckskin jacket. I watched Dexter over my front site as he ran, jumped, zig zagged, and slid in the dry leaves down a steep slope. Unlike this morning, I would have no problem shooting him, but I held my fire as I was sure that I would miss. Around me, I heard the explosive outburst of rifles barking near me and watched the fallen leaves dance harmlessly around Dexter until he disappeared behind a rock outcropping that led deep down into a sheltered ravine.

Critter cursed as he lowered his rifle. He was about to chase after Dexter, but Bryan placed a firm hand on Critter's shoulder, stopping his pursuit.

"Let it go," Bryan sighed. "We need to focus on leaving here before the vampires come out. Darkness will hit soon."

"Hell no," Critter shot back. "If we let that bastard go, he'll just rebuild another army."

"We have our families and friends waiting for us back home," Bryan said.

Critter clenched his jaw tightly in reply. His fierce eyes told Bryan his answer. After a stare-down he said, "We won't have any family or friends if he sets up shop again."

Bryan explained in a deep commanding voice, "It's dark at the bottom of that cove. You can't possibly track him, but the vampires can track you."

Without a word, Critter violently jerked his shoulder to get Bryan's hand off of him. He took two big sprinting steps into the woods, followed by half of our crew, but he suddenly stopped with a hand cupped over his ear.

I heard the faintest, yet unmistakable scream of horror deep in the shaded ravine. The scream started high pitched, lowered in timbre and delved into the deepest pit of pain. Had not Critter stopped, I would have thought that I was imagining it, but others stopped to listen as well. Then abruptly the scream was silenced. So abrupt was the quiet that followed that it gave us the impression of the finality of death. We stared into the darkness of the deep mountain cove.

"Whatcha all stop for?" asked Scott.

I held up my hand for him to be quiet. After a pause, I asked, "did you guys hear that?"

"My hearing's been shot for years," said Scott. "Whadya think ya hear?"

I looked at Critter who had the sharpest ears and gave my opinion, "That sounded like Dexter."

"It sounded like he was in mortal terror and pain," Tomas added.

Critter nodded grimly and then shrugged. "I hope he's dead."

"It came from the direction he ran," Bryan agreed.

"What would cause such terror? A zombie?" I asked.

Critter shook his head, "Not in that terrain. They like flat ground."

"A vamp would almost make me scream like that," Tomas admitted, "but it's still daylight, barely."

"Well, we know of at least one vampire who isn't confined by the sun," said Bryan as he eyed the forest in the direction that Dexter's scream came from.

"Abigail," I finally said.

"And she was pretty pissed off at him," said Scott. "Hell, a man just don't treat a lady like that, even a vampire chick, but I ain't going down there to critique whether she killed him properly or not," he finished with a smart assed smirk.

A few of us, including myself, shuddered. I had seen first hand the evil that the vampires could inflict on the mind, especially when together in a group.

"But Dexter is under The Specter's and ultimately the vampire's protection," I said knowing full well that Abigail tended to operate on her own.

We spent a moment in thoughtful consideration.

"Maybe it was a wendigo," Critter said.

When he had our rapt attention he gave a half grin and a snort as if our discussion was silliness and not worth his time.

He turned his back to us, gathered his dropped MRE boxes, and started marching up the hill without another word. We followed Critter at a light jog. Scott was right. No one had the desire or guts to go into the area shaded from the sun to see what happened to Dexter.

I picked up my boxes as well and started walking. I was out of breath very quickly. All I could do was focus on taking the next running step and taking the next ragged breath. I focused on keeping up with the man in front of me through my sweat blurred vision. The sweat poured down my face but I couldn't wipe it away. You would never have guessed that there was snow on the ground this morning. Now after a warm afternoon, the cooling wind against my face prophesied a night that would freeze my sweat. The twenty pound boxes of food now might as well have weighed two thousand pounds, making my arms feel like they were simply thin, frayed cords tied to the boxes.

When we reached the ridge top, we paused to catch our breath. Down below we saw the Rat Man's army running from the fortress carrying their own boxes of MREs. They gathered together within the walls. It seemed that whoever they fought hadn't scared them that much. Maybe they might even finish the winter in the valley of the mad scientist. They had enough food.

Bryan smiled and nodded. "I'm glad to see that they made it," he said.

"Why?" I asked slightly perplexed. I didn't need to tell him that he was rooting for our enemies and potential competitors for limited resources in the future. Not to mention, he used them mercilessly to port our camp and then to help fight our battle.

"For one thing, Eric, they're people. Brothers and sisters in this world of monsters. Second and most important, although

I did a bit of acting, they entrusted me to lead them to food. I made a promise. I like to keep my word. Besides, if someone follows me, I feel that I owe them good leadership."

I nodded back. I could see he really did feel a bit of a bond with them. I felt one too until they let me charge into the zombie horde alone. I shuddered at the grim reality of his change of heart. He was equally ready to give kindness or death to anyone. What they received was entirely dependent on what they offered Bryan, and he would apply that to me too. With this knowledge, I understood Bryan more. However, I still prepared myself for leaving the tribe to go on my own if necessary.

As we were quickly ascending in height up the mountain trail, it seemed to halt the sun's setting time only slightly. The sun appeared to hover above the horizon like a magical levitating red ball.

At this apex, I watched Bryan and Critter raise their fist and extended their arms to it. It looked like some pagan salute to a sun god. I raised mine as well.

They had taught me earlier that week that you can tell how long before sunset it will be by how many fists away from the horizon that the sun hovered.

Each extended fist is approximately fifteen degrees. There are twenty four, fifteen degree angles in the three hundred and sixty degrees in a circle. So each fifteen degree movement of the sun on the horizon corresponded to an hour of daylight. Each fist length that the sun was above the horizon was an hour. Each knuckle equaled fifteen minutes. With actual vampires around, this knowledge was worth more than gold.

Looking at my fist, the sun was at the top portion of my bottom knuckle. We had about fifteen minutes before darkness settled and the terrors of the night ruled once again.

Nobody said anything. We all knew it already and most were too tired to even waste breath on complaints.

Bryan was the first to pick up his boxes. We followed his example and started to run. The ridge line was pretty smooth. This relatively flat land for the Appalachian Mountains wasn't nearly as bad as that continuous climb up the mountain that we just accomplished, but I kept turning my eyes on the setting sun as if watching a time bomb ticking to its final seconds.

18

Just as dark settled, Critter, who was leading, ran into the woods off the trail. We followed him to a small overhang beneath a cliff. A waterfall trickled over the rocks twenty meters off the path. We dropped our boxes in the overhang and sated our powerful thirst in the cold mountain spring water. We drank at the spot where the stream fell directly in a small pool. We then went downstream and washed ourselves in another small pool. Some of the cleansing was for the zombie goo. Some of it was simply for the spirit. Sometimes splashing cold water over the face works more miracles than any physician.

We went back to the overhang. Critter removed a few stones from the base of the cliff. What had looked like a formidable rock wall soon revealed a hidden cavern. By the weak starlight and remaining traces of twilight, I could see a few crates already inside. I could tell that the Mountain Warriors had used this as a stash point for quite a while. Bryan gave me a few boxes of ammunition for my new AR-15 that he grabbed from this hidden stash.

"You earned it," he said.

We unloaded most of our MREs inside the cavern. From this point on, only half the crew would carry one box of MREs. The other half would only hold weapons at the ready. With night finally here, we wanted the warriors at the front and at the rear, well armed and ready to fight. And the porters ready with a free arm and unencumbered by too much weight.

After we walked back to the main trail, Critter took the time to camouflage our tracks off the path we took to the overhang that hid our loot. All this was done in darkness. A week ago I would have suspected these guys as vampires strictly by their abilities to work without artificial lights, but even with my short stay here, I found my night vision not just getting better, but I acquired a decent instinct for avoiding bumping my head or stubbing my toe on unseen objects.

Just before we resumed our jog back to our new camp, Bryan warned Critter that we had run into Rat Man's group earlier, "We might meet them as they come to meet their fighters."

Critter shook his head. He sniffed the air and looked in their direction. He said, "They never left their camp."

"How do you know?" asked Bryan.

"I'm a tracker. I know my job."

Without another word, Critter led the way as he started to jog back to our new home. I ran just behind Critter. I felt one hundred pounds lighter without the MREs. I only held my new AR-15 and I felt like superman. My old lever action

Winchester that was strapped to my back would act as a good backup rifle or as a trade. I actually felt like a rich man.

We arrived at the Rat Man's camp shortly after full dark to find that Critter was correct, they were still there.

The occupants were terrified as our shapes appeared before them around the fires. Bryan assured them that their fighters should arrive shortly with lots of MREs. They stared at him with a mix of hope at his words and hopelessness of their situation. If their fighters and hunters didn't return due to following Bryan on some quixotical trail, the non-combatants would slowly starve to death. Bryan assured them again that they were on their way with food.

I understood Bryan's sympathy for the people who followed him. I felt it too as I watched and felt the worry in their eyes.

The people asked for our MREs but despite Bryan's feelings for them, his feelings were far more deeper for his own tribe of friends and family. He ignored their pleas and turned to us.

"They're still a ways behind us," he said, "but they'll be here with food soon enough." He turned to us and ordered, "Let's go.".

As quick as we appeared before their fires, we were gone.

When we arrived at our camp, it was nearing midnight and starless. The clouds had moved in and I worried about more snow. We had gone down the hill and I could hear the low rumble from the bubbling of a sizable river nearby. The water sounds brought me a primal comfort that I couldn't explain, similar but different from the comfort brought on by a campfire.

Adam greeted us outside of the fire rings like he expected us at that moment. He always looked mystical to me at night, from his straight confident posture to the way his opaque glasses reflected the flames of the campfires.

Bryan said. "We've got a lot to talk about, Adam. You wouldn't believe what we found—"

Adam joked, "I am not going to let guys go out to play if you keep coming back with new terrors." He then sighed sagely and asked, "Did everyone come back in good health?"

Bryan shook his head, but before he could tell Adam about Nick, Anna flung her arms around her man, Bryan, as his kids jumped all over him shouting, "Daddy! Daddy!"

"I love that word more than any other," Bryan said.

Adam and Shelley quickly inspected the warriors for any bites that could potentially turn us into a monster, but aside from the usual scrapes and bruises, we were all intact.

Friends and family greeted the other warriors. A woman openly cried for Nicholas who had been devoured back at the fortress, but no one rushed to hug me.

It was an odd moment. All the camaraderie that we shared on the walk back evaporated and I was left alone. It's hard to explain, but after the steady rush of adrenaline all day, it was quite a letdown and it felt like someone threw a wet blanket of depression over me. No one would weep for me if I had died. Even with the brotherhood forged by the sword over the last week, I was still alone, an outsider, and feared that I would always be one in this tribe.

I thought of Jennifer, my now obvious ex-girlfriend. I wondered if she held any sadness for my exile. If she did, she found relief in the arms of that jackass and betrayer, Tommy.

I sat alone by the communal fire. After a time, I looked up and realized that Bryan stood next to me. Despite his tall, broad frame, he moved as silent as the clouds above, and like the clouds he had the potential to turn quite tempestuous.

"Hey, Eric," Bryan said.

"Yeah?" I asked. I forced my tone to sound bright. I didn't want to sound like I was moping around. I had a personal dislike for people who seemed to be obsessed and in love with their depression. Maybe it was because I was prone to it myself and I didn't want others to see that same weakness in me.

Bryan replied, "There's a woman waiting to speak to you."

Instantly, I thought of Jennifer. Did she leave Tommy to join me in this wasteland? That was absurd, but for some reason I was hanging onto something to pull me out of my funk.

I stood in answer to his call without him saying anything further. Before I could ask who, he strode into the night. I placed the strap of my newly acquired AR-15 over my shoulder and quickly followed, mystified by the woman's identity.

I followed him past the various fire rings. The ground of the new camp still looked more like the forest floor than a camp. It was covered in loose leaves rather than packed dirt and trails from constant foot traffic like our last camp.

As we left the camp, I felt like cold water poured into my spine. I instinctively touched the sword and handgun at my hip. As I was about to question why we were leaving the camp both hope and terror simultaneously struck my heart. Deep inside I knew who it was and why Bryan didn't mention her name in camp so as not to terrorize anyone who overheard. The absence of the drones also told me. I only knew of one person who could mentally override the electronics. The night was her dominion.

Bryan whispered. "We want to see what she tells you. When you find out what her bosses want, act like you are stretching. When you raise your hands in the air above your head and yawn, that will signal us to get her. I want to interrogate her and find out what the vampires and The Specter are up to."

I nodded, and saw the shadow-like silhouette of Critter, the silent woodsman, in a dark recess off in the forest. He crouched in a sinewy coil, ready for action.

The two men disappeared noiselessly into the gloom off of the trail. All I could hear were my steps, breath, and thundering heartbeat. There was something about being in the woods late after dark. The safe light from the campfires behind me seemed as distant as the cold light from the stars above hidden in the clouds. Not the best time to meet one of the terrors of the Forbidden Zone.

I came upon her. At night with her flowing black hooded cloak her silhouette was witch-like. I'm not talking about the modern idea of a witch: The hippie-like chick who has a penchant for crystals and silly spells, but rather the slim creature from nightmarish legend whose figure stood out in the night only because she was darker than the night itself. Back at

Dexter's, during the daytime and under the fluorescent lights, the vampires looked harmless, almost comical. Now, the situation was deadly serious.

And yet I felt drawn to her. I didn't feel her probing my mind, yet I took the precaution to block off her access. I would communicate purely with spoken words. I knew Abigail's tricks and she wouldn't fool me again.

She addressed me, "My reason told me not to expect you to make it this long. Yet deep inside I knew that you would."

"You thought that I'd hide from you at the firelight this evening despite all that I've been through?" I asked.

"No. I knew that you would see me tonight," she said. "I didn't think you would make it from that first night. When I was supposed to kill you. It is why I warned you in your dreams not to come while you were still in Washington, DC."

"What happened to Dexter?" I asked as I remembered his cries.

"Let's just say that he ran into a woman who his mother should have warned him about," she said with a sly smile.

"You killed him?" I asked.

"He would have brought back the zombie bot army in a matter of weeks. The Specter would have used it as a hammer against your tribe," she said.

"But will they suspect you or us of killing him?" I asked.

"No. I savagely attacked him and drained his blood. They will suspect a coven of failed vampires. Intelligent vampires tend to use a dagger to draw blood. It's more civilized."

"I have no interest in vampire niceties. Are you sure that he's dead?" I asked.

"Oh yeah. I also left his body on the trail. If he simply disappeared, his death would be blamed on you all. I did not want that."

"I thought you only drank the blood of animals?" I asked.

"Do you know of any animal more depraved and more deserving than Dexter?" I couldn't see her face under the hood, but I knew that she smiled with grim humor.

I shrugged. "You have a point," I admitted.

I thought about our first meeting. The paralyzing terror from her unnatural spell. That was only a week ago but it felt like a lifetime, maybe quite a few. Even this very morning when she warned us about the Rat Man's army felt like years had passed.

"Take off your hood, Abigail."

She cocked her head curiously. "Why?" she asked telepathically.

"Talk out loud, not in my head," I nearly shouted. I did not like meeting her in the dark and alone when she was in her full power. I felt like the lion tamer who had to convince the much more powerful beast that the mere man was the one with power, not the four hundred pound feline with fangs and claws and muscle power that only a wild animal can harness.

"Fine," she said out loud.

She let the hood fall over her back. Her long hair spilled past her shoulders. The moon broke forth from a cloud and I realized my mistake. Maybe I should not have told her to remove her hood. It might be better to see her as a monster than a woman. She was naturally beautiful. Seeing her as a woman would cause me to relax. I couldn't let my guard down.

"What do you want? People here want to kill you," I said.

She smirked, "Like your two friends trying to creep up on a creature of the night?"

I nervously looked in the woods around us, but could neither see nor hear Bryan and Critter. It dawned on me that she could have vampiric allies who took them out. I could be alone and at the mercy of the vampires right now.

She opened her red lips to say something. I could see by the sparkle in her eyes that she had something ironic to say, but I cut her off.

"What do you want?" I bluntly asked.

Her smile left her face and she said, "I am supposed to tell you to leave these people and join us, join me."

"No."

She nodded soberly and said, "I thought that would be your answer."

"Then why did you come or better yet, why did The Specter and Richard send you?"

"Don't think you are so smart, Eric."

"Am I wrong?"

She sighed as if speaking to a toddler, "No, but because a scientist understands some aspect of a virus and can even see it under a microscope, he should never think that he has mastered it."

"What do you want?" I asked again.

"Since you won't believe me when I tell you that I want you to be my friend, I will tell you why they sent me. We will come to your village soon on one of these evenings and make you an offer you must accept."

"And what would that be?" I asked.

"Your tribe must give us blood. You can use medical bags like the ones in the equipment we tried to give to you at the meeting in Craigsville last week. No one will die and in exchange your tribe will receive protection from the coven. I understand that it's revolting, but we have no choice. You must remember to convince your tribe to accept. I am sorry."

"How can you tell me that?"

"I am just the messenger," she said.

"And if we don't?"

"You must or they are all doomed. I hate that I must tell you this as much as you hate to hear it, but your tribe must agree," Abigail sounded genuinely worried. Again I could see the deep sorrow in her eyes that I saw this morning when I talked to her. I was guessing that her earlier smiles and taunts were due to elation of her power and drunkenness on the fresh blood of her enemy. Either that or a facade.

"Look. Look at me, Eric. I know you think about me, often," she said with too much confidence for my liking.

"Only because you and Richard put lustful thoughts in my head."

"And none of those thoughts are your own?" she asked with a knowing smile.

I opened my mouth to deny it, but it was pointless. She knew.

"Eric, look at me," she said with a gorgeous smile that seemed to light up the forest like a midnight sun.

I looked into her wide feline eyes. I remembered how stunning she looked in the daylight. I held that image in my mind. I could see how she would smile her love at me. I could see her as we passed the years together, Abigail, with her immortal beauty. I focused so hard on that image of her. Her image took up my full consciousness. I was in paradise.

I felt Critter and Bryan shaking me.

"Where is she?" Bryan demanded.

Slowly the image of her that I had unwittingly conjured in my mind flitted away and I was left standing in the darkened woods with the two men.

"She tricked me again," I said.

Bryan grabbed my shoulder and clenched his fist at me, barely restraining his violence, "What did she want?"

"They're going to make an offer we must refuse," I said. There was no way I could tell them to give the vampires their blood.

I tore away from Bryan's grasp with a wrench of my shoulder and headed back to camp to feel the primal safety of the fires.

I stopped walking and swore.

"What?" asked Bryan as he and Critter stood around me, piercing me with questioning stares.

"I forgot to warn her that there are videos of her helping me, helping us."

"Maybe she knows, and her 'help' is really their bidding. Never forget that she is a monster," Bryan warned.

"No. No, she isn't a monster," I said.

It was at this point that I knew they were wrong. Without thinking I brought my hands to a slight sensation that still lingered on my throat. I felt my blood pulse pounding under my fingers. There were no bite marks, just the dampness on my neck left by the vampiress when she kissed my neck.

***

Tommy smiled. He watched his computer screen as the dark figure of Abigail kissed Eric on the throat. A techie had just hit a few buttons on another computer and opened a backdoor entry to access Eric's video from his vest and cap. Whoever designed the bodycams did so with an eye on the reality of the Forbidden Zone, such as the potential for violence that may disable one transmitter, different frequencies to override jammers, nothing was overlooked and despite Robert disabling one transmitter it took no time to open a new one by remote control.

Another bonus was that Tommy could finally get Abigail out of his hair. She was so full of Dexter's blood that she was careless in her satiation. She overlooked the cameras and basically confessed, and Tommy knew that Dexter would return with a debt to him...

EPILOGUE

Dexter lay in the woods, dead. Only unnatural vampiric life sustained him. Drained of blood, his heart had stopped beating, but he could feel his thoughts shooting through space at infinite speeds in infinite directions. He picked up so many foreign thoughts and he reached for more. He was dead but his brain, mind, and spirit felt more alive than ever, the worst tease. He had his hypotheses of how the vampiric mind worked before, but now that he was infected he sought out what he could explore. He sought out electromagnetic impulses. He was aware of the electric workings of a drone a half mile away. He next picked up the relatively single-minded thoughts of an opossum who headed for the hundreds of his dead zombies at the base of the hill. Dexter suddenly knew that opossums were the only scavengers that would eat a dead zombie. He felt the instincts of earthworms enjoying the consumption of the decaying loam of the forest floor beneath him.

Dexter could understand why lesser human minds went insane and failed with all the extra input from every operating nervous and electric being around him. That overload was too taxing for most people and resulted in death or if they lived, they became failed vampires.

Dexter on the other hand rejoiced in the new input, despite the intense pain. If that bitch had not drained him, he would cry real tears that he could never fully enjoy the new psychic powers. His life was now measured in minutes or hours; he couldn't tell, but it was short. This would be the greatest gift: to live with this power. But instead, he was to get only a taste of this power and die. He had to live somehow! He had to get help, but all he could do was think. Even blinking his eyes taxed his reserves.

In the distance he saw some lights heading his way. Maybe there was hope. He could tell these were humans by their worried fears of the night, but couldn't sense their full thoughts, yet, just emotions. He watched as their path deviated away from his position. He tried to yell, but his muscles were too weak. He sent an impulse of thought and watched them stop walking. He sent another one and they looked in his direction. Despite being naturally dead and vampirically alive, he felt a thrill as he sent a third impulse and they headed in his direction.

He caught a flash of Abigail's mind far away and realized that he was bound to her. She was his matriarch by the bloodline. He realized that she would be aware of his weak life if he kept his connection. He found that he could temporarily cut off that link. He simply willed up a mental wall in his mind to shield himself from her.

The horror of the episode that happened shortly before replayed in his head. He had escaped the Mountain Warriors. Laughing at how he outsmarted them as he sprinted downhill. He ran his tongue over his jagged teeth that Bryan had shattered and laughed louder as visions flashed through his head of the fatal vengeance that he would deliver. He just had to get back to The Specter and the vampires.

As he ran into the deep shadows of the valley, something compelled him to stop. It was a mental command deep in his head. He turned and was relieved to see a figure in a black hooded cloak coming toward him in the twilight. After the initial shudder of terror passed, he relaxed.

"Hey, take me back to The Specter!" he demanded.

He crossed his arms and stood with his chest out. These creeps needed to see a person fully confident and in control, but his arms fell to his side and his jaw fell open.

Abigail walked towards him, nude. Somehow, his mind dismissed that he had first seen her cloaked and the clothing suddenly disappeared. Oh, how he had always desired to see her naked especially after feeling her firm body beneath him. Her confident hips swayed suggestively. Her eyes... Oh, her eyes said more than any spoken words could.

She floated above the leaves. Deep inside, he knew that was impossible. He knew he must be under her spell. Abigail would not walk in the woods naked. She would not offer herself like this to him, but he didn't care. And she wore a perfume that was his favorite. It was aggressively feminine and her hungry eyes... She stood before him and leaned her lips into him. As he brought his lips to meet hers, fully under her power, as her hand slipped up and around his chest, back, up his neck where her fingers interlaced with his hair. She drew him closer to her and then before their lips met, she placed her other hand on his chest.

Her cold voice broke the spell like a splash of frigid water to the face, "Dexter, look at me. I want you to know..."

His eyes snapped open. She leaned over him fully clothed. She wore no perfume and smelled of the forest. Her eyes were indeed hungry but not for sex. She smiled, baring her fangs. She wanted him to know that she would kill him.

He screamed as she sank her fangs deep into his neck with what seemed to be superhuman speed and power. Each time he moved to escape, she took another bite, leaving gaping holes in his neck, chest, and shoulders. She kept eye contact as much as possible. For a moment, she was not a thinking, intelligent vampire, but rather she succumbed to the beast that lies in the hearts of all vampires as the fires of blood madness consumed her eyes.

"I am sorry I treated you like that!" he pleaded.

The tearing at his throat was excruciating. Vampires had a venom that acted like a narcotic that actually placed the victim in ecstasy so that they enjoyed their deaths, making them easier prey. This bitch withheld the venom to make him suffer.

She kept biting, drinking his life, but her psychic mind whispered into his brain that she killed him so he could not bring about another zombie bot army and that she had decided his fate long before they even met. She let him know that she went beast mode so no one would suspect her. The vampire nature in her that she normally suppressed relished the pain she gave him. He looked in her eyes as she looked up from his neck, still drinking. The ancient vampiric bloodlust blazed in her eyes, but beneath the surface, was the intelligent, young woman.

As this went on, he realized that he felt her infection spreading from his gaping throat wound into his heart, which pumped the infection to his organs, to his limbs, to his brain, to his psyche... He realized that he was now reading her. Seeing her most ambitious dreams and greatest fears. A mix of passionate love and hatred for her welled up in him. If he would live, he would have a bond to her, his vampiric mother.

A tearing pain ripped his chest as his heart struggled to pump, but the absence of blood in his veins made it impossible. No. He was dying. He could feel Abigail's heart thundering against him as he fell to the ground with her on top.

Each time he moved, she embraced him tighter and sank her fangs in deeper. It was hopeless.

He felt her intoxication in his blood and wished that he could live to experience killing a person like he was getting killed. She then bit him everywhere she could, sinking her fangs deeply into his body to imitate the attack of a coven of failed and idiot vampires until he had no blood left.

She stood up, leaving him on the ground. Abigail glared at him as she broke a branch so that she produced a ragged sharp point. She then drove it through his chest to pierce his heart to ensure that he could not be revived. He read her thoughts that the sharp stick would give the appearance that he simply fell on the stick. An elation hit him, that it would have worked, but in her feral, intoxicated state, she missed his heart. It pierced an edge of his left lung's lobe and slid against his esophagus without piercing it.

Abigail was not used to drinking human blood and the intoxication that it brought. She was arrogant and sloppy.

She spat at him and then glared into his eyes. He watched her as she carefully cleaned the blood off her face. Then she simply turned and walked away, disappearing in the forest.

She had left him there a few hours ago. He would have been dead, but the vampiric virus kept him barely alive, but bloodless. He would die soon even with the vampiric infection, at least by the time the cursed sun arose.

However, a few hours before sunup, headlamps blinded him with his newly acquired night vision. Now he watched as three soldiers approached him. They squatted around him.

One of them said, "Yep. This is him!"

Another said, "Hang in there buddy. We're from Craigsville. Tommy Laurens sent us. We'll get you a blood transfusion and save you."

"Holy cow! Some animal really ripped up his throat and chest!"

"He's dead. I can't feel his heartbeat," one of the men said as he felt for his wrist pulse.

"Look. His eyes are open and alert."

"But he doesn't have a pulse."

"We're just supposed to take him in. Just do your job."

"Do you think he'll turn into a vampire or a zombie?"

"Shut up! Our orders are just to get him to the safe house."

Dexter was too weak to reply. He listened to their thoughts. He gathered that Tommy hoped to make him an ally, but Dexter had loyalty to no one. He already had plans formulating in his head. How he would get revenge against his vampiric mother, kill Eric, the one she cared for, shake the core of the world's foundations. But first, he had to regain his strength and then he would kill these three soldiers for their sweet blood that he suddenly craved, and then, as a vampire, he'd use his superior intelligence to fulfill the prophecy of the "One." A faint smile spread across his face.

EXCERPT FROM BOOK 4

Beneath The Cavern Of The Vampires

I sprinted down a cavernous passage deep in the vampires' lair. The corridor came to a fork. One path led upward, the other down. Without breaking stride, I took the one that sloped up. I guessed that the only escape from deep inside the Cavern of the Vampires was to go upward. I was quickly disappointed as the slope immediately went downhill again. However I could hear footsteps and heavy the panting of the vampires pursuing me. I had no choice but continued to sprint away from my pursuit although it took me deeper into their stronghold. I rounded a bend and smashed into a vampire.

We were both taken by surprise with the collision. We rolled on the ground together. His face inches from my own. His breath was sour and rancid on my face. Although the vampires smelled similar to people, unlike the rotten smell of the zombies, this one smelled atrocious from a lack of hygiene, and I soon figured out that he was a failed vampire, based on his drooling, grunting, and single-minded desire to bite my throat. His mouth snapped ceaselessly as his fangs flashed in my face.

We struggled. I slammed his nose with my fist careful not to impale my knuckles on his infected fangs. I had to get out of his grip and off the ground as I could hear my pursuers still behind me. I kneed the failed vampire in the testicles without knowing enough of vampiric anatomy to be sure it would work. However I was rewarded when I heard it gasp in pain. It's horrid breath spat on my face. His hands let go and I leapt up to continue my running escape as vampiric faces surrounded me. Their hands reached and grabbed me with their long claw-like fingernails.

However, I lost sense of space as a void opened beneath me. I fell with the failed vampire, and guessed that a trap door had opened beneath us. I realized his abysmal state of idiocy as we fell. He did not succumb to an instinct to right himself, but rather his mouth kept snapping at my unprotected neck. I kept my hands on his throat to keep him away as his nails tore at my shoulder trying to bring me towards his drooling fanged mouth.

I had a moment to realize just how long the fall was and with a savage twist of my body, I flung the thing beneath me as we slammed into the relatively soft sandy soil at the bottom of the pit. My knees were on his chest and that saved them from breaking as his rib cage took the full impact with multiple cringe inducing cracks. In fact, his rib cage was completely smashed. A normal person would have died almost instantly.

There was another loud noise above me. I looked up and saw that the trap door had closed.

My eyes gradually adjusted to the darkness of the pit. I think I was slowly acquiring the vampire's ability to see just through the contact with Abigail. In the total absence of light there was no way I should have seen anything, but the walls seemed to sparkle with a dim iridescence. However, I began to sense a red light was coming up from beneath me.

I painfully stood up. The vampire still moaned in nonsensical gibberish as it slobbered, drooling bloody spittle down its cheek and chin. I stood five feet away, but it kept snapping its jaws at me. The vampire was totally disabled but it desired me, using whatever muscles connected to unshatter bones that still worked. It only had enough boney structure to raise its hideous head and reach with its grasping right arm. I found the single-mindedness of the creature that sought blood over healing even more terrifying than if it had full bodily function and came at me in full health.

The repulsion I felt towards its unnatural life and bloodlust filled me with such rage that I had the urge to destroy and rend the creature as Bryan had done earlier to another vampire. Instead I let out a breath and stabbed its heart with the vampiric sword that Abigail had given me. When it grabbed my ankle with its right arm, I chopped it off. Then I chopped off its head with the belief that there was a limit that life could be sustained with this separation.

I then backed to an opposite corner of the room as far from the failed vampire's head as possible and looked over the pit. It's eyes still hungrily followed my movement from its decapitated head.

The walls were made of the pure crystal that gave Shining Rock its name. I looked above me and doubted whether I could climb out. It was a straight shot to the top with no handholds. Plus the walls were damp and slick with the perpetual underground condensation. I could see a few places that I could climb but worried about getting too high, slipping, and falling to my death or lying injured with the headless vampire that still snapped at me from the corner.

As I mulled my dire predicament, Abigail's voice spoke loudly in my head. I could hear the worry, nearing panic in her telepathic voice.

"Eric! Good, I see you survived the fall. A vampire is descending to your level in the pit. You must kill it at all costs, immediately!"

I looked up as the trap door opened above.

I backed into my corner as a rope descended and was quickly followed by a hooded vampire who slid down with great speed and athletic coordination. The vampire landed like a cat and the rope was withdrawn. I stared at the creature before me. It was not intimidating in a muscular way like David, the vampire enforcer of the coven, but rather it had a quick gracefulness like a panther. Its sword was sheathed, but it struck me as more confident. It saw me as I would see an insect. I would not draw a sword on an insect, but rather, simply squash it.

The trap door above closed again. The thing was trapped with me.

I could not see its face beneath the shadow of its hood, but I felt its eyes on me and wondered what horrible creature lurked beneath the black cloak and hood.

My sword was up, pointing at the face of my strange opponent, but I remembered Bryan telling me never to telegraph my intent to kill. I relaxed my shoulders and lowered my sword so that it pointed at the floor so that I may get closer to launch a surprise attack. However, inside I steeled myself to spring and slice through its neck.

"Do not delay!" Abigail's voice screamed in my head as the thing stared at me. "What it has in store for you is far worse than death."

As I prepared to attack, the creature lowered its hood. What I saw totally took me off guard.

"What the hell, Abigail?" I demanded.

WHAT COMES NEXT

I originally envisioned this in 2012 as a combination of *The Office, Survivor Man,* and *The Walking Dead* but made with the personalities of actual friends of mine. Basically, the idea was a faux-reality show that was originally intended to be more humorous than the dark tone the novels eventually took. I wanted to do a TV series. Unfortunately that involved getting a team together which is not my strong point.

I then went on to write a novel instead. Now, it is something very different and the characters no longer resemble the friends I based them on. I have written the first 6 novels and I foresee the series spanning to 12 or 15 by the time we reach the finale. I plan to get out 1 book every 6 months. So I thank you again for your loyalty.

Writing is at times a very lonely endeavor. A writer suffers from duo personalities. At times we think we are the greatest at what we do. That's a good attitude to have on your first draft–it keeps you going. It also comes with an arrogance that we believe that other people don't just want to hear what we have to say, but that they'll also pay to read it. On the flip side, there's an almost paralyzing doubt that we are the worst writers in the world and maybe we've been wrong about this whole thing all along. So, it is always great to hear from friends and fans who have feedback!

One of the best ways you can encourage and help a writer to keep going is to leave reviews on Amazon, Goodreads etc. I would greatly appreciate that. You can also like me on Facebook and subscribe to me on Youtube as well. That not only is encouraging, but it gets the message out. I am a one man marketer and self-promoter, with some help from my gracious wife who is a great writer as well. Thank you all for reading and I hope you enjoy the rest of the series!

ABOUT THE AUTHOR

R.J. Burle is a former Marine and volunteer firefighter. He's currently and outdoor skills and martial arts instructor, a chiropractor, and a writer. He lives in the mountains near Asheville, NC with his wife and four kids.

Aside from his *Mountain Warrior* series and other horror stories, he also writes comedy. His completed novel, *Jack's Fork*, is the first in a comedic series of crime thrillers set in the wilds of Appalachia. There are goof-balls, crooks, killers, lovable misfits, and a whole lot of hidden loot. Find him online at rjburle.com

CPSIA information can be obtained
at www.ICGtesting.com
Printed in the USA
BVHW041820050622
638962BV00014BA/119